IN THE ARMS OF
THE RANCHER

BY
JOAN HOHL

Published in Great Britain 2010
Harlequin Mills & Boon Limited,
Eton House, 18-24 Paradise Road, Richmond, Surrey TW9 1SR

© Joan Hohl 2009

ISBN: 978 0 263 88188 2

51-1210

Harlequin Mills & Boon policy is to use papers that are natural, renewable
and recyclable products and made from wood grown in sustainable forests.
The logging and manufacturing processes conform to the legal environmental
regulations of the country of origin.

Printed and bound in Spain
by Litografia Rosés S.A., Barcelona

Joan Hohl is a bestselling author of more than sixty books. She has received numerous awards for her work, including a Romance Writers of America Golden Medallion award. In addition to contemporary romance, this prolific author also writes historical and time-travel romances. Joan lives in eastern Pennsylvania with her husband and family.

To:
My new editor, Krista, and her assistant, Shana.
Welcome to my imaginary world!

Dear Reader,

Hello once again. I'm back with another story for you. If you happen to have read a previous book of mine titled *Maverick*, you may recognize the hero in this book as the Maverick's friend Hawk McKenna. Well, it seems after playing a minor role in one book, Hawk decided he needed a book of his own. What's a poor writer to do but obey her imagination? Besides, I really liked the character named McKenna my busy little mind came up with.

So here, then, is Hawk's story about a summer-weary rancher taking a vacation break in Las Vegas for a little R&R and some female company before winter sets in. Instead, he finds Kate, a beautiful female with man troubles.

Although I'm writing this letter on a beautiful spring day in May, I know the holiday season is approaching as you hold this book, which I hope you will buy and enjoy, in your hands.

Happy holidays to all and to all a good read!

Joan Hohl

Prologue

He needed a break, and he was going to take one.
Hawk McKenna stood in the sunlight slanting from
the west onto the covered porch that ran the width
of his ranch house, his hand absently resting on the
head of the large dog next to him.

Though the sun's rays were warm, there was a
nip in the early October breeze. It felt good to Hawk
after the long, hot, hard but productive and prof-
itable summer. Yet he knew that before too long, the
mild autumn would be replaced by snowflakes
swirling, driven by harsh, bitter cold winds.

When the deep snows came, Hawk knew the

work on the ranch would be just as hard as it had been during the summer. No, he thought, smiling wryly as he gazed around him at the valley in which his ranch was nestled, the work in the deep snows of winter entailed numb fingers and toes and being chilled to the bone. All things considered, he'd rather sweat than freeze.

The idea of what was to come sent a shiver through him. He must be getting old, Hawk mused, stepping from the porch into the fading sunlight. But as he was only thirty-six, perhaps it wasn't so much his age as it was tiredness. Other than a run into Durango, the city closest to the ranch, for supplies, he hadn't been off the property in months.

Nor had he been in any female company in all that time, other than that of his foreman Jack's nineteen-year-old daughter and his wrangler Ted's wife.

Not exactly what Hawk had in mind for female company. Ted's wife, Carol, while very nice and pretty, was...well, Ted's wife. And Jack's daughter, Brenda, was even prettier but far too young, and she was becoming a pain in the ass.

A year or so ago, Brenda, who had hung around the ranch every summer since Jack had come to work for Hawk, had begun trailing behind Hawk. Her sidelong, supposedly sexy glances were beginning to grate on his nerves.

He wasn't interested. She was a kid, for cripes' sake. Not wanting to hurt her feelings, Hawk had tried dropping subtle hints to that effect, to no avail. She had gone right on with the sly, intimate looks, at moments even deliberately making physical contact, while making the touches appear accidental.

Frustrated, not knowing what to do other than be brutally honest by telling her to act her age and knock off her flirting, Hawk had approached Jack about her behavior. Treading as carefully as if he were negotiating a mine field, Hawk had asked him what Brenda's plans were for the future.

"Oh, you know kids," Jack said, grimacing. "They want everything. They just can't decide what in particular."

Hawk sighed. Not much help there. "It's over a year since she graduated high school. I thought she was planning to go on to college?"

"She now says she isn't sure." Jack gave him a probing look. "Why? Has she been making a pest of herself hanging around here?"

Drawing a slow breath, Hawk hedged. "Well… she has been kinda getting underfoot."

Jack nodded his understanding. "Yeah, I noticed," he admitted with a sigh. "I've been meaning to say something to her about it, but you know girls… They get so dramatic and emotional."

"Yeah," Hawk agreed, although he really didn't

know girls, as in kids. He knew women, knew as well how emotional they could be. He worked hard at avoiding the dramatic ones.

"I'll talk to her," Jack said, heaving a sigh before flashing a grin. "Maybe I can talk her into spending the winter with her mother, as she always did while she was still in school." He chuckled.

Hawk shook his head. Jack and his former wife had not divorced amicably. Although Brenda had spent only the summers with Jack while she had been in school, mere days after receiving her diploma, she'd taken off, telling her mother she wanted to be on her own, *free*.

Well, Hawk mused, if being on her own and free meant living with her father while bugging the hell out of him, she had succeeded too well. "You handle it any way you want," Hawk said, not bothering to add that Jack had better handle it, and her, sooner rather than later. "Maybe a father-daughter heart-to-heart will help."

"Will do." Jack started to turn away.

"Hold up a minute," Hawk said, stopping Jack short. "I'm going to take off for a couple weeks for a little R and R. Can you hold down the fort, and Boyo?" Hawk ruffled the hair on the dog's head.

Jack gave him a look. "You know damn well I can."

Hawk grinned. "Yeah, I know. I just like riling you now and again."

"As if I didn't know," Jack drawled. "You tellin' me where you're going and when?"

"Sure. No secret. I'm going to Vegas as soon as I can make room reservations. I'll let you know where I'll be staying." He paused before going on. "When I get back, you and Ted can take some time off. While I'm gone, you can decide who goes first."

"Good deal." Jack grinned and went back to work.

Relieved, Hawk drew a deep breath of the pine-scented mountain air. The dog looked up at him expectantly. "Not this time, Boyo," he said, ruffling the dog's thick hair. "You'll be staying with Jack."

If a dog could frown, Hawk thought, that was exactly what the big Irish wolfhound was doing. With a final hair ruffle, he turned to the porch steps.

A smile on his lips, Hawk walked into the house, picked up the phone and began punching in numbers.

One

Kate Muldoon was behind the hostess station, checking the reservation list, when the restaurant entrance door opened. A smile of greeting on her lips, she glanced up to see a man just inside the door and felt a strange skip beat in her chest.

The first word to jump into her mind was *cowboy*. Kate couldn't say why that particular descriptive word came to mind. There wasn't a pair of boots or a Stetson in sight. He was dressed the same as most patrons, casually in jeans that hugged his hips like a lover, a pale blue button down shirt tucked into the narrow denim waistband, the sleeves rolled up to mid-forearm.

His height was impressive. Kate judged him to be six feet five or six inches tall at least, maybe more. He was lean, muscular and rangy. He had a head full of thick, straight dark, almost black, hair with strands of deepest red glinting under the lights. It was long, caught at his nape and was tied with a narrow strip of leather.

He was striking—sharply defined features, a squared jaw and piercing dark eyes. His skin was tanned, near bronze. Part Native American, perhaps? Maybe.

But he wasn't what she would call handsome, not in the way Jeff was....

"May I help you?" Kate asked brightly, pushing away errant thoughts of her former lover.

"I don't have a reservation, but I'd like a table for one, if you have it." His voice was smooth, low, rather sexy and alluring.

Telling herself to grow up, Kate said, "Yes, of course. If you'll follow me." Scooping up a menu, she ushered him to a small table for two set in a corner between two curtained windows.

He arched a dark brow with visible amusement when she slid out a chair for him. "Thank you."

"You're welcome," she replied, handing him the

menu. "Tom will be your server today." Feeling oddly breathless, she added, "Enjoy your dinner."

He smiled.

Kate felt the shivery effects of his smile all the way back to her station. Ridiculous, she chided herself, dismissing thoughts of the tall man when she noticed a line of unexpected guests waiting for her.

Greeting and seating the hungry patrons who had suddenly shown up snared Kate's focus. After seating a party of four nearest the corner table, she heard the tall man quietly call to her.

"Miss?"

The shivery effects began all over again. Sighing through her professional smile, she stopped at his table. "Can I get you something?" she responded, noticing his half-empty beer glass. He smiled, this time with a suggestive hint. Kate felt the shiver turn into an unnerving shimmering heat.

"Is Vic in the kitchen this evening?"

His question threw her for a moment. She didn't know what she had expected, but an inquiry about her boss wasn't it. "Yes, he is," she answered, instantly regaining her composure.

"Would you give him a message from me?"

"Yes, of course." What else could she say?

"Tell him Hawk would like to talk to him." He smiled again, revealing strong white teeth.

"Hawk...just Hawk?" she asked. Lord, the man had a killer smile.

"Just Hawk," he said with a soft laugh. "He'll know who you mean."

"Uh...right. I'll tell him," Kate said, turning away to head for the kitchen. It was a good thing Jeff had immunized her against men, she thought, pushing through the swing door to the kitchen. That kind of man would get under an unwary woman's skin in a hurry.

That was one appealing package of femininity, he mused, his gaze fixed on the subtle yet intriguing movement of her hips as she pushed through the door to the kitchen. Of average height, she was all woman from the riot of loose curls in her long dark hair to her slim ankles, and everywhere in between. And he had noticed she wasn't wearing a ring on the third finger of her left hand.

Of course, that didn't necessarily mean she wasn't married. Hawk knew of many men as well as women who didn't wear their bands of commitment. Cramped their style, he supposed. He was wondering if she might be one of those women when a familiar voice broke into his musing.

"Hawk, you old dog, when did you get into town?" Vic Molino came to a stop next to Hawk, a big smile of welcome on his handsome face, his right hand outthrust.

Rising, Hawk grasped the hand and pulled the shorter man into a buddy embrace.

Stepping back, Hawk flicked a hand at the empty chair opposite his. "Got a minute to talk…or are you too busy in the kitchen?"

Vic grinned. "Always got a minute for you, Hawk. How the hell are you?" He arched his dark brows. "It's been a long while since your last visit."

"Yeah, I know." Hawk grinned back. "Been too busy making money. Now, before winter sets in, I aim to spend a little of it."

"I hear you." As he spoke, a server came to a stop at the table. Vic smiled at him. "I'll take care of this customer, Tom, but you'll still get the tip." He lowered his voice dramatically, as if to prevent Hawk from hearing him. "And he's a big tipper."

Tom smiled. "Thanks, Vic." He turned to leave but Vic stopped him before he could take a step.

"One thing, Tom. You can bring me a pot of coffee." He shot a glance at Hawk. "You want a fresh beer?"

Hawk shook his head. "No, thanks. I'm going to have wine with dinner, but I would like a cup of coffee."

"Coming right up, sir," Tom said, hurrying away.

Hawk glanced around the dining room. "Business looks brisk, as usual."

"It has been good," Vic said, a touch of gratitude in his voice, "even with the slump in the economy." He pulled a frown. "I didn't even get a vacation this year."

Hawk gave him a droll look. "Poor baby. Lisa cracking the whip over you, huh?"

Vic flashed a white grin. "Never. My bride is too much in love with me to find fault."

Hawk felt a touch of something—longing, an empty sensation. Surely not envy for his friend and the bride he'd married over five years ago.

"In fact," Vic went on smugly, "Lisa's too happy at the present to find fault with anyone." He paused, waiting for the look of confused curiosity to bring a frown to Hawk's face.

"Well," Hawk said. "Where's the punch line?"

Vic gave a burst of happy laughter. "She's pregnant, Hawk. After all this time, all the praying and hoping, we're going to have a baby."

Hawk lit up in a smile. "That's wonderful, Vic. When's the baby due?"

"In the spring. She's in the beginning of her second trimester."

"Damn! Damn, that's great, for both of you. I know how much you've wanted a child." Even as he congratulated his friend, Hawk again felt that twinge of empty longing. He brushed it off as he shook Vic's hand.

"Yeah," Vic said, grinning like a kid. "We were almost at the point of accepting that there would never be a baby for us."

Grinning back at him, Hawk raised his glass of beer. "Well, here's to perseverance." Bringing the glass to his lips, he downed the beer remaining in it. As he set the glass down, the hostess came to the table with a full fresh pot of coffee.

"Tom was busy at another table," she explained. "So I brought this over. Is there anything else, Vic?"

"No thanks." Vic shook his head. As she started to turn away, he stopped her by taking her hand. "Wait a minute. I want you to meet an old friend."

"Okay." She smiled at Hawk.

He felt an instant of breathlessness. He stood up as Vic rose from his chair.

"Hawk," Vic said, "this lovely lady is Kate Muldoon, my hostess and Lisa's and my friend." He smiled at her. "Kate, Hawk McKenna. We've been friends since college, and he's been Lisa's friend since our wedding." A teasing gleam shone from his eyes. "I suspect she'd have grabbed him if she'd met him earlier."

"Right," Hawk drawled, offering his long-fingered hand to her. "Nice to meet you…Kate?"

"Of course," she answered. "Hawk?"

"Of course," he echoed.

"Have a seat, Kate," Vic said, rising to grab an

empty chair at the next table while beckoning to someone.

Kate shook her head. "I can't, Vic. There are custom—"

"Yes, you can," Vic interrupted. "You haven't had a break yet."

Kate gave him a dry look. "I started working only two hours ago."

"Long enough," Vic said, turning to the young woman who had come to a halt at the table.

"You employed the imperial wave, sire?" the woman said, her blue eyes fairly dancing with amusement.

Vic laughed as he watched her give a quick glance at Hawk, her eyes widening with surprise. "Hawk!"

"Hi, Bella." Hawk said, getting to his feet just in time to catch her as she flung herself into his arms. "Subdued as ever, I see." Taking her by the shoulders, he set her back a step to look at her. "And beautiful as ever."

"I bet you say that to all your friends' sisters," Bella said, laughing. "You look great, Hawk."

"Thanks." Hawk smiled. "So do you."

"If this ritual of mutual admiration is over," Vic said, "I'd like you to take over at the desk for Kate for a while."

"Sure." Bella gave Hawk another quick hug before turning away. "Will I be seeing you while you're in town, Hawk?"

"Of course." Hawk smiled.

"Good." Bella smiled back. "Take your time, Kate. I can handle the ravenous crowd."

"Thanks, Bella," Kate said. "I'll only be a few minutes."

Her soft, almost smoky-sounding voice, along with her smile, caused an even stronger searing sensation in Hawk's stomach and sections south.

"So," Vic said, "how long are you going to be in town this time, Hawk?"

"I haven't decided yet. I have a room for a week." Hawk shrugged. "After that…depends."

"On what?" Vic laughed. "The weather?"

Hawk grinned. "Yeah, the weather. You know how much it concerns me." He shook his head. "No, actually, if I'm tired of the whole scene at the end of a week, I'll head home. If not, I'll make other arrangements."

"And where is home, Hawk?" Kate asked.

"Colorado," Hawk said. "In the mountains."

She laughed. "Colorado is full of mountains."

A tingle skipped the length of his spine. He drew a deep breath, willing steel to chase the tingle from his back. "I'm in the southwest corner, in the San Juans, a double jump from Durango."

"A double jump?" she said.

Vic answered for him. "Hawk's got a horse ranch in a small valley in the foothills there," he said. "I gotta tell you, this guy breeds and trains some gorgeous horseflesh."

"And I'm damned good at it, too," Hawk drawled around a quick smile.

Once again he felt that strange reaction to the conversation, a reaction he had never felt before. Hawk wasn't sure he liked it.

They chatted for a few moments longer. Then Kate excused herself to get back to work.

Unaware of his surroundings, Vic, or the soft sigh he expelled, Hawk watched Kate walk back to the hostess station, head high, her back straight, as regal as any queen.

"Attractive, isn't she?"

Vic's quiet voice jolted Hawk into awareness. "Yes," he said, shifting his gaze to his friend.

"And you're interested." It was not a question.

"Yes," Hawk admitted without hesitation.

"A lot of men are." Vic shrugged.

"I did notice she was not wearing a ring on her left ring finger." Hawk lifted his brows. "Is she attached?"

Vic shook his head. "No."

"Why do I have the feeling that if I said I wanted to ask her to have dinner one evening with me, you'd tell me she'll refuse?"

"Because she very likely would." Vic gave him a half smile. "She always does."

"She doesn't like men?" Hawk felt a sharp pang of disappointment.

"She used to," Vic answered cryptically.

Hawk's eyes narrowed. "Are you going to explain that murky statement, or am I going to have to call you out?"

Vic grinned. "Pistols at dawn, eh?"

"No…" Hawk drawled. "My foot in your rear right here in front of all your customers. So you'd better start explaining."

"There was a man…" Vic began.

"Isn't there always?" Hawk said in disgust.

"The same as there's always a woman with bitter men," Vic said. "Isn't there?"

"I wouldn't know." It was not a boast. Hawk had never been in love. He had no experience of how a relationship gone sour could rip a person up.

"You're a lucky man." Vic sighed. "Well, Kate knows in spades. She was head over heels with a guy, enough to let him move in with her after they got engaged."

"He dumped her for another woman?" Hawk asked at the thought of any sane man dumping Kate.

"No, worse than that. Not long after he moved in with her, he became abusive."

Hawk stiffened, his features like chiseled rock. "He what?" His voice was low, icy with menace.

"Not physically," Vic said. "Verbally, which is just as bad, if not worse. Bruises heal pretty quickly. Emotional scars take a lot longer."

"The son of a bitch."

"That's my take on him."

Hawk was quiet a moment. "I'm still thinking of asking her to dinner one night." He frowned at Vic. "What do you think?"

"Well..." Now Vic was quiet a moment. He shrugged. "It can't hurt to give it a try."

"You wouldn't mind?"

"Why would I mind?" Vice shook his head. "I think it would do Kate good to get out... She hasn't been since she tossed the creep out." He grinned at Hawk. "And I know you'd never do anything to hurt her."

"How do you know that?"

Vic's grin grew sinister. "Because if you did, I'd have to kill you."

Hawk roared with laughter. "Get outta here and get me something to eat...and make it good."

Standing, Vic leveled a stern look at Hawk. "You know damn well everything I cook is good. Excellent, even."

"I know," Hawk admitted. "So, go cook."

Moments later he was served a glass of red wine. Soon after the wine, the server set a steaming plate of pasta before him, with a short, folded note on the side. Hawk opened the note and chuckled. Vic had written just seven words.

Kate's days off are Monday and Tuesday.

Two

Kate didn't have time to think of anything except greeting and seating customers for over an hour. When she again returned to her station, she was both disconcertingly disappointed and pleased.

She needed a breathing break. What Kate didn't need were the thoughts of the attractive Hawk McKenna, which immediately flooded her mind.

He was just another man, she told herself. And yet he invaded her mind and senses the minute activity around her slowed. Shaking her head, as if she could physically shake the thoughts aside, she busied herself by fussing with the station. She straightened the large menus and made a production out of studying the names not crossed off on the long list of reservations. The few parties left on the list were not due to arrive for a while.

Sighing, she glanced up from the list, right into the dark eyes of the very man she had been trying her best not to think about.

She managed a professional smile. "How was your dinner, Mr. McKenna?"

He gave her a slight frown. "I thought we had agreed on Hawk and Kate."

"Okay. How was your dinner, Hawk?"

"Superb, as Vic's dinners usually are."

Kate felt the effects of his breathtaking smile all the way down to her curling toes.

"That's true," she managed to articulate around the sudden tightness in her throat. "Vic is a very talented chef. One of the best."

"I know." He nodded, a shadow of his smile lingering at the corners of his too-attractive mouth. "He was taught by another very talented chef…" He paused for effect. "His mother."

Kate laughed. It felt good to laugh with him. Too good. She quickly sobered. "I know," she said, sneaking a glance around him in hopes of finding a waiting patron. The entryway was empty.

"You expecting someone special?" he asked, obviously not missing her swift look behind him.

"No." She shook her head. "Why?"

Hawk studied her a moment. Kate felt strangely trapped, as if pinned to a board like a butterfly or some other species of insects.

"You're afraid of me, aren't you?" He was frowning again, this time in consternation.

"Afraid? Me?" She gave a quick and hard shake of her head. "That's ridiculous." She raked a slow look down the length of him, the long length of him. "Should I have a reason to fear you?" Kate was babbling, and she knew it. She just didn't know how to stop. "Do you mean me harm?"

"You're right. That is ridiculous, Kate." There was a note, a bit angry, a bit sad, in his soft voice. "I mean no harm to any woman. Why would you even think that?"

Kate bit her lip and closed her eyes. "I…I don't know…I…"

"Yes, you do." He cut her off. He drew a deep breath.

"That bastard really did a number on you, didn't he?" His voice was low, as if to make sure no one could overhear him.

Kate froze, inside and out. How did he know? Who told him? Vic, it had to have been Vic. The mere thought of Jeff, his nasty temper and his accusations caused a cold sensation in her stomach.

Dammit, she thought. She had believed she was over it, free of the memories.

"Kate?" Hawk murmured, his soft tone threaded with concern.

Steeling herself, Kate looked him square in the eyes. "My personal life is not open for discussion, Mr. McKenna. I'd like you to leave, please. I have a party of four due any minute."

As if on cue the party swept into the lobby, laughing and chattering. His face unreadable, Hawk stepped to one side, standing firm.

Kate conjured a pleasant smile and turned to face the new arrivals. "Good evening." Lifting four menus from the neat pile, she added, "Right this way."

After the patrons were seated and perusing their menus, Kate started back to the hostess station. Spotting Hawk—how could she miss him?—leaning against the side wall, she couldn't help noticing again how tall and lean and…

Don't go there, Kate, she advised herself, trying and failing to ignore the tiny twist of excitement curling around her insides.

She began feeling edgy as she approached the station. There wasn't a single person waiting in the foyer. She lifted her chin, prepared to glare at him for still being there.

Hawk didn't move but remained standing there,

leaning one shoulder against the wall, his gaze fixed on her, a small, enticing smile curving his masculine lips.

His smile set off a new sensation in her body, one so intense she reached for anger in defense.

"You still here?" she said, inwardly cringing at having stated the obvious.

Hawk glanced down, then at the wall he was lounging against, then at her. "I do believe so. At least, it looks like me." His smile broadened, his eyes grew bright with a teasing light.

Kate suppressed a shiver of awareness as he pushed away from the wall and strolled to stand directly in front of her.

"Will you have dinner with me Monday or Tuesday evening?" he asked softly.

Nonplussed, Kate stared up at him. Surprise kept her silent. Raking her mind for a reply, she decided that she simply couldn't brush him off. He was a good friend of Vic's, besides being a customer. Still…the nerve of the man. She scowled at him while fighting a sudden urge to agree.

Foolish woman. She didn't even know him, trust him. She was afraid to trust any man, other than her father and Vic. Yet she was tempted to say yes to him.

"How did you know I was off Monday and Tuesday?" she said in a sad attempt at irritation.

He cocked his head.

She couldn't blame him, when the answer was so evident. Damn him. "Vic," she answered for him.

"Yes." Hawk nodded. "I can be trusted, Kate," he said, voice soft, tone sincere. "And Vic will vouch for me. I promise not to step out of line."

Dilemma. What to do? Kate knew what she wanted to do. It had been so long, months since she'd been to dinner with a man.

Looking up at him, she stared into his dark eyes, seeing admiration and concern...for her.

Hawk leaned closer, against the station, his voice a bare, husky whisper. "Word of honor, I'll be good."

Kate relented. "Okay, Hawk, I'll have dinner with you Monday evening."

"That has got to be the hardest I have ever worked to get a date. What time and where can I pick you up?"

There was no way Kate was giving him her home address. "You can meet me here. Is seven-thirty okay?"

"Fine. I'll see you then." He raised a hand as if to respectfully touch his hat, which wasn't there. Grinning at her, he lowered his hand, gave a quick wave, turned and strode from the restaurant.

Bemused by his attractive smile, salute and even more so his laughter, Kate stared after him, kind of scared, kind of excited. Had she done the right thing in accepting his invitation, or should she have refused? Should she stay firmly hidden behind her barrier of mistrust for men?

Fortunately, Kate was temporarily relieved of the weight of the conundrum by the door opening to a family group exactly on time for their reservation.

By eleven forty-five, Kate, along with the other employees and the boss, had finished getting the place cleaned, the tables set and everything ready for the next day, Saturday, one of their busiest days.

As he did every night while the other male employees escorted the waitresses out, Vic walked Kate to her car, which was parked in the employees section of the parking lot. Kate used those few minutes to question Vic.

"Why did you tell your friend Hawk my days off?" She kept her voice free of inflection.

Vic slanted a wary look at her. "He asked. Are you angry at me for telling him?"

"No." Kate shook her head as she came to a stop next to her car.

"Just annoyed with me," he said. "Right?"

Kate met his direct gaze and smiled. "A bit, yes," she admitted. "You know how I feel about…" She paused, giving him a chance to speak over her.

"Yes, Kate, I know how you feel about men in general and what's-his-name in particular. And I respect that." He shrugged. "But Hawk isn't any man in general, and not just because he's my friend. Hawk's one of the good guys, honey." He grinned. "You know, the ones who wear white hats in the cowboy movies." His grin widened. "Besides, I warned him that if you happened to accept his invitation, and he got out of line, I'd have to kill him."

Kate had to smile. "Well, I…um…I did agree to have dinner with him Monday evening."

"Good. It's time for you to get out and about again. Flirt a little. Hawk will love it, after being stuck in the mountains all summer."

"I'm sure I'll enjoy his company, Vic." Kate said. "But I don't believe I'm ready to flirt yet, if ever again."

"Well, if not this time, then sometime. Just relax and enjoy a little." He glanced at his watch. "Now, I'd better be getting home to Lisa…before she starts getting suspicious."

"As if." Kate laughed. "Thanks, Vic. I'll see you tomorrow."

He waited until she had slid into the car, locked the doors and started the engine. With a quick wave, Vic headed for his own car.

Kate sat for a minute before pulling out of the lot. Although Vic's recommendation helped, she still felt a little nervous about the date with Hawk.

Drawing a deep, determined breath, she released the hand brake and drove away.

* * *

Two more days until Monday.

Excitement and trepidation pushed at her mind. Fortunately for Kate, Saturday evenings and Sunday brunches were always the busiest times in the restaurant. She barely had time to take deep breaths between greeting and seating patrons, never mind long enough to let herself indulge the nervous twinges playing havoc with her stomach.

Kate was relieved when it was finally time for her break Sunday evening.

She felt her entire body tighten with nerves when Vic joined her in the small employees' break room next to the noisy kitchen.

"Instead of enjoying a quiet break," he said, eyeing her critically, "you look as if you just heard terrifying news." His tone was only half kidding. "Would you like me to get in touch with Hawk and tell him you've changed your mind?"

Yes. The word immediately slammed into her mind. But Kate gritted her teeth, damned if she would chicken out.

She gave her head a quick shake. "No. I'll confess I'm a little nervous." She tried on a smile; it didn't fit. "But I have no intention of backing out of the date. I'm going to go and I'll enjoy the evening, as well." What a liar, she chided herself.

Vic's slip tightened as if to suppress a smile. She

could tell he knew exactly how ambiguous she felt about spending the evening with Hawk…or with any other man, come to that.

Fortunately, Vic changed the subject and Kate managed to maintain her composure until quitting time.

Monday, 7:25 p.m.

Kate stood next to the hostess station, chatting with Bella. She was early. She had arrived at the restaurant soon after seven. She was also nervous. She felt foolish about her anxiety, but there it was, like it or not.

Bella was seating customers. Kate was casting quick glances at the doorway, chiding herself every time she did, which by now was too often.

Kate glanced up as Bella returned to the station, just in time to see the young woman's face light up with a bright smile.

"Hi, Hawk," Bella said, quickening her step to launch herself into his open arms.

For an instant, a heartbeat, Kate felt the strangest emotion. She couldn't describe it exactly, but then, she didn't want to examine it, either, refusing to even think the word *envy*.

She allowed another word into her mind. *Breathtaking*. Hawk looked absolutely breathtaking. This evening he was dressed casually elegant in dark gray slacks, a crisp white shirt, no tie and a navy blazer.

Kate was relieved that she had taken extra time with her own attire. She had chosen a frilly-collared, long-sleeved sage blouse, a long, swirly nutmeg skirt and three-inch heels. While the days were still warm and even sometimes hot in October, the evenings dropped into the fifties and even the forties, so she had brought the same smooth fleece shawl that she had worn at work the previous night.

Bella swung out of Hawk's arms as a party of two entered. Hawk switched his dark gaze to Kate.

"Hi." His voice was soft, enticing.

Kate had to swallow before she could manage a rusty-sounding response. "Hi."

He slid a long glance the length of her body. "You look lovely."

She swallowed again. "Thank you. "Y-you look lovely, too." Good grief, Kate thought, feeling fool-ish. Had she really said that?

Hawk strolled to the hostess station, a smile flick-ering on his temptingly masculine lips. "Hungry?"

Watching his lips move, Kate felt as if the bottom had fallen out of her stomach. And in that moment she was hungrier than she'd ever been in her adult life. Yet the last thing on her rattled mind was food.

"Yes." She tried to unobtrusively wet her parched lips. "Are you?"

His eyes narrowing, he watched the slow movement of the tip of her tongue. "You have no idea," he murmured, reaching out a hand to take hers.

"W-where are we going?" Kate felt a flash of annoyance, not at Hawk, but at herself for the brief stutter again. Damn, she didn't stutter. Never had, not even briefly.

Hawk grinned. "Right here. Vic's creating something special for us."

"Here? We're staying here for dinner?" Kate had to laugh. "Why?"

His brows drew together in a dark frown. "You don't like Vic's cooking?"

"I love Vic's cooking," she protested. "It's just, well, I thought you would want to…"

"What I want, Kate," he declared, "is for you to feel comfortable with me, and I figured you would here." He smiled, then added, "With Vic to defend you."

"Right," Vic drawled, leading them to the same corner table for two that Hawk had been given a few days before. "As if I could defend her against you. I'm a chef, not a warrior."

"Cute. You're the one who works with knives." Hawk shot Vic a wry look as he held a chair for Kate. "Wine?" he asked, folding his long body onto the chair opposite her.

Pondering their odd exchange, Kate nodded. "Yes, thank you." She glanced at Vic. "What do you recommend with the meal? White or red?"

"White for you," Vic said. "I think nothing too dry, nothing too sweet. You're both at my mercy with the meal tonight."

Hawk smiled dryly. "Right. I'll have the red. Room temperature."

"You know each other very well, don't you?" Kate said as Vic retreated to his kitchen.

"Hmm." Hawk nodded, taking a sip of his water. "We roomed together at college."

"Did you serve in the military?" Her question, seemingly coming out of nowhere, brought his eyebrows together in a brief frown.

"Yeah, after college I served in the air force. What made you ask that?"

Kate shrugged. "Vic called you a warrior, so I assumed that's what he was referring to."

His brows smoothed as he gave a soft chuckle. "I flew a Black Hawk chopper, but that wasn't what Vic was referring to," he said. "The warrior reference was to my heritage. You see, my father is Scottish, but my mother was a full-blooded Apache Indian."

"Was?"

"Yes, my mother died giving birth to my younger sister, Catriona." His smile was bittersweet. "I was two and never got to know her. All I have of her are pictures of her lovely face."

"I'm sorry," Kate said, at a loss for any other words of sympathy.

The bitter tinge vanished, leaving only the sweet. "Kate, it was a long time ago. I'm thirty-six years old. Though I'd have loved to have gotten to know her, I'm over it."

Somehow Kate doubted his assurance, but she didn't push. "Catriona. That's different," she said, changing the subject.

"It's Scottish for Catherine."

"What about your father?"

"He, with help from my mother's parents, raised me and Cat. After college I joined the air force. And after Cat graduated two years later, she moved to New York, and then Dad moved back to Scotland, where he owns several business holdings." A server appeared and Hawk took his glass. "He and his second wife raise Irish wolfhounds."

"Oh," Kate said. "They're really big and kind of mean, aren't they?"

Hawk's head was shaking before she finished. "They are big, but certainly not mean. I have one. His name's Boyo, and he's a pussycat." He hesitated before clarifying. "Of course, he can get ferocious if I'm in any way threatened. The breed is very protective of his people."

Kate had to laugh. "His people?"

"Oh, yeah." He laughed with her. "Boyo believes I belong to him."

They grew quiet when their meal was served,

enjoying the sumptuous dinner Vic had prepared for them.

"Dessert? Coffee?" Hawk asked when they had both finished eating.

Kate shook her head. "No thank you. I'm too full for even coffee."

"Good." Hawk drew a quick breath. "It's nice here, but…" He took another breath. "I have tickets for a show on the strip. Would you like to go?"

Kate was quiet a moment, stilled by a little flicker inside, a combination of anxiety and expectation. As she had before, she drew a quick breath and made a quick decision. "Yes, thank you. I would."

Hawk shot a look at his watch, pushed back his chair and circled around the table to slide Kate's chair back for her to rise.

"We'd better leave. It's after nine and the show starts at ten." Hawk waved for their server. He said, "Check, please," when the server hurried over.

"No check," the server said. "Vic said this meal is on the house."

"Tom, you tell Vic I said he's a sweetie," Kate said, smiling as the young man's cheeks flushed.

After quick goodbyes to Bella, they exited the restaurant.

Three

Taking Kate's elbow, Hawk steered her to the first parking space in the parking lot. Noting the make-shift Reserved sign tied to the light pole in one corner of the lot, Kate raised an eyebrow and looked up at him.

Hawk grinned at her. "It's good to be the king," he declared quoting from an old Mel Brooks movie.

The car he guided her to was midsize. After she was seated, Kate watched, a slight smile on her lips, as he crammed his long body into the seat behind the wheel. Settled in, he slanted a look at her.

"This king needs a bigger carriage."

"You do appear a bit cramped in that seat."

He rolled his eyes dramatically. "You have no idea." He heaved a put-upon sigh. "At home I drive a big-boy truck, with a large seat and lots of legroom."

"This car is easier to fit into a parking space," she said.

"Granted, but..." He smiled at her, smugly, as he started the engine. "I don't have to park it. I'm going valet." He paused an instant before adding in a gotcha tone, "So there."

Kate lost it. Her laughter poured out of her with genuine amusement. She couldn't recall the last time she had laughed so hard, with such ease. It was even better that Hawk was laughing right along with her.

As promised, he drove them to the valet parking at one of the casino hotels. The show, by a comedian Kate had never heard of before, was in one of the smaller entertainment rooms. The room was already full when they were escorted to their table just ahead of the burst of applause as the comedian strolled onto the stage.

The man wasn't merely funny; he was hilarious...and he worked clean. He didn't tell jokes. He told life, everyday things that just about every person in the room could relate to and appreciate.

The few times Kate shifted a quick glance at Hawk during the show, she found him laughing, too. One time he winked at her.

A simple wink, and yet it made Kate feel warm all over. Silly woman, she chided herself.

Now, the show over, Kate moved to get up. Hawk stopped her with a shake of his head. "Want to go into the casino, play awhile before we leave?" he asked.

Kate hesitated. Then, remembering this was one of Jeff's favorite gambling sites, she shook her head. "Not tonight. I hurt from laughing," she said, smiling at him to soften her refusal. "He was very funny."

"Yes, he was," Hawk agreed, leading her outside. He handed over his parking ticket to the valet before adding, "And you're a lousy liar."

Kate opened her mouth, but before she could utter a protest, he said, "No insult intended."

"What would you call that remark?" Kate didn't attempt to conceal her annoyance.

The valet area was crowded with people waiting for their vehicles. Hawk moved closer to her. "Kate," he said, his voice low, private, "I'm not unconscious. I saw the flicker in your eyes when you uttered that lame excuse. For some reason of your own, you don't want to go near that casino." He raised one dark brow. "Care to tell me why?"

He stood there, so close to Kate that she could smell his cologne and the pure masculine scent of him, and the tang of wine on his breath, teasing her lips. It played havoc with her nervous system.

"No?" He smiled.

She smiled, surrendering to his smile. "It's a silly thing, I guess," she said, sighing. "I didn't want to go in there, because that is one of Jeff's favorites." She shrugged. "I prefer not to run into him."

The instant she finished speaking, as if she had conjured him up, Jeff's practiced, cultured voice sent shivers of revulsion through her.

"Well, Kate. Beautiful as ever," he said, his voice and smile much too smooth. "Imagine seeing you here. I thought you didn't like the casinos." He acted as though Hawk wasn't there.

"You thought a lot of things, Jeff," she returned, her voice as cool as she could make it. "Most of them wrong...no, all of them wrong."

Jeff's pale blue eyes went cold; his smooth voice grew a jagged edge. "Not all of them." A leer twisted his lips as he ran a quick look over her. "I wasn't wrong about your response in the bed...."

"If you'll excuse me," Hawk interjected in a menacing drawl, sliding one arm around Kate's waist. "The car's here, Kate."

Relief washed through her, but only for a moment. Jeff caught her by the arm, keeping her from moving away with Hawk. She stiffened, angry and embarrassed.

Jeff glared up at Hawk. And *up* was the word, as Hawk had a good six inches on the man. "Who the hell do you think you are?" he demanded.

"I don't think who I am," Hawk said. "I know who I am. And I don't want to know you." His drawl vanished, a soft warning taking its place. "Now, little man, take your hand off my lady."

"Little man! Your…your lady…" Jeff sputtered in anger. "You dare—"

Hawk sighed. "I. Dare. Anything." He enunciated very softly. "Now, back it up, buster, before I'm tempted to get real nasty."

To Kate's near amazement, Jeff took a step back, looking not at all like a cock of the walk, which was how he regularly portrayed himself. She watched him stare narrow-eyed at them as Hawk helped her into the car. But he blinked and took another step back as Hawk turned to stare back at him.

Although Kate couldn't see Hawk's face, she thought his expression must have looked meaner than hell, for turning on his heel, Jeff quickly strode back into the casino.

Turning her head, Kate watched, expecting to see a man ready to explode with anger, as Hawk came around the car and slid behind the wheel. To her utter surprise, she saw the brightness of inner laughter in his eyes and a grin on his rugged face. Amusement danced in his voice.

"I bluff at poker, too."

It started as a chuckle from Kate and developed into full laughter. "You're something else," she said, her laughter subsiding.

"Oh, lady, you don't know the half of it." Hawk slid his glance from the wheel after starting the car to toss a smile at her.

The tension of the previous minutes drained from Kate's body, leaving her relaxed and comfortable. For the first time since throwing Jeff, cursing and arguing, out of her apartment, and her life, she felt at ease in the company of a man.

Kate couldn't quite decide if that was good or not. She knew too well that being at ease with a man was not the same as trusting one. At this point in time, she wasn't sure she would ever again be able to trust a man, any man. It was sad, really, that one nasty male... She gave a mental shake. Forget him, she thought. He wasn't worth the effort it cost her to dwell on him. Resting her head back, she allowed her thoughts to drift.

They drove for several minutes, Kate content and mellow, before Hawk broke the mood.

"Er...Kate, are we going to drive around aimlessly for the rest of the night, or are you going to tell me where you live?"

Kate knew the mood was too good to last. "I

parked my car at Vic's," she said, straightening from her near lounging position.

"Um," he murmured, making a turn at the next intersection. "We're a little past his restaurant."

Kate gave him a startled look before glancing around at the area. She frowned when she didn't recognize where they were. "How little?"

A smile twitched the corners of his mouth. "Oh, only a couple miles or so," he said. "You looked so comfortable, I hated to mention it. Fact is, I wasn't certain you were awake."

She felt her cheeks grow warm and was glad for the dark interior of the car. "I wasn't sleeping but I was drifting a bit. It must be the wine."

"All two glasses of it," Hawk drawled. Then he sobered. "Were you thinking about that clown who was giving you a hard time?"

"His name is Jeff," she said, tossing off the name as if it didn't matter, and it truly didn't.

"He grabbed your arm." His voice had changed. It was now close to a growl, almost scary. "And if he tries something like that again, touches you again when you're with me, his name will be sh—er—mud."

She had to chuckle at his quick word switch. "I do know the word, Hawk."

"I know. Everybody does." He shrugged. "My father is a stickler for speaking politely in front of or to a lady. I feel the same way he does."

"That's nice." Kate said as he drove into the restaurant parking lot. He came to a stop next to her car in the otherwise empty lot.

Unfastening the seat belt, she turned to face him, offering her hand for him to shake. "Thank you, Hawk, for a lovely evening."

Although he took her hand, he shook his head. "I'm following you home, Kate."

"But…"

That was as far as he allowed her to get. "It's late, so I'll follow you and make sure you're safely inside." His voice was firm; he would brook no argument.

Shaking her head, she sighed and didn't argue. She got out of his car and into her own. True to his word, Hawk stayed on her tail, nearly tapping her bumper, until she pulled into the parking area of her apartment complex.

Once again he parked next to her. He got out of his car as Kate stepped from hers.

"I'll see you to the door," he told her.

"Really, Hawk, it's not necessary," she protested. She might as well have saved her breath. Without replying, he strolled beside her to the entranceway.

"Thanks again, Hawk," she said once more offering her hand to him.

"You're welcome." He took her hand and used it to gently draw her close to him. "Will I see you again?"

"Yes," was all Kate was capable of saying due to her suddenly dry throat.

"Tomorrow evening?"

She swallowed, hesitated before repeating, "Yes."

"Good." A mixture of relief and satisfaction colored his voice. "I'll pick you up here at seven-thirty, okay? We'll do something fun."

She nodded, her heart skipping when he raised his hand to cradle her face, his thumb slowly stroking her cheek. "That creep was right about one thing, Kate," he murmured, gently lifting her chin with the heel of his hand. "You are one very beautiful woman."

Now Kate's heart wasn't skipping; it was thundering.

"Hawk…I…"

"Shh," he murmured, lowering his head to hers. "It's all right. I won't hurt you." His breath whispered over her lips an instant before his mouth brushed over her mouth in what was not a kiss, but more a promise. "Good night, Kate." He stepped back. "Now, go inside and lock up."

Barely breathing and not thinking at all, Kate went inside, unlocked the lobby door and ran up the stairs to her second-floor apartment, completely forgetting the elevator.

As Hawk slid behind the wheel of the rental, he glanced up at the building just as lights went on in the second-floor front apartment.

Staring at the glow through the sheer curtains on the windows, Hawk propped his elbows on the steering wheel.

Kate.

Surprisingly, as his lips had barely touched her own, there was still a shimmering trace of her taste on his mouth, an unfamiliar twinge in his chest. He rather liked it. Smiling as a shiver raced up his spine, Hawk switched on the engine and drove back to the hotel he'd booked on the Vegas Strip.

Not twenty minutes after leaving his car key with the valet, Hawk was in bed, lost in fantasies of Kate, her lithe, equally naked form close to his.

Hawk woke suddenly, his skin chilled beneath a fine film of perspiration. He was cold, hot and frustrated. He hadn't even realized he'd fallen asleep, only to suddenly awaken right at the most intense part of his fantasy dream. He was aching with need.

Knowing he had to take drastic measures to cool the passion pouring through him, he dragged his body from the bed and headed for the bathroom.

Damn, he hated cold showers.

Kate stood at a side window, one hand flicking the curtain aside an inch or so. Gliding her tongue over her lips, she watched until she could no longer see the car.

She could taste him.

Ridiculous, Kate told herself and let the curtain

fall back into place. That mere brush of his mouth over hers had been the furthest thing from a kiss she had ever experienced. She walked to the bedroom. Why in the world would she think she could taste him? Testing, she again slid her tongue along her bottom lip and snivelled.

No, it wasn't ridiculous; she really could taste him, and she liked the taste very much. Kate feared that a real deep kiss from Hawk could very likely be addictive…like rich dark chocolate.

A real deep kiss from Hawk. She replayed the thought inside her head. Swallowing to moisten her suddenly parched throat, she began to undress, her hands fumbling with the simple routine. She mumbled a mild curse to herself.

She had just managed to remove her blouse when the phone rang.

Hawk? Kate froze, her heart beating wildly. It rang again. Not bothering to look at the caller ID, she snatched it up, nearly dropping it. Drawing a quick breath in an attempt to keep a tremor from her voice, she said, "Hello."

"Who was he?" Jeff snarled.

Kate went cold and stiff. "That is none of your business." She wouldn't so much as say his name.

"Yes, it is," he snapped back at her. "You're mine and you know it."

"I never was yours," she said icily. "And I broke up with you months ago, as you well know."

"You were in a snit." He was back to the snarl. "And—"

"No," she said, cutting him off. "You were being verbally and emotionally abusive…again."

"I'm not giving up, Kate. I know you love me." His voice was suddenly soft, cajoling, "I'll get you back."

"I've been patient up until now, Jeff," she stated flatly, finally saying his name, anger stirring in her voice. "If you bother me again, I'll report you to the police. And this time I mean it."

"Sure," he said in honeyed tones. "You mean it every time, which only tells me you don't mean it."

Kate drew a deep breath in an attempt to control her anger. How in the world had she ever thought that syrupy tone was attractive? Now it repulsed her. *He* repulsed her.

"I have only three words for you, Jeff," she began.

"Yeah, I know," he replied smoothly, interrupting her. "Like I told you, you love me."

"Go to hell." She hung up on him.

Kate stood trembling, staring warily at the phone as if it might attack her.

Damn him. Damn him. Damn him.

She had had enough. Tomorrow morning she would see a lawyer about reporting him to the authorities and would take out a restraining order against him.

Although Kate had never done so before, in case there happened to be an emergency in her family, she was so uneasy that she disconnected the landline and turned off her cell.

After she was ready for bed, she still felt shaken by the call and so she checked the locks on the front door, even though no one could go beyond the lobby without a card key. Then she double-checked the locks on the patio door and on every window.

Kate lay in bed for some time, unable to sleep. When she finally drifted off, she drifted right into a dream. Not of Jeff and fear, but of Hawk and unbelievable pleasure.

He came to her softly, murmuring of the exciting delights to be found in the joining of their bodies. She sighed in her sleep, her body moving in sensual restlessness.

She wanted, needed, ached for his touch, the feel of his mouth taking passionate control of hers, for his hard body possessing, owning, her own.

Kate woke, trembling, quivering deep inside her body, her breathing harsh and uneven. She kicked the covers away from her perspiration-slicked body. Never had she had a dream so real, so vivid that it actually brought her close to release in her sleep.

Her breathing slowly returning to normal, she

sat up, staring into the dimness of her bedroom, her mind and senses still reeling.

While it was true that it had been some time since she had been intimate with a man—she would not think his name—it seemed unreal to Kate that a dream of a man she had so recently met and knew practically nothing about, not simply a dream of a fantasy man, could affect her to her very core. Her thoughts ebbed as sleep claimed her once more.

To her surprise, Kate woke later refreshed, if still a bit anxious.

What was with her, anyway? Kate asked herself, musing on her unusual reaction to Hawk. Yes, he was extremely attractive and fun to be with, not to mention sexy as hell. But he was just another man…wasn't he?

Shying away from the thought, Kate centered her attention on the business at hand. Going to the phone, she reconnected the landline and dialed Vic's home number.

Lisa was happy to oblige with the name of a good attorney, as she had been after Kate to swear out a restraining order against Jeff ever since Kate had thrown him out of her apartment.

Minutes later, Kate had an appointment for the next morning with the attorney Lisa had recommended, an older-sounding man named Edward Bender. It was a start.

Four

Even though she knew the time of Hawk's arrival, Kate jumped when the buzzer rang from the intercom in the lobby. Fortunately she had just finished swiping her lashes with the mascara wand, or she would have had a very strange black streak across her temple.

Grabbing her purse and a Black Watch plaid wrap that complemented her off-white dress, she flipped the button and spoke into the wall-mounted receiver.

"Hawk?"

"Yes." His sexy, low voice gave her an all over tingly sensation.

"I'm coming right down."

Without waiting for a response, Kate switched on a night light, locked the door and headed for the elevator.

She had felt an attraction to him from the moment he had walked into Vic's, standing there all tall and lean and ruggedly masculine.

On the other hand, even from the beginning Jeff had appeared almost too handsome, cultured and charming. Almost too good to be true. Of course, before long, his real character had come through.

Kate snorted derisively as she pressed the elevator button. Handsome, cultured and charming was an act hiding Jeff's true nature.

As Kate stepped inside the elevator, an old adage of her mother's came to mind. *Handsome is as handsome does.* Well, for Kate, handsome had proved to be a nasty jerk when things didn't go exactly the way he wanted them to go.

"Hi," Hawk said as the elevator doors parted. "You look lovely." His eyes held a teasing gleam. "How did you know the Black Watch was my favorite of the clan plaids?"

Kate laughed. "I didn't. It just happens to be my favorite, too. And hello yourself." She grinned.

"Where are we going this evening?"

Shaking his head, Hawk cupped her elbow and led her to the car. "I thought we'd pick up where we were, before we were so rudely interrupted. Do you avoid all casinos or just the one we almost went in last night?"

"Just that one," she said and buckled her seat belt. "But I don't go to casinos very often." She smiled. "As the old song goes, I work hard for my money. But I do play occasionally."

"Table games?" He arched his brows.

"No, I play the machines only." Kate arched her brows back at him. "What about you?"

"Poker, Texas hold 'em," he answered, shrugging. "And some blackjack now and again. Ready to go?"

"Whenever you are," Kate said, and he pulled out of the lot.

He was quiet for a moment as they drove. "I don't know what scent you're wearing but I like it…a lot."

Kate grew warmer and more tingly. "Thank you, Hawk. It's the only scent I wear."

"Whenever or wherever I smell it, I'll think of you." He flashed a smile at her.

Kate was certain everything inside her was melting. She told herself she had better be careful, because this man wasn't merely dangerous, but he was dynamite. Compared to Hawk, she thought, Jeff wasn't even a firecracker.

Playing with firecrackers was one thing, but playing with dynamite… Kate shivered.

"Are you cold?" Hawk asked, noticing her shiver even though he never took his eyes from the road. "I can turn on the car heater." He reached to do so.

"No...no." Kate shook her head while offering a weak smile. "I'm fine, really, and we're almost to the strip." Jeez, she thought, if he turned on the heater, she'd melt right there in front of him.

"It does seem strange," he said. "In October here in Vegas in the afternoon, the temp can go into the seventies and even the eighties, yet in the evening it can drop down into the fifties and forties."

"It's different where you live?" she said, wanting to know every little thing about him, about his life.

He grinned. "It depends what part of the state you're in. In Denver it can get very warm during the day and cooler in the evenings. But in the mountains where I live, while we might get some warmth in the daytime, it can get damned cold at night."

"I like the mountains," she said, unaware of the wistful note in her voice.

"You're not from here originally?"

"No." She shook her head. "I'm from Virginia, near the Blue Ridge Mountains. My father runs a small horse farm."

He slanted a quick smile at her. "There you go. We have something in common."

"Horses?" She laughed.

"Hey, don't knock it. It's a start."

Kate couldn't help wondering exactly what he meant by a start. A start of what? He was only going to be in Vegas for a while, wasn't he?

Hawk surprised her by avoiding the Strip, driving to one of the older hotel casinos in town, one she had never been inside before. That is, old in comparison to the unbelievably expensive palaces forever under construction.

Kate liked it even better than the much more elaborate pleasure palaces with which Vegas abounded. For one thing, it wasn't nearly as crowded as the others.

"So," Hawk said, "what do you want to do?"

Kate was quiet a moment, glancing around her. "I think I'll wander around a bit—" she flashed a smile at him "—until one of the machines calls to me."

"Fine," he said. He paused before adding, "I think I'll wander to a blackjack table. Suppose we synchronize our watches and meet right here in, say, an hour?"

Grinning, Kate looked at her wristwatch. "Right. If I don't see you before, I'll see you then."

They had no sooner separated than Kate began to feel lonely. Silly, she chided herself, checking out the lines of machines as she strolled around.

In a bid to distract herself from thoughts of Hawk, she sat down at a machine at the end of a row. She spent several minutes studying the instructions on the three-coin machine before feeding a twenty into the money slot. She racked up eighty credits in the credit window.

Kate had played the machine for almost the full hour when she became aware that someone new had taken the machine beside her. She did not spare a glance at the person.

"Hello, Kate." Jeff's smooth voice gave her a start. "I saw you sitting here all alone and came to keep you company."

Jeff, here? Kate could hardly believe it. This casino was not the kind he frequented; he preferred the glitzy new ones that drew all the celebrities. The thought that followed sent a chill down her spine.

Was he following her, stalking her?

Scared but determined not to reveal her fear to him, Kate turned a cold look on him. "I'm not alone. I have company, and even if I didn't, I would never want yours."

"Now, Kate, we both know you don't—"

That was as far as she allowed him to go. "You know nothing, Jeff, but I'll enlighten you." She drew courage from the cool tones she had achieved. "If you aren't gone from my sight within the next few seconds, I will begin screaming for security."

"You wouldn't dare," he said. "You forget I know you hate making a scene."

"Perhaps," she admitted, "but I'll gladly make an exception in your case." She made a show of glancing at her watch. "You have exactly two seconds to disappear." She didn't look away from her watch. "One...two..."

He was off the stool and moving away from her, swearing a blue streak. Shaken by the encounter, she drew a calming breath, and the minute he was out of her sight, she hit the pay-out button and walked away with five dollars more than she'd started with.

She was hurrying back to the place where she'd agreed to meet Hawk when she spotted him at a blackjack table. She hesitated a moment but then decided to approach him, certain Jeff wouldn't try anything again so long as Hawk was near.

Coming up behind him, Kate laid a hand on his shoulder to let him know she was there. "Hi. I see you're winning." There were several stacks of chips in front of him.

"Yeah." He turned to smile at her. "You ready to leave?"

"No hurry," she said. "I'd like to watch awhile, if you don't mind me standing in back of you as you play."

"Not at all," he said, managing to keep an eye on the play of cards at the same time. "I'm not superstitious. Fact is, I like you there."

Feeling inordinately pleased and warmed by his

comment, especially after that unpleasant encounter with Jeff, Kate lightly flexed her fingers on his shoulder. The warmth flowed stronger when he raised a hand to cover hers briefly, his fingers lacing with hers.

The feeling of his touch remained on her even as the evening continued. Would his touch bring such torrid dreams again? She hoped it would banish those nightmares that only Jeff could inspire.

Five

The idea was to tire himself out enough to sleep. Hawk knew that was the only reason he found himself back at the poker tables until after two in the morning. As he had earlier in the evening, he won. But that wasn't the purpose.

He didn't even doze off, not until after four. Hell, he thought, prowling around the spacious room, popping the top off a can of light beer, he might as well have stayed at the poker tables. He stopped at the floor-to-ceiling window to stare at the glaringly bright lights along the Strip. On the street below, the traffic, both human and vehicular, was almost as heavy as in the afternoon or evening. He took a swig of the cold beer. Obviously there was more than one town in the country that never slept.

His thoughts swirled continuously, every one about Kate. Hawk sighed, "Kate." He didn't realize he had whispered her name aloud or finished off the beer. Shaking his head at his wandering mind, he tossed the can into the wastebasket.

He wanted to be with her so badly, he ached with the wanting, the raw need. His back teeth hurt from clenching them together. There were other women in Vegas; there had been plenty of them in the casino and the restaurant yesterday morning. Several of them had cast unmistakable looks of availability at him. He had ignored them.

Just any woman wouldn't do. Hawk was always selective when it came to the females he spent time with, despite the fact that he so seldom left the ranch.

This time around was different. Hawk was coming to the reluctant conclusion that the only woman he wanted to spend his time with was Kate.

And Kate had man problems, dammit.

She appeared to resent the oily guy more than fear him…but one could never really know what another person was thinking, feeling. Vic had said Kate had thrown the creep out of her apartment for verbally abusing her. And last night he had been far from pleasant.

Hawk frowned. Was the jerk harassing her? Had he been harassing her since she dumped him? Hell, that was months ago now.

When Kate had joined him at the blackjack table earlier that night, she had seemed different than when they had separated, he to play the tables and she to play the slots. It had been nothing overt or obvious. She had been quieter and slightly more reserved, not at all the woman who had laughed so easily earlier.

The wheels in Hawk's mind were rolling full speed. Had that creep approached her again between the time they parted and when she joined him at the blackjack table? Had she come to him for protection? Hmm, it was possible, and now that he thought about it, probable.

Confused by her sudden change in mood, he had slightly withdrawn. He had had such high hopes for a kiss, a real kiss, with her before she went into her apartment building.

Hope in one hand and spit in the other.

The old saying of his father's slipped through his mind. Hawk rejected the very idea that he gave up hope. Sliding beneath the covers again, he thought he had better get some sleep if he wanted to be sharp enough to catch any slight change in her attitude, because he *could* see her tomorrow.

This time he was unconscious within minutes.

* * *

Kate entered Mr. Bender's office with a heavy step that morning. The lawyer was older—close to sixty she judged—and he appeared to be the classic prototype of an old-fashioned gentleman.

She told him her problem. In turn, Mr. Bender had questions.

"Did he ever hit you, even the lightest slap?"

"No." Kate shook her head. "But...I must admit there were times when he was the most angry, swearing...I began fearing he might."

"I see. Did he ever threaten you?"

"Not outright," she said, "but in a vague, oblique way." She sighed. "I don't know how else to describe it, but he frightens me."

"Now, don't you worry, Miss Muldoon. The law will take care of this..." He hesitated, his lips pursed as if from a sour taste. "This lowlife."

Sighing with resignation at her predicament, Kate pushed herself through the revolving door.

Directly into reality. Her cell phone rang. Kate hesitated, eyeing the instrument as if it might leap into the air and bite her. It wasn't a number she recognized.

Thoughts whipped through her head, one tripping over another. Jeff...the bastard. She knew; she knew he'd track her to the lawyer's. He must have followed her.

What to do?

The phone rang for the third time. Kate opened the phone, determining to rip a verbal strip off him.

"Hello?" Her mouth was bone-dry; her voice, sharp with impatience. She fully expected to hear Jeff's angry voice in response.

"Kate?"

A silent sigh of relief slipped through her lips. "Hawk! I, uh, I'm glad to hear it's you. I had a lovely time last night," she said, trying to forget the unwanted and unwelcome appearance of Jeff, and the doubts assailing her now.

"I'm glad." Now she could hear the relief in his voice. "I wondered whether something had upset you."

"Well, you wondered wrong," she said, her tone firm. "It's been a very long time since I laughed the way I have with you these past two evenings, Hawk. It felt good." Too good.

In all honesty, and as much as she would have liked to deny it, she felt shaky at the awareness it was him on the line. She felt as if everything was smoldering inside her—and breathless, shivery. She had felt somewhat the same at first with Jeff almost two years ago. This time the feeling was stronger, more intense. No, she didn't like it at all.

She had believed herself immune to any other charmer. For Jeff had been charming and gallant for many months, right up until she had agreed to him moving in with her, his ring on her finger. For a while she had been content. Her contentment had lasted all of three months. A bitter taste filled her mouth. First Jeff had become possessive, questioning her every move when they weren't together. Then he had become verbally abusive, cursing, accusing her of being with other men, even Vic.

The warm sensations that had been inside Kate faded to cold determination. She could not, would not, go through a situation like that again.

He jumped on her last remark. "In that case, lunch?"

She had no choice but to smile, and it did feel good, dammit. And she couldn't resist, didn't want to resist, even though she feared she'd regret it.

"I've got to stop by my apartment to change. Do you want to meet me there?"

"Sure. What time?"

Kate glanced at her wristwatch, noting it was not quite twelve-thirty. "Would forty-five minutes work? You realize I'm not going to even ask whether Vic gave you the number."

He chuckled in reply. "See you then."

Within fifteen minutes, Kate was entering her apartment. Slipping off her jacket as she went, she headed for her bedroom. She removed the rest of her suit, hung it back in the closet and made a beeline for the bathroom, wanting to wash up before applying fresh makeup.

She smoothed her hair with a brush, giving it a healthy sheen. Makeup was fast and easy. She kept it light, natural looking. Back in the bedroom she was reaching into the closet for one of the outfits she wore only to work when the buzzer sounded on the intercom.

Hawk? Kate shot a look at the bedside clock. Only thirty-five minutes had passed since she'd talked to him. Pulling on a lightweight robe, she went running to the intercom.

"Yes?" she said on a quick breath.

"Ready for lunch?"

A flutter tickled her stomach, clutched at her throat. "Err…" she said, "not quite. Sorry."

"That's okay, I'll wait."

"You don't have to wait in the lobby," she said, feeling uncertain that inviting him up was wise. Still, she did. "I'll buzz the lock on the lobby door. I'm in the second-floor front apartment. Just walk in. I'll be ready in a few minutes."

"Gotcha."

That was what she was afraid of, and if he did have her, what did he intend to do with her?

Thinking she must either be nuts or self-destructive, Kate unlocked the front door and, turning, dashed back into her bedroom, shutting the door behind her.

She heard the front door open and Hawk call out, "I'm here, Kate. Take your time. I'm in no hurry."

In the process of fastening her belt, Kate had to smile. Hawk was—or at least appeared to be—so nice, pleasant. But then appearances, she reminded herself, were deceiving. She sighed, fully aware that she knew that better than most.

When she entered the living room, Hawk was standing with his back to her, perusing the books on her five-shelf bookcase. He looked gorgeous from the rear.

"See something you like?" she asked, her face growing warm from merely thinking about his tight rear.

He turned to smile at her before replying. "Now I do." He ran a slow look over her, which parched her throat and moistened other places she didn't care to think about at the moment.

"Ready to go?" she asked brightly, perhaps a bit too brightly.

"Ready for anything," he said in a tone that was darn close to a purr. "What about you?"

So am I. The thought zapped into her mind and she immediately zapped it back out. "Uhh…" She stalled, trying to think of a reply, then improvised. "Well, if you don't mind, I'm not ready for lunch…at least not in a restaurant." She dragged up a facsimile of a smile. "I'll be spending most of the rest of the day in a restaurant."

He shrugged. "Okay, what would you rather do?"

She didn't have to think about that one. "It's such a mild and beautiful day. "I'd like to spend some time outside. What do you think?" Kate watched as he pondered her suggestion for all of a few seconds.

"I think it's a great idea," he said and arched one brow. "Do you like hot dogs?"

Kate had to smile. "I love hot dogs, especially dogs loaded with chili."

"Well…" he said slowly, "how about we drive to town, park and stroll around the outside of the casino hotels. Some of the grounds are beautiful. When we're ready, we can go into one of the hotel food courts, have our dogs and, if we still have time, maybe check out some of the upscale shops."

Kate came to a halt, staring at him as if he had two heads.

"What?" Hawk said, frowning.

"You like to shop?" She managed a fake note of awe.

His frown turned into a wry expression. "I wouldn't go so far as to say I like it, but I don't mind shopping occasionally…like two or three times a year." He grinned at her.

Even as she shook her head in despair at him, Kate grinned back. "Okay. Let's roll before you change your mind."

"Good idea." As if unconscious of his move,

Hawk curled his hand around hers, laced their fingers together and led them out the door.

Kate's hand tingled with warmth as they rode the elevator to the ground floor. When the doors slid apart, she immediately felt both chilled and angry all over at the sight that met her eyes.

Jeff… What was he doing there? Her earlier fear coursed back. She could hardly miss his hand reaching for the buzzer to one of the apartments. She felt Hawk stiffen beside her, as if readying for a fight, either verbal or physical.

"What are you doing here, Jeff?" she said, trying to tell Hawk to keep his cool by squeezing his hand.

Without taking his hard-eyed gaze off Jeff, Hawk tightened his grip on her fingers.

"I came to invite you to brunch," Jeff answered, his tone of voice demeaning. "But I see you obviously have already eaten."

Steel infused Kate's back and her head lifted, propelled by pride and anger at the insult in his double entendre. A low, almost growling sound in his throat, Hawk took a step forward.

"Don't," she said, yanking his hand to hold him back. "He's not worth your time and energy." She looked at Jeff with distaste. "I saw a lawyer today. He is going to swear out an order of restraint against you."

"You bitch," Jeff snarled. "And you think that

should worry me?" His laugh was harsh, demeaning. "I should have taught you who's boss long ago."

Kate felt the simmering anger inside Hawk with the tremor that flashed through him from his rough hand in hers.

"You gutless bastard." Hawk's voice was very soft, controlled and somehow terrifying. He again took a step forward, loosening his fingers to draw his hand away from hers.

Kate clasped his arm with her free hand, holding him in place next to her.

"I'd advise you to leave, Jeff, while you are still in one piece," Hawk growled.

Though Jeff sneered and put on an act of bravado, as if unimpressed with the six-foot-six-inch Hawk, he cast a disparaging look at Kate as he turned, yanked open the lobby door, then paused to glance back this time in clear fear and anger. He glared at Hawk. "You have no idea the trouble you're going to be in." He sneered. "I have friends in this town."

"Yeah, yeah," Hawk drawled, obviously neither impressed nor intimidated. "And all of them in low places, I'm sure. You know what you can do with your threats and your friends. Get lost."

His face looking like it was about to cave in on itself, Jeff tore out of the lobby. The swiftness of his steps as he headed for his car was proof that the bigger man had more than intimidated him. He had scared the hell out of him.

"Son of a bitch," Hawk said softly between his teeth, harsh anger in his voice. Tension hummed through his taut body. He made another move, as if to follow after Jeff.

"Hawk, please don't," Kate said, tugging his hand.

He paused, but his hard-eyed gaze remained fixed on the other man until he drove away. Only then did he shift his gaze to her. "I'm not a violent man, Kate," he said, his voice still threaded with anger. "But I'll take only so much, be pushed only so far…."

"Not today," she said, smiling in hopes of cooling his temper.

"No?" Hawk raised one brow. "Says who?" The tension and anger were gone; his eyes teased her.

"Me…I…" She shook her head. "Whatever. I'm ready for a walk in the sunshine… I need a breath of fresh air after that nasty encounter."

Hawk's expression was sober, but his eyes continued to tease. "Okay, but this jaunt better be good."

"Or?" Kate asked in challenge.

"Or it won't be," he said, grinning, an invitation for her to join him.

Her relief palpable, Kate laughed.

The tension gone, they had a brief tug-of-war

over whose car they were going to use. Hawk won with the simple offer to drop Kate off at work afterward.

The hours they spent together seemed to fly by. They talked practically the entire time, except while they were devouring the chili dogs, sharing one order of French fries and sipping on iced tea.

In a boutique in the Forum Shops at Caesars, they discussed the array of colorful cashmere scarves since Hawk was considering giving one as a Christmas gift to his sister, Catriona. Kate didn't hesitate giving him her opinion.

"This is beautiful. Perfect for winter," she said, holding up a scarf in swirling shades of forest green, russet and antique gold.

His lean fingers lightly stroked the length of the soft material.

As if he were touching her, a tingle slid the length of Kate's spine in time with the stroking of his fingers. She drew a quick breath before asking, "Yes? No?"

He nodded. "I think you're right. "It's perfect. Is there anything else you want to look at?"

"No." She shook her head.

"You wouldn't like one of these scarves for yourself?"

"I'd love one," she said ruefully. "But my clothing budget doesn't stretch to cashmere anything."

From the expression that flittered over his face, Kate was afraid for a moment that he was going to offer to buy her one of the gorgeous scarves. She softly sighed with relief when he shrugged.

"Are you ready to go, then?"

"Yes," she said, glad he hadn't made an offer she would have to refuse, even one involving a simple, if very expensive item.

Kate was happy to get outside again and barely noticed where they were walking until they were in sight of where Hawk had parked the car. It was only then that she glanced at her watch for the first time since they had left her apartment complex.

An odd sensation, almost like sadness, settled on her as they drove to Vic's restaurant. Their day together was almost over. Kate doubted there would ever be another one, as he would soon be leaving for his ranch, his vacation over.

"I had a lovely day, Hawk. Thank you," she said when he brought the car to a stop in the restaurant lot. This time she waited until he opened the car door for her.

"You're welcome, Kate." His hand on the door handle, Hawk looked at her as she emerged from the car, an endearingly soft smile curving his tempting mouth. He leaned toward her. Without a thought, she met him halfway.

Hawk's kiss was as soft as his smile and gentle, with no sudden hungry pressure or demand.

Naturally, Kate wanted more, a lot more. Obviously, Hawk did, too. A low groan of protest slipped into her mouth as he reluctantly drew away.

Moving back, away from her, he dragged a deep breath into his body. Looking her straight in the eyes, he said, simply, "When?"

Kate didn't need to question him. She knew exactly what he meant. The heat radiating through her body was a dead giveaway. He wanted her. Always honest with herself, she acknowledged she wanted him just as badly. But... Why did there always have to be a but? Nevertheless, there it was. Feeling she had known him forever didn't change the fact that she had met Hawk less than a week ago, and she didn't really know the inner man, the unvarnished person.

Oh, Kate was well aware that there were women who "hooked up" with a man the same day or night of meeting him. Yet as hackneyed as it sounded, she was not one of those women.

"Kate?"

At the soft sound of his voice, Kate blinked to meet his direct stare.

"I'm sorry, Hawk," she said, disappointment tingeing her tone. "I...I'm just not sure...I..."

"Shh," he soothed, raising a hand to glide a finger along the curve of her cheek. "It's all right. I can wait." A self-deprecating smile played over his lips. "Well, I think I can wait." His smile turned teasing as he added, "I'll suffer in silent agony."

Kate had to laugh, but she felt like crying. "You really don't need to come back for me tonight. Vic will drive me home."

There it was, her feeble declaration of independence. Hawk stared at her for a moment, but she knew he had understood. She was feeling pressured and was asking him to give her some room.

He gave her a wry smile and circled the car to the driver's side. "May I call you tonight, after you get home from work?"

"Yes, of course." She glanced at her watch. "I've got to go, Hawk, or I'll be late."

"Tonight," he said, standing by the open car door.

"Tonight," she echoed, softly sighing as he slid behind the wheel and swung the door shut.

Kate made it to Vic's just in time, not that Vic would have said anything if she had been a few minutes late. While he was easygoing—the employees didn't even have to clock in—she was a nut about punctuality. Although she admitted she had plenty of human flaws, being late wasn't one of them.

Big deal, Kate thought, hanging her jacket on the coat rack in the employees' break room. So she was never, or hardly ever, late for anything. What was so great about that? She would be better served by being tough rather than prompt. If she were tough, she would have had Jeff hauled into court for abuse and harassment long ago.

But, no, she hadn't done that. She had tried reasoning with him. Ha! A lot that had got her. She should have realized early on that there was simply no reasoning with the self-indulgent, narcissistic jerk.

And Kate knew Jeff would ignore any restraining order and would do exactly as he pleased, which meant the continued harassment of her, especially after Hawk returned home.

There was only one thing she could do. Though Kate had thought of it many times, she now felt certain she had to leave Vegas. She had put off the decision because she liked it here, liked her job and the people she worked with. And she loved Vic, Lisa and Bella like family.

No, as much as she wanted to stay, she couldn't take a chance of putting her friends in danger. Kate heaved a sigh of regret and hurried to the hostess station to relieve the older woman who worked part-time handling the lunch patrons.

She was afraid the day would drag by. It didn't. The restaurant was so busy, time just flew. Kate also expected Hawk to amble in for dinner. He didn't. So, of course, not only was she disappointed, but she couldn't help but wonder where and with whom he might be spending his evening.

After they closed the restaurant, Vic walked Kate to his car. "Are you all right, Kate?" he asked, sounding concerned. "You've been awful quiet tonight."

"I'm fine," she answered, managing a smile for him. "At least I will be after tomorrow."

Vic frowned, opening the car door for her. "What's happening then?"

Kate sighed. "Jeff's been bothering me again," she said, touching his arm reassuringly when she saw him grow stiff. "It's all right, Vic. Nothing happened. Hawk was with me at the time."

Vic cocked an eyebrow. "And nothing happened? Hawk didn't do anything?"

She smiled, if faintly, looking at her hand on his arm. "He couldn't. I held him back."

Vic actually laughed. "Yeah, right. Honey, if Hawk wanted to go for him, you wouldn't have been able to hold him back."

"I said please." She gave him a sweet smile and fluttered her eyelashes at him.

"Yeah." Vic nodded. "I can see that would have stopped even Hawk." Shaking his head, he ushered her into the car. Although she knew he was bursting with questions, Vic didn't voice even one as he drove her home.

She had no sooner entered her apartment than the phone rang. Hawk. Dropping her purse onto a chair, she hurried to the phone and snatched it up.

Six

"Hello?" Somehow she managed to keep her voice calm, concealing the eagerness she felt.

"I'm sorry, Kate."

She froze, hand gripping the receiver. "I won't speak to you, Jeff."

Before she could hang up on him, he went on. "Please, Kate, listen. I mean it. I'm so sorry for what I said to you today in the lobby. I was just so shocked to see you step out of the elevator with that man, I…" He paused as if to catch his breath.

Kate frowned. He had made an odd noise. Was he crying? Jeff? Ha! Was she crazy?

He babbled on. "Baby, I can't—"

"I told you before, over and over again, not to call me that," she said, cutting him off.

"I know, and I'm sorry. I forgot. Geez, Kate, I love you so much, I can't stand it."

"Jeff. Restraining order," she said, striving for patience. "I have nothing to say to you except leave me alone."

"Damn you, Kate!"

The call waiting signal beeped. Relief washed through her.

Hawk.

She had to get rid of Jeff. "I have another call. I'm going to hang up."

"*Kate*, you will be *very* sor—" Kate pressed the flashing button. Drawing a quick steadying breath, she said, "Hello?"

"Hi." His voice was soft, intimate.

Shivering in reaction to the nasty note in Jeff's voice, Kate dropped onto the chair beside the phone table and curled into herself, trying to contain the shakes. "Hi, yourself," she said as calmly as possible. "Have a nice evening?"

"You want the polite answer or the truth?"

She dredged up a quivering smile. "The truth." Or maybe not, she thought, but it was too late to change her mind.

"Well…" He exhaled a very long sigh. "I ate

dinner…alone. I went to the pool…alone. I played some poker. I won…alone." He sighed again, so sad and forlorn. "I took a nap…alone." That last comment was followed by a groan.

Kate was holding her hand over her mouth to keep from laughing—or was it sobbing?—out loud.

He went on. "I had a late snack…alone. I played blackjack…alone." Now, as if he was having difficulty controlling his voice, a sliver of humor broke through. He cleared his throat. "I won again…alone. You get the picture?"

She opened her mouth.

He didn't wait for an answer. "Dammit, Kate, I was missing you like hell the whole time."

Kate couldn't hold it in any longer; instead of sobs, laughter poured out of her.

"Sure, you can laugh," Hawk groused, very close to chuckling. "You had friends and customers around all day and evening to talk to. You were probably even flirting with some of those nice old gentlemen I've noticed watching you as you walk away from the tables."

"What?" Kate blinked. Confusion overrode a lingering fear. "What are you talking about?" She drew an easier breath. "What nice old gentlemen?"

"The ones with the nice old ladies who aren't paying attention," he shot back at her, pausing before clarifying. "I mean, those regular patrons I've seen there every time I've been there."

"The regular old gentlemen customers watch me walk away from their tables?" How funny, she mused. She really hadn't known.

"Sure they do," he answered. "The younger men do, too, when their dates or wives aren't paying attention." He gave a short laugh. "I've been sending quite a few glares their way."

"Really?" she asked, pleased and surprised. "Why?"

"I had rather hoped I was the only one watching the gentle, sensuous sway of your hips," he murmured.

Oh my. Kate grew warm—no, hot—all over. She drew a deep, silent breath and let it out softly, all thoughts of Jeff banished.

"Kate?"

"Yes, Hawk?" Her voice was little more than a whisper of air through her suddenly dry lips.

"When?"

She swallowed to moisten her dry throat and took a look at her watch. "Hawk, it's nearly one o'clock in the morning."

"Yeah, I know...and I'm starving."

For you.

He didn't need to say it. Kate heard it loud and clear. Not allowing herself to hesitate, consider, she murmured, "I am, too, Hawk." Starving and scared.

"So?" His voice was quiet, calm, without a hint of pressure.

Kate wet her lips, swallowed again and said, "How soon can you get here?"

"Twenty-five minutes or so, maybe less if the traffic has thinned," he responded at once, sexual electricity sizzling in his tone.

"I'll be counting the minutes."

"I'm on my way." He hung up.

Determined to push Jeff's not-so-veiled threats from her mind, Kate replaced the receiver and disconnected the phone cord from the wall jack. Digging her cell phone out of her purse, she turned that off, too, before rising to go into her bedroom.

Hawk had said around twenty-five minutes or so. That was just enough time for her to have a quick shower and slip into something a little more comfortable. Simply thinking about that made her smile as she undressed and headed for the bathroom. Tossing off her clothes, she stepped into the shower, careful not to get her hair wet.

Kate was excited but nervous, as well. She hadn't been with a man in some time, and in all truth, she had never thought the act of sex was the end all and be all it was made out to be.

What if she disappointed Hawk? On the other hand, what if he disappointed her? An image of him swam into her mind. Somehow she doubted he could disappoint any woman.

Why was she taking this course now, with this particular man? She had had offers before, many times. Why Hawk? Oh, sure, he was very attractive, masculine and made her laugh.

He made her feel safe and secure.

Was that enough reason to go to bed with a man? They were practically strangers…and yet. Kate shook the thoughts away as she stepped out of the shower and stuffed the wet towel and her clothing into the wicker laundry basket in the closet.

Why was she analyzing her reasons? She was thirty-one years old; she didn't need reasons to go to bed with a man. What she needed was the man, this man, simply because he turned her on something fierce.

She opened a dresser drawer and reached for a nightshirt. No. Why bother? she thought, slipping into her silk, wide-sleeved, knee-length robe. If you're going to do it, do it right, she told herself, staring into the mirror to smooth her hair.

Makeup? Kate shook her head. No. No artifice. This was the way she looked. It was take it or leave it, Mr. Hawk McKenna.

The intercom buzzed. Kate froze, frowning at her reflection. Maybe she should quickly apply a bit of makeup, if only blush.

No. No backing out, she thought, backing away from the dresser and walking to her bedroom doorway. Drawing a deep breath, she rushed to the intercom to buzz Hawk through the lobby door.

The next instant she nearly panicked. Good grief! What if it wasn't Hawk? What if it was Jeff, coming to back his threats up physically?

The doorbell rang. Standing rigid, Kate said softly, "Hawk?"

His answer came back as softly. "Who were you expecting? The big bad wolf?"

Close, she thought. Dragging a smile to her lips, she unlocked the door and opened it for him, one brow arched. "Aren't you? The big bad wolf, I mean." Swinging the door open wide, she moved back.

Stepping inside, he shut the door, locked it, tossed aside the windbreaker he carried and stood there, leaning back against the door frame. His heated gaze took note of every inch of her body. "I wish I were," he murmured, closing the short distance between them. "You certainly look good enough to eat."

"Hmm…uh…would you like something to drink?" Her throat was dry; her voice low, raspy.

His mouth took hers, ending her question. His kiss was every bit as soft, gentle and undemanding as before…for a moment. With a soft growl deep in his throat, Hawk parted her lips with his tongue, delving, tasting every part of her mouth before plunging deep inside.

Afraid her legs would fail her, Kate grasped him at the waist, hanging on for dear life. His kiss was hot, devastating. Drowning in sensations, she slid her hands up his chest and curled her arms around his neck.

Without releasing her mouth, Hawk slowly rose to his full height, taking her with him. Her feet dangling a foot or so off the floor, he carried her into the bedroom, closing the door with a backward thrust of one foot.

Still he held her lips and her mind in thrall as he lowered one hand to the base of her spine, drawing her hips in line with his own.

Hawk's purpose was apparent and successful. Kate felt the hard fullness of him. Lost in the fiery world of sensuality, needy and wanting, she held her hips tightly to him.

"I know," he said at her sudden movement, ending the kiss to allow them both to breathe, pressing into her body.

Kate drew a deep breath before trying to speak. "What do you think we should do about it?" she said, surprising herself with her brazen response to him. Never before had she felt like this, and certainly never with…oh, the hell with *him*. He was a nothing compared to Hawk. No, he was a nothing, period.

"I suppose I could think of a few things," he drawled, his lips a hair's breadth from hers. "We could start with losing our clothes." His tongue tickled the corner of her mouth.

She hadn't known a touch so simple could cause such a burning reaction. Kate couldn't wait to find out what else she hadn't known. Eager to learn, she cupped his head with her hands, and whispering, "More, please," she roughly drew his mouth to hers.

Hawk was quick to comply. This time his kiss wasn't as long, but it was just as powerful. Breathing deeply, harshly, he murmured, "I'm going to burst out of these jeans if I don't get them off soon."

Having no idea that the smile was seductive, Kate lowered her arms and stepped back, looking directly at the spot he indicated.

"This I want to see," she murmured.

Shoes, socks and pants were removed and kicked aside before he answered.

"Well, I didn't mean literally." His gaze devoured her as he dug into a pocket of the discarded jeans, withdrew a foil packet and laid it on the nightstand.

Kate's breaths were coming out of her body in tiny puffs. Her throat felt parched. Curious, she shamefully lowered her gaze to his boxer shorts, her breathing halting altogether at the sight and size of the bulge there. She tried to swallow, was unable and had to try again. She never even saw him pull off his golf shirt.

"Not fair," he said, his own voice sounding desert dry. "I'm doing all the undressing."

Raising her glance, she gasped for breath at the sight of the width of his flat, muscled chest. She blinked as it and he moved closer. She looked up and immediately down again as he pushed down the boxers and kicked them aside.

Good grief! The man was big, absolutely beautiful in form, and perfectly proportioned. Reluctantly returning her gaze to his face, she found him watching her, as if studying her reaction to his nakedness.

"You're…you're beautiful," she whispered, staring into his smoldering gaze.

"Men aren't beautiful." There was a trace of pleasure in his voice at her compliment.

"Sure they are," she said, a wave of her hand brushing aside his rebuttal. "At least you are." She hesitated a moment before blurting out, "Anyway, *I* think you are."

Hawk stepped up close to her, his hand reaching for the belt of her robe. "I disagree with you, but I confess I did like hearing it." The belt knot loose, he gently parted the sides of her robe to glide a slow look over her body. "Now, that's my definition of beauty." Slipping the silky cloth off her, he let it drop to the floor.

Kate was hot and cold. She was shivering on the surface of her body, but a fire blazing inside.

"Hawk?" It was the only word she could manage from her dry throat. It was enough.

"Anything you want, Kate. Anything," he murmured, throwing back the bedcover and sweeping her into his arms to lay her in the middle of her bed. The next instant he was beside her, drawing her to the heat and hardness of his body.

"Another kiss," she said, moving with him as he flipped onto his back, drawing her over his chest. His hands cradling her face, he slowly drew her lips down to his. His tongue was ready for the meeting of mouths, laving her lower lip, driving her wild for more.

Feeling like a column of flames burning only for him, she shuddered at his intimate exploration of her body...every inch of her body. And all the while he murmured to her about what he would do next, sending her anticipation, excitement and tension higher and higher.

Her breathing as rough as his, moaning softly, Kate matched him kiss for kiss, stroke for stroke, thrilling at the sound of his own deep-throated moans.

"That feels so good," he whispered when at last

she took him in her hand, marveling at the thick length of him. "But be careful. Don't go too far."

"Are you sure?" Kate didn't need to ask him what he meant; she knew very well. Still, obeying an impish urge, she wriggled down his now sweat-moistened body and took him into her mouth.

Hawk's body jerked as though he had been touched by a live wire. "Kate…I…" His voice gave way to a groan and he arched into her as she laved him with her tongue. "Damn, Kate. You've got to stop now." His voice was ragged yet his hands were gentle as he grasped her shoulders and pulled her body up the length of his.

"I thought you might like that," she said, the same impish feeling driving her to tease him.

"Like it?" Heaving a deep breath, he rolled both of them over until he was on top of her. "Oh, you have no idea. I loved it."

"But…" she began, enjoying teasing him.

"But I want to be inside you," he said, settling his body between her legs.

Kate sighed as she watched him tear the foil packet, sheath himself. She arched her hips as he slowly, too slowly, slid himself inside her, joining them as one.

Dragging harsh breaths into her chest, Kate sighed with pure pleasure as he began a steady rhythm, slowly building the tension coiling inside her.

Catching him by the hips, she pulled him deeper inside her quivering body, needing more and more of him until, with a soft cry, the tension snapped, flinging her into a shattering release.

A moment later she heard Hawk exhale a gritted "whoa." And felt the shudder of his body as he exploded within her.

With a heavy sigh, Hawk settled on top of her, his face nestled in the curve of her neck. Drained, satiated, Kate idly stroked his shoulders, his back, and kissed his forehead in thanks for the pleasure he had given to her, a pleasure she had never before experienced.

She sighed with utter contentment.

"Yeah," he said in complete understanding. "That has never happened before. An orgasm as strong as that," he murmured close to her ear, which he proceeded to nibble on. "I thought the top of my head would blow off."

"If it does, you'll clean it up," she said, tilting her head to give him better access to her neck, where he was dropping tiny kisses.

Chuckling, he lifted himself up so he could look down at her. "You're something else. You know that?" Without giving her time to respond, he kissed her in a way that was every bit as hot and arousing as before.

Where did the man get his stamina? Kate wondered hazily. Feeling him growing again against the apex of her thighs, she went warm all over. How was it possible for him to be ready again so soon? she mused, every bit as ready as he was. She moved against the hardness pressing against her.

"More?" he asked, his tone soft and hopeful.

"Oh, yes, please." Kate surprised herself with her immediate and pleading answer.

This time Hawk took his time. Slow and easy, he caressed, stroked, kissed every inch of her, lingering on her breasts with maddening attention.

Moving sensuously against him, moaning low with pleasure, she speared her fingers through his long hair, holding him to her as she arched her back.

"Like that?" he said, flicking his tongue over one tight nipple.

Kate was barely able to speak but she managed to sigh, "Oh, yes." Without warning him, she pushed against him until she could slide out from beneath him.

"What—"

"Shush," she said, turning on her side to face him. "I want to play, too." Leaning against him, she gently kissed one of his flat nipples.

Hawk sucked in a breath, then let it out on a laugh. "I did say we could do anything you want. My body's your playground for the rest of the night."

Gliding one palm down his chest, Kate laughed, too.

"Sounds tempting, but I doubt I'll last that long."

Her teasing hand found its destination. "From the size of you, I doubt you can last that long."

Hawk's hand was also moving, curving over her small waist and rounded hips to the apex of her thighs. He drew a quick gasp from her with his exploring fingers.

"Oh my God!" she cried. "Hawk, stop. I can't wait much longer. I want you now."

"That's good." His voice was raw. "Because I can't hold out much longer, either."

Rolling her onto her back, he slid between her thighs and entered her. Within moments they cried out their release simultaneously.

It took longer this time for Kate to come down from the sexual high. Slowly her breathing returned to normal. She smiled as Hawk flipped onto his back, his breathing still labored.

"That was fantastic," he said, turning his head to grin at her.

Although Kate blushed, she felt a sense of deep satisfaction and just a bit of pride. She felt so very pleased, in fact, that she returned his compliment with complete honesty.

"Know what? I've never, ever experienced anything even vaguely like that." Pleasantly exhausted, she curled up against his warm, moist body and closed her eyes.

"Hey, don't go to sleep on me," he said, sitting up. "Well, you may go to sleep on me, but not until we've cleaned up under a shower."

Kate groaned in protest as he took her by the shoulders to sit her up next to him. "Hawk, please. I don't want a shower. I just want to sleep."

"Oh, c'mon, my Kate," he coaxed, sliding off the bed with her in his arms. "A quick wash, and then you may sleep till it's time to get ready for work tomorrow." Cradling her in his arms, he strode into the bathroom as if he weren't a bit tired.

He let her legs slide to the floor. "You have the silkiest skin," he said, stroking his hands over her shoulders.

"Thank you." Kate shivered with the thrill of his words and his caress. "Can we get a shower now? I'm freezing and still sleepy."

Hawk heaved a deep sigh. "Oh, okay," he groused, picking her up again and stepping into the shower stall. He turned the water on full blast, and for a few minutes it was very cold.

"Hawk!" she yelped as her shivering intensified.

He wrapped his arms around her shoulders, drew her against his still warm body. "Better?"

She sighed when she felt the heat of him and the warming water. "Much better. Now let's get this over with."

True to his promise of a quick wash, he impersonally soaped and rinsed them both. Picking her up by the waist, he lifted her out of the shower, set her feet down on the shower mat and joined her there.

Kate was the first to dry off. Dashing into the bedroom, she pulled a thigh-length, baseball-style nightshirt from a dresser drawer and slipped into it. She was diving under the rumpled covers as he left the bathroom.

Smiling gently at her, he reached for his boxer shorts and sat on the edge of the bed to put them on. When he grabbed his jeans, she stopped him.

"What are you doing?" she asked.

He slanted a curious look at her, as if his actions should be obvious. "Getting dressed."

"Why?" She frowned.

"Why else?" he answered, frowning back at her. "So you can get the sleep you were whining about."

"I was not whining," she said indignantly. "Anyway, I thought you'd stay, sleep with me." She was beginning to feel hurt and, ridiculously, used.

Hawk went dead still. "You want me to stay the night?" Hope coated his voice.

"Isn't that what I just said?" She smiled.

"You talked me into it." Smiling back, he dropped the jeans to the floor and crawled into the bed, beside her. "I'm sleepy, too." With that he settled, spoon fashion, behind her, smiling when he heard her soft sigh.

Warm and cuddling, they were both asleep within minutes.

Seven

Kate woke, immediately aware of three things: the bed beside her was empty, the clock on the nightstand read 11:42 a.m. and the tantalizing aromas of fresh coffee brewing and bread toasting were drifting into the bedroom.

She felt wonderful, better than she had in over a year or even longer. There was no tightness or tension inside her, no dread of what the day might bring.

She sat up and stretched, and discovered the ache in her thighs. She was stiff, and understandably so, after the workout she had indulged in with Hawk.

Standing by the bed, she noticed his clothes and shoes were gone. Well, at least she didn't have to worry about walking into the kitchen and finding him naked!

Hawk. Kate smiled at the mere thought of him. He was a fantastic lover and a gentle friend. He made her laugh and it felt so good just being with him.

So, go to him, she told herself. Enjoy being with him before he goes back to the mountains. Walking a bit stiffly, she went into the bathroom. After washing her face and brushing her teeth, she looked at her hair in the mirror. Disaster. Too hungry to care, she went back to her room, thinking that Hawk could just deal with it, messy or not.

Pulling on a different robe, one that actually was warm, she slid her feet into satin mules and headed for the kitchen. Hawk was standing at the counter, two plates, a knife, butter and a jar of marmalade in front of him, carefully removing two pieces of golden-brown bread from the toaster.

"Good morning, Hawk," Kate said quietly. "Did you sleep well?"

Turning to look at her, Hawk threw out one arm in an invitation for her to join him. "Good morning, Kate. I love your do," he said teasingly. "I slept very well, thank you," he added, curling his long arm around her shoulders when she stepped up beside him and tangling his fingers into her flyaway curls. "You?"

"Yes. Deeply. I don't even remember dreaming." She raised her brows. "Is one of those pieces for me?"

"There's a price," he said, smiling down at her.

"Hmm." She hummed as though considering his offer. "And the price is?"

"A kiss," he said at once.

"Oh, all right," she said impatiently. "But you should be darned glad I'm hungry." She raised her mouth to him, her lips parted.

Wrapping his other arm around her to draw her tightly against him, Hawk accepted her silent offer. Expecting one of his deep, ravishing kisses, Kate was pleasantly surprised by his sweet and gentle morning greeting.

"The toast is getting cold," he said, releasing her to tend to the bread.

Kate made a production of pouting.

Hawk laughed. "Don't start anything. You have to be at work in about three hours."

They laughed together and it struck Kate that they laughed together a lot. She and the jerk had rarely laughed easily—or together.

They sat at the kitchen table and chatted about things, common things, important things, until they had finished their toast and two cups of coffee each.

Then Hawk shoved his chair back. "I'm going to get out of here to give you time to do whatever you have to do before going to work."

He pulled her into a crushing embrace and kissed her until her senses were swimming. She was breathless and thrilled when he stepped back from her to draw a deep breath.

"Do you want me to help you with the dishes?" he asked after a moment.

"You don't have to help, Hawk." She wore a suggestive smile. "But you could give me another kiss…if you don't mind."

"Mind?" He drew her back into his embrace. "I'll show you how much I mind." He took her mouth, owned it for long seconds before again releasing it, stepping back, drawing another deep breath.

"I'll see you tonight at dinner, okay?" he said in a dry croak. "Right now I'd better get outta here before I do something I'd never be sorry for." Turning, he strode from the room, her laughter following him to the door.

After setting the kitchen to rights, Kate went back into the bedroom to remove the sheets from the bed and wash them. She paused beside the bed, then began making it instead. The scent of Hawk was on her sheets, and she wanted to sleep between them again, surrounded by his masculine smell.

Kate was all but ready to go to work when the intercom buzzer sounded.

Hawk? She frowned when she realized that his name was the first thing to flash into her mind. Well, she told herself, it was understandable.

Going to the intercom, she pushed a button and said, "Yes? Who is it?"

"Florist," a young male voice answered. "I have a delivery for a Ms. Kate Muldoon."

Hmm, she thought. Hawk? Already? Suddenly she flushed with pleasure. "I'll be right down," she said into the intercom, grabbed her purse to extract several dollars for a tip, then opened the front door and ran down the steps, too eager to wait for the elevator.

A young man stood on the other side of the lobby door, smiling at her. She flipped the lock and opened the door. "Hi. Is that for me?" she said, eyeing the large cellophane-wrapped bouquet he held in one hand.

"Yep. Enjoy your flowers."

"I will," she replied handing him his tip and closing the door behind her as she stepped back with the bouquet.

Back in her apartment, Kate went into the kitchen. Setting the pale green glass vase on the countertop, she carefully removed the cellophane to reveal dark red roses.

"Oh, my," she said, unaware she had whispered aloud. The roses, her favorite flower, were just beginning to open, and each bloom looked perfect.

Suddenly realizing she had pulled the florist's card away along with the cellophane, she rummaged until she found it. Her pleasure turned to anger as she read the card.

Kate,
I am so very sorry for my obnoxious behavior last night and recently and before, when we were together. It's just that I love you so much, the fear of losing you made me wild and I reacted badly. I know that but I beg you to please forgive me. I love you and know you love me, too. And, please don't go to a lawyer. You'd lose.
Jeff

Kate's first thought was, How did he get all that on that small card? Her second thought was, The son of a bitch.

Her anger growing into full-blown fury, she tore the card into tiny pieces, dropped them into the kitchen trash can and tossed the beautiful roses in on top of them, slamming the lid shut.

Shaking, she forced herself to take deep breaths and slowly let them out until she had calmed down.

Her gaze landing on the wall clock, Kate strode from the kitchen. She had to go to work.

Hawk made an appearance mere minutes before her meal break. The sight of him as he entered the restuarant and strolled to the hostess station, where she stood, brought a sigh of sheer relief from the depths of her being. Everything would be all right now. The thought startled her. But only until he went back to Colorado, she reminded herself.

"I'm going to miss you when you're gone," she blurted. With her surprising words, an idea popped into her head. Ridiculous, she thought, mentally shaking her head. Forget it.

"Thanks, Kate." Hawk smiled back, not a bright smile but temptingly, slumberous one. "I'm going to miss you, too. You are going to join me for dinner, aren't you? I'm not heading to Colorado this second."

Still recovering from the force of his smile, Kate had to swallow before she could answer.

He picked up two menus and arched a brow. "Will you join me?"

"Yes, yes, I will." Circling around the hostess station, she led the way to a table.

"Is something wrong, Kate?" he said after he'd seated them both. "You seem far away, distracted."

"I am somewhat. I…" she began, halting when

the server came to take their order. She raised her brows at Hawk. Strangely, he appeared to know what she was asking of him.

"We'll both have the special of the day," he said, glancing at her. "Wine?"

Looking up at him, she smiled. "No wine. I'm working." She looked at the server, Gladys, a middle-aged woman with a great sense of humor. "I'll have coffee, Gladys. Before dinner, please."

"Got it," Gladys said, turning her gaze on Hawk. "What about you, Mr. McKenna?"

"Yes, ma'am," he said. "I'll have coffee, also."

Gladys was flushed with pleasure from his respectful address when she moved away from the table.

"What's the matter, Kate?" His voice held concern. Hawk paused before continuing. "Is it something I can help you with?"

Go for it, a small voice inside her said. Kate drew a deep breath, then explained everything that had happened.

She concluded by saying, "I tore up the card and threw it in the trash and dropped the flowers in with it. Hawk…I…" She stopped when Gladys came to the table, bearing a tray with their coffees, cream and sugar.

"Your dinners will be here shortly," Gladys informed them.

Kate added cream to her coffee, gnawing on her lip as she reconsidered her decision to share her idea with him. She was certain that if she did, he'd think she'd slipped over the edge of reason.

"Hawk...I...what?" he said, gently nudging her.

Kate opened her mouth, closed it again, swallowed, then softly and quickly asked, "Hawk, will you marry me?"

Hawk was thrown for a loop by Kate's proposal. He stared at her in dead silence for a moment. She had just finished relaying the details of the harassment and the threats that Jeff, the jerk, had been using to frighten her. And then she tossed the proposal at him out of left field.

"Kate—" he began, but she cut him off.

"No." She was shaking her head. "I'm sorry. I don't know why..." The arrival of Gladys at their table with their dinners silenced her.

She started again the moment Gladys moved away.

"Hawk, forget what I—" she began, but he cut her off.

"No, I want to discuss this matter with you," he said, raising his hand, palm up, to keep her from talking. "Let's eat our dinner. We'll talk afterward."

Kate didn't say a word. She fidgeted. She drank her coffee in a few deep swallows. She picked at her food with a fork but ate little of it.

Watching her, Hawk silently decided that was enough. Reaching across the table, he laid his hand over hers, ending her mutilation of the fish on her plate. She glanced up at him, which had been his purpose.

"Kate." His voice was soft, gentle. "The poor fish is already dead. Calm down and eat. The food is delicious." He smiled. "You don't want to hurt Vic's feelings, do you?"

She exhaled and he could see the tension drain out of her rigid body. "Okay," she said, offering him an apologetic smile. He accepted it with one of his own before returning his attention to his meal.

Hawk cleaned off his plate, along with two rolls from the basket Gladys had set on the table with their dinners. He was pleased to note that Kate had consumed over half of her meal and part of one roll.

"Dessert?" he asked, wiping his mouth with his napkin. "More coffee?"

"Coffee. No dessert," she said, offering him a tentative smile.

He smiled back, feeling relaxed, hoping she would relax also. "Coffee it is." Before he could so much as glance around to locate Gladys, she was there, a coffee carafe in hand. She refilled the cups, collected the dinner plates and was gone again, leaving them alone.

As there were diners at the next table, Hawk kept his voice low. "Okay. What's the deal?"

"Forget it," Kate said, once again shaking her head. "It was a stupid brainstorm. That's all."

"C'mon, Kate," he said, lowering his voice even more. "We were lovers last night. You can tell me anything, even your stupid brainstorm." His smile was sweet. "I promise I won't laugh."

His efforts paid off when she returned his smile. "Okay. Thanks, Hawk." Kate took a deep breath, as if drawing courage into herself and quickly blurted out, "I asked you to marry me to get out of Vegas for a while and away from Jeff. I'm sorry. I am at the end of my rope and scared. I didn't give a thought to the fact that I'd be using you, and that was unfair of me."

"Why not just report Jeff to the authorities?" Hawk asked reasonably.

"I did." Kate shuddered. "I should have done something when he continued to bother me after I tossed him out. I realize that now. But I was so sure he'd eventually give it up and leave me alone. I thought the restraining order would finish it." She drew a tired-sounding breath. "My mistake and now I'm paying for it."

Hawk was shaking his head. "But you talked to that lawyer yesterday. Call him or the police and tell them Jeff has threatened you."

She shook her head. "You don't understand. Jeff told me he has contacts, friends, some in court, so to speak. This is Vegas. Some of those friends might not be so friendly."

That gave him pause. His expression turned stony.

"So you decided to skip town for a while...with me?"

"No." She heaved a sigh. "The idea that stormed my brain was to ask you to marry me and remain married for a while, maybe four months or so, and to make sure Jeff hears about it. I guess I was hoping that after a time, he'd give it up and find someone else to abuse."

"Uh-huh," Hawk murmured, pondering her explanation. "And did your brainstorm come with any information for me as to how this would work?"

Kate frowned. Damned if she wasn't gorgeous, even with a scowl on her face. "Such as?" She was now staring at him through narrowed eyes.

"Hey, kid, don't look at me as though you want to strangle me." He narrowed his eyes right back at her. "You started this, you know."

Closing her eyes, Kate seemed to deflate. "Yes, I do know. I'm sorry, Hawk. Just forget it. I know I have no right to dump my troubles in your lap."

Deciding he was a damn fool, Hawk smiled and said, "I didn't say I wouldn't do it, Kate. I just want to know what exactly you had in mind."

Eight

Kate was stunned and couldn't find her voice for a moment. "I…uh…as I said, I was thinking about a temporary arrangement, say four to six months."

Hawk's brows went up in question. "You're not suggesting we get married and stay here in Vegas for that amount of time, because if—" That was as far as he got before she cut in.

"No, of course not," she quickly said. "I know you have a ranch to run."

"That's right," he said before she could say any more. "And I'm going to have to get back soon." He only paused a second before continuing. "Look, I was thinking of leaving this weekend…."

"Oh…" she replied, disappointed.

"No, don't go jumping to any conclusions, Kate. Let me finish. Okay?"

She nodded in agreement and flicked a hand, indicating he should continue.

"Good." He smiled.

Kate felt some of the tension leak from her spine. She smiled back at him.

"First of all, though I said I was thinking about flying out this weekend, I don't have to go. I have an open-ended ticket." He paused again, this time to take a swallow of his cooling coffee. "Now, tell me what you have in mind."

"Thank you, Hawk," she said and rushed to convey the details before he could change his mind. "If you're agreeable to my proposal, I thought we could get married here in Vegas, making sure Jeff hears about it. You could then go back to Colorado immediately if you wanted to."

Hawk narrowed his eyes at her. "And you stay here in Vegas? That's not going to convince anybody."

"No, no. If you'd prefer I didn't go with you, I would find another place to stay. Maybe my father's farm in Virginia, although I'd really rather not go there."

"Why not?" he asked. "It seems reasonable to me for you to go there without the farce of a wedding."

Kate was starting to feel queasy. He wasn't going to agree to her plan, which she was starting to think was a bad one from the beginning. Smothering a sigh, she went on to explain.

"My mother died when I was in high school," she said, her voice dull. "I didn't go to college as planned but stayed home to keep house for my father. I liked the work. Cooking, cleaning, keeping the farm accounts on the computer." She paused to sip her coffee.

"You didn't resent not going to college?" Raising his coffee to his lips, Hawk watched her over the rim of his cup.

"Oh, for a while, sure, but I accepted it." She smiled. "I didn't want my father to do everything around the farm and the house by himself."

"No siblings?"

"No, at least not then. I now have two, a brother, Kent, and a sister, Erin."

Hawk smiled in understanding. "Your father remarried, and you found out you were not an exception to the rule."

Kate frowned. "What do you mean? What rule?"

"That two women can't live in harmony in the same house."

"I did try," she said defensively. "Well, maybe I didn't try hard enough." She gave him a wry smile. "I had everything the way I wanted it." She sighed. "But you know the old saying…a new broom sweeps clean."

"Hmm…" Hawk nodded. "So you took off for parts unknown. Right?"

"Yes. My father had insisted on paying me, and since I really had nothing much to spend money on, I had quite a bit saved." She shrugged. "I had a car of my own and took off to see something of the country. I landed, all but broke, here in Vegas and got lucky." She smiled. "Not in the casinos but by meeting Vic."

"And your brother and sister?" he asked, lifting a brow.

"Oh, I hung around, gritting my teeth, until after Erin was born. She's the youngest."

"You don't like kids?"

"I love kids," she said. "I just didn't want to spend years raising another woman's kids, or even helping, to tell the truth."

"Okay, so you don't want to go back to Virginia," he said. "And that brought on the idea to go back to Colorado with me?"

"Hawk, really, let's just forget it," she said, now feeling sorry for presenting the idea. Pushing her chair back, she stood up before he could rise to help her. "Look, Hawk, I'm an idiot. Just forget I said anything. Okay?"

"No," he replied mildly. "I'm still ready to hear

the rest of your plan. I'll be waiting in back tonight when you go for your car."

"But, Vic will be there," she protested.

"So?" Hawk shrugged, drawing her gaze to his wide shoulders. "I'll say hello and good-night." He grinned. "That is, if I may follow you home."

Like the fabled phoenix, Kate's hopes rose from her ashes of defeat. "All right, Hawk. Not only may you follow me home, but you may come in for a drink."

"Now you're talkin'," he said. "You'd better get on the ball before Vic fires you."

"As if," Kate shot back at him as she hurried back to the hostess station.

Hawk left soon after. He didn't stop at the hostess station but rather touched his fingertips to his lips and blew a kiss at her. "See you later," he called, striding from the restaurant.

Kate couldn't wait. She wanted this over with. Her nerves felt like a mass of tangled live electrical wires. Fortunately, the rest of the night passed swiftly. There was only one hitch.

Close to quitting time, Kate's cell phone beeped with a text message. It was from Jeff and contained the same garbage as before: I'm sorry. Forgive me. I love you. And I know you love me. So don't do anything stupid, and call off the lawyer.

Exhaling, she lifted her hand to delete the message, then paused, deciding to keep it instead. She'd show the message to Hawk. Maybe, just maybe it might convince him to help her.

Hawk was leaning against his rental car when she walked across the parking lot. Good heavens, he was one hunk of a man. Kate felt a chasm yawning inside her, a crevasse of longing and want. Being with him last night had been more than she had ever imagined making love with a man could be.

Love? Kate nearly staggered at the thought and came to an abrupt stop. No. She shook her head and straightened her shoulders. Love was an illusion; she had learned that the hard way. What she and Hawk had shared had been sex, great sex, but sex all the same. And in all honesty, she wanted to share it with him again.

"Hey," he called, drawing her from her musings. "Why are you just standing there?" Pushing himself upright, he started toward her. "Are you all right?"

"Yes," she answered, getting herself moving again. "I'm fine. I...er...was thinking."

"Where's Vic? I thought he always walked you to your car." The gentleness in Hawk's eyes had been replaced by a frown.

"He's doing some paperwork. He was going to escort me out here, until I told him you would be here." Smiling, Kate unlocked and opened her car door. "I think I'll go home now," she added, sliding behind the wheel before glancing up at him. "Are you going to come?"

Hawk groaned. "Oh, lady, that is a loaded question, especially as I'm feeling loaded for bear already."

Cringing inside due to the unintentional double meaning of her question, Kate flushed with embarrassment. She felt foolish and not too bright. Not having a clue how to respond, she turned the key in the ignition, firing the engine to life, and began backing out of the space.

Laughing softly, Hawk strolled back to his car. Kate saw him squeezing his long body inside as she drove past him and into the street.

Although Kate couldn't tell if he was following her during the drive home, Hawk pulled his vehicle alongside her car just as she was stepping out of it. The devil was still smiling.

"I amuse you, do I?" she asked, swishing by him to the entrance to the building.

"Oh, Katie, you have no idea what you do to me," he said, standing close to her, whispering in her ear.

Kate's heartbeat seemed to skip and her breathing grew shallow. Inside the lobby her hand trembled, so she had trouble getting the key into the lock.

"You want me to get that for you?" Hawk's expression was somber, but amusement laced his voice.

"No, thank you," she said through gritted teeth, stabbing the key into the lock, turning the knob and striding through the lobby to the elevator.

Hawk was blessedly quiet until the elevator doors slid shut, closing them in together. "You angry at me?"

Growing warm inside, Kate shot him a glaring look. "Are you trying to make me angry?" Her attempt to sound harsh failed miserably.

The elevator jerked to a stop, the doors slid apart and Hawk stepped out of the car, turning to hold a hand out to her. "You want to come?" he said, his lips twitching with laughter.

Ignoring his hand, head held high, Kate walked past him, saying smartly, "Grow up, McKenna."

His lips no longer twitching, Hawk roared with laughter. He laughed all the way through the living room to the kitchen, where Kate stopped, spun around and placed her hands on her hips.

"Do you want a drink or not?" she demanded, trying mightily to control her voice.

"Yes, ma'am," he replied nicely.

Kate shook her head. "You are something, Hawk," she said, her mock frown giving way to a flashing smile.

He strolled to her, shrugging off his jacket and

tossing it over a chair on the way. Coming to a halt in front of her, he lifted the wrap from her shoulders, sent it flying on top of his jacket and raised her head with his hand to rub his rough thumb over her parted lips.

"You think so, huh?" he said, low and sexy. "Well, I think you're something, too. Something special."

Oh…oh…Kate's senses were going crazy. Her lips tingled from his touch, burned for the taste of his mouth on hers. Her entire body ached for his. Hawk. His name echoed through her mind. Hawk.

Closing her eyes to shield herself from the heat glowing in his, Kate gave herself a mental shake, telling herself to get it together. Before anything else, they had to talk, discuss the suggestion she was now sorry she had ever thought of, never mind mentioned to him.

"Uh…a drink," she said, her heart racing as she stepped back and turned to the refrigerator. "What would you like? Beer, wine or something stronger?"

"What are you having?" He smiled. She feared his smile was for her sudden ineptness.

"Well, as I don't often drink beer and never drink the stronger stuff, I'm having a glass of wine." *And I can't get to it soon enough,* she thought. Opening the fridge door, she withdrew a bottle of white zinfandel. "What can I get you, Hawk?"

"Do you have any red?" He was close, too close, peering over her shoulder.

"Yes, on the rack at the end of the countertop." Kate sighed with relief when he moved away from her.

They carried their wine into the living room. Kate motioned for Hawk to have a seat, while she kicked off her shoes before curling up on a corner of the couch. Her pulse rate increased when he chose to settle at the other end of it.

"Okay," he said, taking a swallow of his cabernet. "Tell me exactly what you had in mind."

Kate set her glass on the table next to the couch because her hands were shaking again. "I did, Hawk. I asked you to marry me."

One of his brows shot up. "Kate, tell me what you had in mind," he repeated concisely. "Were you thinking of a convenience marriage, one that is purely platonic?"

"Oh, no," she said at once. "I'm… I wouldn't dream of asking that of you. I had thought, as we seemed to be getting along so well, we could deal with each other for maybe four to six months."

"Live together, work together, share the same bed for half a year? Then go our separate ways, still friends, no harm done?"

Feeling her face grow warm and wanting to look away from his direct, riveting gaze, Kate held her head high, drew a steadying breath and answered, "Yes."

He was quiet for a moment, a long moment, staring into her eyes as if searching her soul. Kate held her breath.

"Okay, you've got a deal." Smiling, Hawk raised his glass to her in a silent salute.

A tremor still rippling through her body, Kate grasped the stem of her glass and returned the salute. "Thank you." Her voice was rough, barely there. She gulped a swallow of wine.

His nearly empty glass in his left hand, Hawk slid down the length of the couch to her. He held out his right hand. "Shake on it?"

Shivering, almost giddy with relief, Kate set her glass aside and placed her palm against his. His fingers curled around her hand. They shook, and then with a light tug, Hawk pulled her to him. He murmured, "A shake and a kiss. That will really seal the deal."

After reaching across her to set his glass next to hers, he drew her into his arms and captured her mouth with his own in a searing kiss.

Sealed indeed. The thought, recognizable if fuzzy, floated through Kate's mind. Or was she herself floating? She didn't care, not while Hawk was igniting a fire deep inside her with his devouring kiss.

When Hawk drew his mouth from hers, Kate

found herself stretched out on the long couch, with Hawk stretched out next to her, or rather practically on top of her.

How did she get into that position when she didn't remember moving? How had Hawk managed the move without her noticing? Did it matter at all?

No. The answer was there, at the forefront of her mind. The only thing that mattered was that she was there with Hawk, secure and safe in his arms.

"That was some seal," he murmured close to her ear, stirring all kinds of delicious sensations throughout her entire body. "But maybe we should do it again…just to make sure."

He didn't give her time to answer. She didn't need time. Kate's lips were parted, ready and eager for the touch of his mouth to hers.

A second later there was a muted beep. Breaking off the kiss, Hawk raised his head to frown at her. "Was that your cell phone, or am I hearing things?"

Heaving a sigh, Kate pressed her palms against his chest. "Yes, please let me get up."

He groaned. "Can't we ignore it?" Still, he shifted, sliding from the couch to the floor.

Scrambling over him, she searched around for her purse, which she'd dropped absentmindedly when she'd come in. Finding the purse on the chair just inside the door, she dug out her cell, certain about who was calling before she looked at the display.

She was right. Softly echoing Hawk's groan, she returned to where he was lying on the floor, now with his hands behind his neck, cradling his head.

"Don't tell me," he drawled. "The sky is falling and we must run and tell the king."

Flipping to the text message she'd received earlier from Jeff, she handed the phone to him.

Hawk skimmed the text message and snorted, but before he could speak, she took the cell phone from him and flipped to the text message she'd just received, then handed the cell back again.

Before reading the new message, Hawk jack-knifed to sit up. Shaking his head, he skimmed the text message. Then, tilting his head, he glanced at her and said wryly, "This clown has a one-phrase song, doesn't he?"

"Yeah," Kate answered, sighing. "He always has. Cyrano he's not. More Scarface. Now, do you see why I'm ready to skip town, so to speak?"

"Yes, but can't this lawyer you've hired take care of it?"

"Hawk, you've read those text messages. If Jeff has the powerful friends he claims to have and I feel certain he does, I really don't believe he'd spend more than a few hours in the lock-up, if that."

Hawk smiled. "Look, Katie, actually don't look so down and defeated. We've just sealed a contract of sorts. We can be in Colorado within a week."

"It will seem awful quick to everyone." She tried a smile and was pleased when it worked. Hawk was very reassuring. "I'll talk to Vic tomorrow at work. I'll explain the situation to him."

"No, you won't." His tone was flat, adamant.

Kate blinked. "Why not?"

"We're going to pull this off like the real thing," he said in the same tone as before. "You know, love at first sight, head over heels, the whole razzle-dazzle. We do have this physical attraction going for us. I'm sure we can appear the picture of not-so-young love."

"I beg your pardon," Kate said indignantly. "Speak for yourself when it comes to age, mister."

Hawk grinned. "You know what I mean, woman. Neither one of us will see our early twenties again. Hell, I won't see my early thirties again."

Suddenly relaxed and easy with him, Kate nodded. "I suppose you're right. That would be the best way to go about it. While I do want the news of our marriage to get back to Jeff, and it will, the chances of the truth getting to him as well are too high even if I tell only Vic."

"I know." Hawk nodded. "Vic would tell Lisa, and who knows where the information would go from there."

"You're right," Kate agreed. "I certainly wouldn't want Jeff showing up at your place."

"Ahh…Katie, you won't have to worry about that. I'm certainly not afraid of him. Besides, I'm a crack shot with a pistol or rifle. I have a foreman and a wrangler who are almost as good with a weapon as I am. Added to that, I have a dog, a very big dog that can bring down a wolf…or a man if necessary."

Kate stared at him warily, not sure if he was putting her on or not. "You wouldn't…" She didn't finish; she didn't have to. Somehow she knew he would if necessary.

"Shoot a man?" he asked. "I did, while I was in the air force. I didn't like it. It was him or me. Sucker lived."

Kate could accept that answer. She nodded. "Okay, we do it your way. I'll simply say it didn't work out when in four or six months I return to Vegas…if I decide to return to Vegas." Before she could as much as raise a hand, she yawned.

"The mood's gone, isn't it?" Hawk looked and sounded disappointed, but his smile held understanding.

"I'm afraid so," Kate admitted. "I'm very tired. Stress, I suppose."

"I can imagine, being bugged and frightened by that SOB." He got to his feet. "Okay, I'm leaving now. I'll meet you at the restaurant tomorrow. We should be together and have our act together when we talk to Vic. That work for you, Kate?"

"Yes, Hawk, that works for me."

He went to the door, Kate behind him. At the door he turned to gaze into her eyes.

"One kiss?" he asked.

Her answer came with the lift of her head. His kiss was warm and gentle and comforting.

"Sleep well, Kate."

"You, too, Hawk."

Right, Hawk thought. He'd be lucky if he slept at all. What had he just committed himself to? Marriage? Sure, he had thought maybe someday, with the right woman. But he had never met that right woman.

Pulling into the line of cars at the valet service at his hotel, Hawk unfolded himself from the car, handed his keys to the valet, accepted his receipt and strolled into the casino.

Since he was positive he wasn't going to sleep well, Hawk decided to pass some time playing poker. Within less than an hour, and with the loss of a couple hundred-dollar bills, he pushed away from the table and went to his room.

Standing sleepless once more at the floor-to-ceiling window overlooking the busy Strip, Hawk sipped the beer he had removed from the small in-room bar, contemplating his future, at least the next four to six months of it.

Starting tomorrow afternoon he had to play a man madly in love with Kate Muldoon. He smiled. Well, it shouldn't be too onerous. Kate was a lovely woman, easy to be with, a comfortable companion and fantastic to be with in bed. In truth, she was a wonderful woman to make love with.

Love.

Was it possible for a man used to being on his own for the most part ever to find real love...if there was such a thing? And, if he should find that woman, would she be willing to spend the major part of her life stuck with him in the lee of mountains located in the back of beyond?

Hawk sighed, wondering if Kate, never mind any other woman, would even last as long as four months.

Hawk was, at that point in time, firmly stuck between anticipation and a strange sensation of something he couldn't put a name to.

A wry smile shadowed his mouth. If nothing else, Kate being at the ranch should discourage Brenda, the daughter of Hawk's foreman, Jack, from her intentions, whatever they were, in regard to him.

Nine

Fortunately Hawk had warned Kate that the ride would be bumpy after they left the macadam road. His truck was a big workhorse, and it had been comfortable up until he turned onto the private dirt road.

"Almost home now," he said, smiling at her while keeping his eyes on the excuse for a road. "Are you okay?" Obviously he had noticed her death grip on the handle mounted above the door window.

"I'm fine," Kate answered. "Or I will be as soon as we're there and I can move around again."

"Won't be long now." He hazarded a quick glance at her. "I imagine you're tired."

"A little," she said wryly. "It's been a pretty hectic day."

He laughed. "It's been a hectic week."

"Yes." A tire hit a pothole, and Kate's butt lifted from the seat for an instant, landing with a painful jar to her spine.

To her mind, they couldn't get off this miserable road fast enough. But, all things considered, the past week had gone by smoothly and swiftly.

The day after Hawk had agreed to her marriage idea, he had shown up at the restaurant moments after she had arrived for work. Together they had sought out Vic. They both knew he had to be convinced that they had almost immediately fallen in love, which wouldn't be a snap, as Vic was a very shrewd man.

The performance began with Hawk asking Vic if they could talk in private. Readily agreeing, though eyeing both of them with a curiosity bordering on suspicion, Vic led them into his small office.

"What's up?" he asked, getting directly to the point.

Encircling her waist with his arm, Hawk took over. "I'm stealing your hostess away, Vic."

Vic looked from one to the other, his suspicions now completely awakened. "What exactly do you mean by stealing Kate?" His gaze settled on her. "You want the day off to spend with the warrior here?" He indicated Hawk with a jerk of his head.

Pulling her closer to him, Hawk answered for her. "No, Vic, she doesn't want the day off to spend with me. Kate's going to leave to spend the rest of her life with me at the ranch."

"What the hell?" Vic exclaimed, his expression a mixture of shock and disbelief. "What are you talking about, Hawk? Is this some kind of a joke?"

"You know me better than that, Vic," Hawk answered. "I wouldn't joke about something this serious. I love Kate, I'm going to marry her as soon as possible and I would like you to be my best man."

His expression now oscillating between delight and confusion, Vic stared at Kate. "Is he serious? No, I can tell he's serious. What about you, Kate?"

"I'm very serious, Vic," she said, her voice soft but rock steady. "I love him." Kate turned to gaze up at Hawk in what she hoped was close to adoration. In truth, it wasn't difficult....

She had no time to contemplate the questions rising to nag at her mind. Without further probing, Vic let out a whoop and snatched Kate from Hawk to give her a big brotherly hug.

"Of course I'll be your best man, chump," he told Hawk. "Hell, I always was the best man."

"Not in this lifetime or any other," Hawk retorted, extending his right hand to Vic. "We want to get married as quickly as possible." He pulled Kate gently from Vic and back into his arms. "Don't we, Katie?"

"Yes, we do," she whispered, lowering her eyes and easily managing a soft sigh.

Vic was grinning and rubbing his hands together. Kate thought she could almost see the wheels rolling inside his head. "Okay, I have an idea."

Kate smiled. Vic always had an idea and was usually dead right with it.

"Go on," she said.

"I was sure you would," Hawk drawled.

Vic looked at Kate. "Were you thinking of getting married in one of the hotels or chapels?"

"Lord no," Kate yelped.

Vic smiled happily. "I was hoping you'd say that. Now, would you like to be married right here, in the restaurant, with the customers as witnesses?"

"Yes!" Kate and Hawk declared in unison.

"Then go do what you have to do," Vic said, flicking a hand to send them away. "I'll take care of everything."

"But…" Kate protested, "don't you need me at the hostess station?"

"We'll manage." Vic hugged her again. "Go. Be together. I have things to do, people to talk to, the first one being Lisa."

"Oh, that reminds me," Kate said. "I must call Lisa to ask her to be my matron of honor."

"I'll take care of that, too." Vic grinned. "She is

going to be so excited. I can't wait to tell her. So, kids, get lost. Come back for supper."

Kate and Hawk went shopping, though not together. She went shopping for a special dress. He, she found out later, went shopping for wedding bands…plural. Kate couldn't have been more surprised days later, when after Hawk placed a gold band on her finger, Vic handed her a matching band to slide onto Hawk's finger.

It was a beautiful wedding. After sending Bella shopping for decorations, Vic had drafted all the employees, and any of the customers who wanted to help, to festoon the restaurant with yards of white tulle and dozens of white silk flowers. Everyone had enjoyed every minute of the fun, and when they had finished, the decorations had looked so good, Vic had decided to keep them up permanently.

Kate smiled in remembrance of the serious, fun but long wedding day. She and Hawk had left the party, still in full swing, just in time to catch the flight to Colorado that he had booked them on.

Now, tired to exhaustion, Kate was relieved when Hawk steered the truck onto a smoother surface before coming to a stop in front of a large ranch house with a deep porch that ran the entire width.

Pulling the hand brake, Hawk heaved a deep sigh

and turned to smile at her. "I'm dragging, Kate. What about you?"

"I feel the same," she said, sighing as deeply as he had. "Why are there lights on in the house?" she asked, frowning. "I hope you don't have company, because I'm light years away from entertaining tonight."

"I only rarely get company, Kate, and never without forewarning." Pushing his truck door open, he jumped to the ground. "I contacted my foreman to ask him to turn on the lights for us."

"Oh, okay." She turned to open her door only to find him coming to a halt beside it. He offered his hand to help her out, and she gratefully accepted, knowing full well there was no way she'd jump out the way he had. She'd be happy if she could walk straight after the long and bumpy ride from the small airport.

Kate didn't need to walk. Hawk swept her up into his arms, drew her from the truck and carried her up the porch steps. He paused to turn the doorknob and nudge the door open with one foot before carrying her into the house, which would be her home for the next four to six months.

"You left the truck door open," she said after he set her feet firmly on the floor.

"Yeah, I know." Hawk smiled. "Welcome home, Kate. And make yourself at home. Walk around to

lifting from her suitcase the gorgeous off-white dress she had found in one of the upscale shops in Hawk's hotel, she shook it out and neatly draped it over the back of the club chair. Quickly stripping off her jeans, sweater and underwear, she stepped into the shower. She gave a long sigh of pure pleasure as the water flowed over her tired body. Oh, it was sheer heaven.

Kate could have stood under the spray forever if it hadn't been for the water beginning to run cold and for the fact that Hawk was waiting for her.

After drying off and quickly blow-drying her hair so that it was only slightly damp, Kate pulled out the panties, nightgown and lightweight, thigh-length robe she always packed in her carry-on bag. Digging out a brush, she smoothed her riot of curls the best she could. As she left the bedroom, she decided she owed it to Hawk to sleep there that night and every night, and she realized that she wanted to, as well. Kate quietly walked barefoot to the kitchen.

Although she didn't know how Hawk heard her enter, he must have, because he turned, raising that one brow as he gave her robed figure and still damp hair the once-over.

"I couldn't resist your shower," she explained. "I felt kind of yucky."

"Yucky, huh?" He smiled, warming her from the outside in. "You smell good…like soap or shampoo."

Kate returned the smile. "Both, I think." She inhaled. "Something else smells good."

"It's what my father always calls comfort food. I'm heating soup and making grilled cheese sandwiches."

"Tomato soup," she said, inhaling again. "The best comfort food."

He shot a quick grin at her. "It's about ready. Have a seat."

Kate was about to ask him if there wasn't something she could do to help when she glanced at the table and found that it was set for two, with wine in stemmed glasses and water in sturdy, heavier glasses.

"It looks like you're pretty handy in the kitchen," she observed, seating herself at the table.

"I've been here alone, except for the occasional guest or two, for almost ten years." Carrying two soup bowls, he crossed to the table and set one in front of her and the other at the place setting opposite.

"Ten years," she repeated, surprised.

"I quickly learned to cook and take care of myself."

He smiled, turning to the countertop to pick up two luncheon plates. "I've got a shelf full of cookbooks *and I use them, too.*"

"Books…books, damn," Kate said, grimacing. "I packed up all my books to go with the things I put into storage." She glanced at Hawk, to find him watching her in apparent bemusement. "Like Jefferson said, 'I cannot live without books.'" She quoted the author of the Declaration of Independence. "And I'd wager the closest bookstore is in Durango. Right?"

"Most likely. I've never checked," he drawled. "But don't fret, Katie. There's always Amazon. Besides, I've got a bookcase jammed with both fiction and nonfiction hardcover keepers." He smiled. "You can spend the winter curled up with a book, warm and safe from the elements."

"Not on your life." Kate gave him an indignant look. "I never intended to have a vacation here. I haven't the temperament or the patience to lounge around all day while other people work." She paused for a breath, noticing Hawk appeared mildly taken aback by her outburst.

Kate lowered her voice. "I'm sorry," she apologized. "But I want to help out with whatever I can. Be useful, you know? Don't forget, I was raised on a working farm."

His lips twitching, Hawk held up his hands in surrender. "Okay, if that's what you want, I'll put you to work." The twitch gave way to a smile. "So, now, do you want to negotiate salary?"

Kate's head snapped up, chin thrust out; her spine stiffened. "Are you looking for a fight?"

Leaning back in his chair, Hawk erupted with laughter. When he could breathe again, he teased, "Ahh, Kate Muldoon McKenna, you are a fiery one, aren't you?"

Kate flushed and smiled at the same time. Hearing him call her McKenna sent a tingling chill through her. After the past crazy days reality finally hit her. This wasn't a dream or make-believe. She was Hawk McKenna's legal wife, if only on a temporary basis. *His*. In a weird way, after knowing him not even two full weeks, Kate kind of liked the idea.

The ghost of his smile still played over his mouth. "What's going on in that busy mind of yours?"

Kate returned his smile. "I was just thinking how strange it sounded to hear you call me Kate McKenna," she said.

"You'll get used to it." He chuckled. "What you'll hear after I've introduced you to my men is Ms. McKenna whenever they address you."

"How long will that last?" she asked, frowning. "I'd much rather they call me Kate."

"Oh, they will in time." He grinned. "They'll have to get used to you first. Take your measure."

"In other words, they're going to be judging me." Kate wasn't sure she liked that idea.

His lips quivered. "Sure, they'll want to make sure you're good enough for me."

"Good enough!" Kate said, anger sparking until she saw him silently laughing at her. "You are a devil, aren't you? Well, I'll show you and your men how good enough I am."

"I already know," he reminded her. "As for my men, go to it…after we've taken a few days for, as my foreman called it, honeymooning."

Kate rolled her eyes.

Hawk laughed.

Together, they cleared away the supper dishes, all but the wineglasses. When the kitchen had been set to rights, he asked, "As you already had your shower, food and wine, are you now ready for sleep?"

"The shower, food, wine and conversation gave me my second wind. I'm not nearly as sleepy as before." She held her glass out to him. "I'd like to have a little more wine, crawl into bed, prop myself up against some pillows and relax while I finish my drink."

Hawk half filled both glasses before saying, "There are two other bedrooms and a central bath on the left side of the hall, opposite my bedroom. Have you decided where you're going to sleep?"

She gave him what she hoped was a sexy, come-hither smile. "My toiletries bag is in your bathroom."

He sent a smile back at her that heated her blood as it tap-danced up her spine. She reached for her glass. He held it aloft.

"Lead on, Kate. I'm right behind you."

She set off for the hallway.

He followed her. "And, since the word *behind* is out there, you have a very enticing one."

In retaliation, Kate wiggled her hips. With a low wolf whistle, he followed her into his bedroom.

Hawk plumped the pillows for her, waited while she crawled into the bed then handed the glass of wine to her. "Comfortable?" he asked.

"Very," she replied, snuggling against the pillows. She felt almost lost in the wide expanse of bed. "Oh, Hawk, this is heaven."

"Not yet, but I have hopes," he said, his gaze seeming to touch her in very delicate spots.

Kate drew a quick breath. "Oh, my." She took a quick sip of the cold wine in hopes of dousing the heat shimmering through her.

"My sentiments exactly." Inhaling, he turned away, setting his glass on the dresser. "I'm going to have a shower. I won't be long."

Reclining against the pillows, too warm all over, Kate kicked the comforter and top sheet to the bottom of the bed. Raising her left hand to take another sip of wine, her gaze caught on the gold band circling her third finger. Unlike Hawk's plain gold ring, the band he had chosen for her was covered with pavé diamonds.

It was beautiful and felt oddly right on her finger, as if it belonged there. Taking more swallows of wine, she continued to gaze at the ring, contemplating the intrinsic, sacred meaning behind the exchange of marriage bands.

Dear Lord, what had she done?

Catching her lower lip between her teeth, her gaze locked on the ring, she felt the sting of incipient tears in her eyes. In her determination to get away from one man, a nasty, possibly dangerous man, she had talked a good man, a decent, wonderful man, into a loveless marriage. It was terribly unfair of her. He deserved better.

The tears overflowed her lower lids just as Hawk, a towel wrapped around his hips, came into the room. He stopped short by the side of the bed.

"Tears," he said, his voice and expression concerned. "Are you feeling regrets?"

"No... Yes, but it's not what you think," she said, sniffing.

Without a word, he walked to the dresser, opened a small side drawer and withdrew a man's snowy-white handkerchief and a foil-wrapped packet. Moving around to the side of the bed she was lying on, he handed the hankie to her and laid the packet on the nightstand.

"Now, what is this 'no...yes'? It's not what I think it is?" Holding the towel with one hand, he took the glass from her trembling hand and set it on the nightstand, next to the foil packet.

Blinking to disperse the tears, which didn't work, she sniffed again and brought the hankie to her nose. "I...I'm sorry. I had no right."

Holding on to the slipping towel, Hawk carefully sat on the edge of the bed, next to her. "If I heard correctly, you mumbled that you had no right." Taking the hankie from her hands, he mopped away the tears. "No right to what?"

Kate sniffed twice, drew a couple deep breaths and shakily answered, "I had no right to talk you into this farce." She sniffed once more. "I'm sorry."

"Kate." Hawk's voice was soft, soothing. "You didn't talk me into anything. If I hadn't wanted to do it, you could have talked your head off, and I'd have said, 'No, thank you, but no.'"

"Oh..." She blinked again.

"Right. Oh." He smiled. "Now, in case you haven't noticed, I'm shivering here. That's because I'm cold. Move over and share the warmth."

Kate shimmied over to let him in.

His gaze skimmed the top of the bed, from her head to her waist. "Where's the sheet and comforter?"

"I was already warm, so I shoved them to the bottom," she admitted. "I'll get them."

"Stay put," he said, turning to grab the covers with his free hand and pull them up and over most of her. "Do you want your wine?"

"No, I'm finished for tonight." Kate quickly lowered her eyes as he lifted his rear off the bed to yank off the towel and toss it to the floor.

"I've had enough, too," he said, sliding into the bed, next to her. "Why are you looking away, Kate? You've seen me naked before."

"Yes, I know," she said, her voice barely a whisper. "But that was before we were married."

Silence. Dead silence. Kate was getting jittery. All of a sudden laughter rumbled in his chest before roaring from his throat.

"Kate, oh, Kate, you are a joy to be with." Rolling to and over her, he cradled her face with his big hands and kissed the nervousness out of her.

She didn't respond, well not verbally. But she kissed him back as if her very sanity depended on his kiss. Then again, maybe it did.

Their lovemaking was even more intense, more exhilarating than before. This time Kate and Hawk reached the summit together.

Completely exhausted, refusing to get out of his bed for any reason, she curled her arm around his waist when he returned from the bathroom, rested her cheek on his still moist chest and closed her eyes.

Hawk slid his fingers into her loose curls, holding her to him. "Good night, Kate." He kissed her hair.

Kate sighed with contentment. "Good night,

Hawk." Closing her eyes, she immediately began to drift.

The marriage was consummated. It was her last thought before drifting into a deep sleep.

Ten

Hawk had set aside four whole days for them to honeymoon. They didn't spend the entire four days in bed, or even three days. But they did spend three of those days in the house, hanging out, reading, eating, having sex, unbelievable, breathtaking sex.

The fourth day they went outside. Unlike the mild, warm October days in Vegas, in the mountains there was a definite chill in the air in the afternoon and the nights were cold, a harbinger of approaching winter.

Hawk had mentioned showing her his horses, at least some of them. She had no idea he had so very many. Kate supposed she should have realized this, as Vic had told her that Hawk bred beautiful horses.

It was a glorious autumn day. There was a nip in the air, but the sunshine was brilliant in a gorgeous deep blue sky. The leaves on the mountain's deciduous trees had begun to fall but the sight was still spectacular.

Caught up in the beauty of this valley nestled in the mountain range, Kate was startled when Hawk, curling his hand around hers, broke her reverie.

"We're having company, Kate," he said, turning her a half step.

In the near distance Kate saw two men riding toward them. "Your men?"

"Yeah," he answered, raising a hand in a welcoming wave. "Coming to meet the Mrs., so please stay in wife mode."

"Well, of course," she said, both hurt and mad, glaring up at him. She could have saved herself the display of annoyance, because beneath the wide brim of the Western hat he had settled on his head before leaving the house, his gaze was fixed on the riders. She now knew the reason he had at times reach to touch a brim that wasn't there while he was in Vegas.

Before he had donned his hat, Hawk had plopped one on her head. Now she was glad he had, as the wide brim shaded her eyes from the dazzling sunlight.

The two riders slowed to a walk as they drew near her and Hawk and pulled up a couple of feet in front of them. Jumping down from his mount, a middle-aged man of medium height and with a sturdy body strolled over to Hawk, his hand outstretched.

"Mornin', Hawk. Ted and I came to meet the wife. I hope we're not intruding."

Hawk gave them a droll look. "Figured," he drawled, turning to her. "Kate, I want you to meet my foreman, Jack, right here, and Ted, the fellow next to Jack, is the best wrangler in the state."

She smiled and nodded at both men. "Jack, Ted, I'm pleased to meet you both." She noticed that Ted was younger than Jack, taller and as slim as a whip.

"Nice to meet you, ma'am," the men said in unison. "We were wonderin' when the boss here was goin' to find a good woman to keep 'im in line," Jack added.

Kate laughed. "Needs to be kept on a short leash, does he?" she said, grinning up at Hawk.

"Yessum, Ms. McKenna," Ted chimed in. "The boss here has a tendency to work too hard."

"That's right," Jack confirmed. "Forgets there's more to livin' than babyin' horses."

Kate laughed, already liking the men.

"Okay, you two, knock off the comedy and get back to work." Hawk interjected. "I'll be with you in a little while."

Both men chuckled, then remounted and rode off in the direction of a pasture with a good number of horses moving around in it. Jack called back, "Take your time, Hawk, if you have better things to do."

Hawk shook his head. Kate smiled. "I like your men, Hawk," she said. "They seem very nice."

"They are good men," he said. "You'll be seeing them again this Saturday. We've invited them to a reception, of sorts."

Kate shot a startled look at him, but he continued speaking.

"Ted and his wife, Carol, and Jack and his daughter, Brenda, will be here Saturday evening, after we've packed it in for the day. Jack's been divorced for close to seven years now. Brenda has spent most of her summers here, at least five, during those years. Carol's a lovely woman. She and Ted have been married two years." He arched that same brow again. "Okay?"

"Okay what?" she asked. "Okay that we have a reception or okay that Ted and Carol have been married two years?" Somehow she managed to keep a straight face.

Now he shook his head in despair at her. "Can you ride?"

"Yes, I can." She put on a haughty expression. "Rather well, too. But first I have a question."

"Shoot," he said.

"Do you…we…have the makings for a party on Saturday night?"

"Plenty of stuff in the pantry and freezer," he answered. "And plenty of beer, wine and soft drinks. Do you have any favorite foods?"

"I'll give it some thought." She smiled. "Now I'm ready for a ride."

"Good." Taking her hand, he led her to the stables. "Let's saddle up, and I'll give you a short tour of the place before I get to work with the men."

Walking by Hawk's side to the stables, Kate was struck by the sudden realization of how completely different her life and lifestyle had been since leaving Vegas. Where she used to sleep in because of working the late hours, now she was up before dawn to prepare Hawk's breakfast. At first, she wasn't too happy about it, but now she enjoyed cooking for him, watching him dig in to the food she had made.

Hawk needed to spend time on ranch chores despite the honeymoon, and he always showered before dinner. He came to the table smelling of shaving cream and pure male. Before the first week was over, Kate was showering with him while the evening meal simmered.

"So, what do you think?"

The sound of his voice drew her from bemusement and Kate glanced up to look at the horse he was saddling. He had picked out a gentle roan mare for her and told her Ted had named the mare Baby-cakes. Kate was happy with his choice and the name. She was surprised when she saw the horse he saddled for himself. It was the biggest horse she had ever seen, other than draft horses.

As they trotted side by side to the pasture, one of several she later learned, she felt like a child on a pony next to Hawk on the tall, sleek animal.

As they circled around, both she and Hawk waved to Jack and Ted as they worked the horses, before heading on to the pasture beyond.

With the sunlight playing on their sleek coats, the horses looked beautiful, well kept and cared for. "Have you always been a horse man?"

Hawk smiled. "Yes, I fell in love when my father bought me my first horse, a filly." He slanted his head, his smile morphing into a grin. "And here comes my second animal love." Pulling up his mount, he jumped down and turned just as a large animal streaked by Kate's horse and leapt straight at Hawk.

"Hawk, watch out…" Kate cried just as the animal made the jump. Fear caught her breath. Gulping in air, she couldn't believe her eyes or ears.

Hawk was on the ground, laughing. She could now see that the animal on top of him was a very big dog. The dog's tail was swishing back and forth a mile a minute, its tongue lapping every inch of Hawk's face.

"Yeah, Boyo, I love you, too, but get off me now. You're crushing my ribs."

To Kate's surprise, the dog immediately jumped to the side, as if he understood every word. Hawk ruffled the dog's wiry-looking coat before getting to his feet. Walking to the side of her horse, he grinned up at her.

"Boyo?" was all she said.

He laughed. "Yep, Boyo. It's Irish slang for *boy.*" The dog came to stand next to him. Hawk placed his hand on the dog's large head. "This is the Irish wolfhound I told you about."

Kate gave the dog a dubious glance. "Does he resent competition?"

Hawk caught on at once and grinned at her. "No, or at any rate, he tolerates it, and that includes every person on the property."

The sigh Kate exhaled wasn't all show. "That's a relief. He's kind of frightening."

"Nah," Hawk said, shaking his head. "He's a pushover for anyone willing to scratch his head."

"I'll keep that in mind," she said.

Nevertheless, she made sure she didn't ride too close to Boyo on the way back to the stable. This time Kate noticed a large white circle between the stable corral and the pasture.

She looked at Hawk. "Is that a helipad over there?"

"Yes, I put it in for rescue purposes, in case of an emergency with either the people or the animals."

"Do you own the chopper?" she asked as she dismounted.

"No, I use a rescue service," he explained as he jumped off his horse. "But I could fly a chopper. I flew a Black Hawk in the service, and I practice now and again."

"Cool," she quipped, giving him a high five.

Kate learned that her wariness of the dog was unnecessary once they were in the house. Boyo nudged her leg with his long snout twice until she hesitantly lowered her hand to his head to give him a brisk scratch. He was immediately her best friend. Kate fell in love with the big, ferocious-looking baby.

Kate spent the next few days getting ready for the reception. While Hawk was outside working with his men, she prepared numerous dishes. Some she had found in his cookbooks; others she had learned from her mother.

She was nervous Saturday evening, before their guests arrived. Hawk came into the house and brushed his mouth over hers on his way to the bathroom for a shower. As he swept by, she caught a whiff of fresh air, horse, sweaty male and Hawk's personal scent. For a moment, she was tempted to join him in the shower.

Kate gave a heartfelt sigh. Living with Hawk was so good…but it was not permanent. The physical life they shared in bed almost every night was wonderful. His sudden quick kisses made her head spin. She knew she wasn't falling in love with him, because she was fathoms deep already.

She knew Hawk loved kissing her, making love with her, but she also knew he was skeptical about the very word *love*. He simply didn't believe in romantic love, the forever after kind. She wished…

The realization of time passing sent her back into the kitchen. Hawk was beside her in record time. "How's it going? Can I do anything to help?"

"Fine and no," she answered, stirring the mouthwatering, aromatic beef barbecue, one of her mother's recipes.

"Lordy, that smells good, and I'm starving." He caught her chin in his hand to turn her to face him. "Hungry, too," he murmured, kissing her senseless.

Kate shoved him away after a few heavenly minutes. "I've got to get this together," she said, grabbing a breath between each word. "Pitch in, lover."

Hawk gave a fake shudder. "Oh, Katie, hearing you call me lover turns me on."

"Later," she said, flashing a smile at him. "Right now I do believe our guests have arrived."

"I'm going to hold you to that," he said, moving away from her.

"I certainly hope so," she replied, laughing as he tossed a wicked grin back at her.

The reception was wonderful. Everyone chattered, laughed and even sang. Kate liked Carol at once. She was young but mature with a great sense of humor.

After Carol, Hawk led Kate over to Jack to introduce her to his daughter. Brenda was a pretty girl, in her late teens, Kate judged.

With a murmured "excuse me, ladies," Jack wandered to where the men were gathered, Hawk handing out cans of beer.

"I'm glad to meet you, Brenda," Kate said, extending her hand to the girl.

"Likewise," the girl replied, a sweet, miss-innocent smile on her face as she took Kate's hand in a crushing grip.

Managing to keep from wincing in pain, Kate tightened her own fingers harder around the girl's hand.

Glaring at her, Brenda gave in, withdrawing her hand.

Despite the tingle of pain in her fingers, Kate met Brenda's glare with a serene smile. "Now, if you will excuse me, I have to check on the food cooking on the stove."

Oh, boy, Kate thought, making her way to the

kitchen. In her estimation, Brenda was walking, talking, snotty trouble. There was something sly and petulant about her that sounded an alarm inside Kate's mind. But why had the girl targeted her? Hawk's soft laughter came from across the room.

Of course. Kate sighed. Brenda was infatuated with Hawk. Kate couldn't blame Brenda. Hawk was all the things of many women's dreams, but he was way out of the young girl's league.

A sense of foreboding rippled through Kate, a warning of unpleasant things, scenes to come.

The festivities lasted long into the night. Finally, but reluctantly, the party broke up. Kate stood next to Hawk on the porch, grateful for his arm around her to ward off the night cold, still talking to the others as they made their way to their vehicles.

"You throw one hell of a party, lady," Hawk said, praising her efforts once everyone had left. "Thanks."

"You're welcome, and thank you for the compliment, sir." Standing on tiptoes, she kissed him on the side of his sculpted, hard jaw. "Now you may help me clear the mess away inside."

"Aw, gee, Kate," he groused like a kid. "Can't we leave it till morning? I gotta work, ya know?"

But Hawk pitched in right beside her, heaving deep, put-upon sighs every few minutes. By the time they were finished, Kate was laughing. She wasn't laughing a short time later, after they were in bed. She was crying out in delicious pleasure.

Kate had dinner ready for him when he came in to eat as the sun went down the next day. While he dug into his food like a starving man, they did a postmortem of the reception the night before.

"I like your friends," she said, handing the dish of mashed potatoes to him for a second helping. "And I could tell at once that they are friends as well as employees."

Nodding, Hawk swallowed before replying. "They are," he said. "Good thing, too, especially during the winter months. We get together often...." He smiled and took another roll from the bread basket. "If we didn't, we'd likely all get antsy with cabin fever."

Kate laughed and gave him an arch look. "And here, all this time I was thinking you were a loner."

"I don't mind being alone," he said, picking up his coffee cup. "Fact is there are times I prefer it."

"Like when you want to read?"

"Yes, and when I'm watching football."

"Uh-huh." Kate tilted her head, fighting a smile. "Is this your way of reminding me there's a game on tonight and you don't want to be bothered?"

"No, because you don't bother me." Standing, he took both their plates, carried them to the sink and came back to the table with the coffee carafe. "Do you like football?"

"I can tolerate it," she admitted. "But I'd rather read."

He was pensive a moment. "I could go into the bedroom to watch the game on the set in there," he offered, pleasing her with his thoughtfulness.

Kate was shaking her head before he'd finished. "That's not necessary. If I'm into a story, I don't even hear the TV unless it's blaring."

"It won't be." Hawk slanted a slow smile at her. "I could watch the game in the living room and you could read your book in bed," he suggested.

Kate laughed. "No, you may watch in the game in bed. I can't get comfortable reading in bed."

He heaved a sigh. "Will you sit next to me and read if I watch the game while sitting on the sofa?"

"I will if you'll refill my cup," she said, reminding him he was still standing there with the carafe in hand. "Can we get back to our discussion about the reception now that our seating arrangement for tonight has been confirmed?" She grinned.

He grinned back, causing a melting sensation inside her. "Sure we can." He frowned. "Something about it on your mind?"

"Well…it's about Brenda."

Hawk groaned. "What about her? Was she rude to you? Did she insult you in some way?"

"Not exactly." Kate paused, searching for the right words. "I tried to draw her into a conversation. She seemed so, oh, I don't know, almost sullen." She sighed. "She wasn't very responsive."

He drew a deep breath. "I was going to talk to you about Brenda. I should have done it before the party. She is, and has been for some time, a pain in the neck and parts south." He ran his fingers through his long hair, loosening it from the leather thong.

Kate smiled at his ruffled strands of hair. His expression serious, Hawk untied the thong and shook his head, freeing the long locks.

"As I was saying," he went on, ignoring her obvious urge to laugh, "Brenda has been coming to the ranch for a long time. When she was younger, she was a high-spirited kid. Jack and I taught her to ride." He grimaced. "When she arrived here after graduating from high school, a year ago this coming summer, she was different."

"In what way?"

"Kate, the only way to describe it is that she began hanging around me too much." He shook his head. "Understand she had always hung around, but that summer it was different. At first I thought she was just using me to practice her wiles to use on younger men. But it wasn't that. She started *accidentally* brushing against me...with her breasts, touching me, hugging me." His smile was wry. "I'm not stupid. Her actions were not the same as when she was a young girl. She was coming on to me. I did talk to Jack about it before I left for Vegas, and he assured me he'd take care of it. Looks like his lecture went in one ear and out the other."

"And now," Kate said, "I suspect Brenda, the temptress in training, resents the woman you brought home with you from Las Vegas."

Sighing again, Hawk finished his coffee and began to clear the table. Kate got up to help him. "That's the way I figure it," he said. "I suppose I'll have to talk to her, tell her a few home truths."

"Ahh, no, Hawk, I'll talk to her, at the right moment." She knew her smile wasn't sweet. "I'll be gentle, but firm."

The right moment appeared the following week. Kate was on the phone. She had received a call from her father, the fourth since Kate had told him she had married Hawk and moved with him to his ranch in Colorado. She was actually gushing in an attempt to finally convince him she was safe, well and over-the-moon happy.

No sooner had she cradled the phone, with a sigh of relief, when it rang again. It was Vic calling from Vegas. After chatting a bit, enquiring about Lisa, Bella and everyone at the restaurant, she told him to hang on while she searched out Hawk who, for-tunately, was working in the stables that day.

At a near run, she went to the stables only to stop short at the low, supposedly sexy sound of Brenda's voice.

"You know, Hawk, it would be fun to take a ride when you're finished here," she said, moving so that the side of her breast made contact with Hawk's arm as he brushed down the mare, Babycakes. "Just you and me. Wouldn't It?"

"Brenda..." he began, strain underlying his tone.

"I don't think so," Kate said, striding forward to wedge herself between Hawk and the girl. "Vic's on the phone, Hawk," she said, taking the brush from his hand. "I'll take over here."

He frowned with concern. "Lisa?"

"No, no," Kate shook her head. "Just a friendly call."

"Good," he said, loping from the stable as he headed for the house.

Kate began applying the brush. She imagined she could hear Brenda getting ready to explode. "I thought you were going for a ride, Brenda." Kate continued brushing. "I'm afraid you'll have to ride alone now." She shifted to level a warning look at the girl. "And in the future...if you get my drift?"

With a snort almost as loud as Babycakes could make, Brenda stormed from the stables.

A few minutes later Hawk startled Kate by silently stepping up next to her. "How can a man walk so damned quietly in those heeled boots?" she demanded.

He grinned. "Practice." He lowered his voice. "Is the temptress in training gone?"

Kate nodded, sighing. "She wants your body."

He tossed his head, exactly as his stallion did. "Who doesn't?"

She rolled her eyes, and changed the subject. "Did Vic want anything in particular?"

"No," he shook his head and gave her a wry look. "He said you sounded okay and told me flat out I'd better make sure you remained okay."

"Or what?" Kate had to laugh. "Vic's in Vegas and we're here. What was he intending to do about it?"

"He said he'd have to come rescue you from me."

"Right," she drawled. "I can just see Vic, running off to the mountains to rescue me, leaving his precious, pregnant Lisa at home alone." Shaking her head as if in despair of the silly men, Kate went back to the house.

Fortunately, they didn't see hid nor hair of Brenda for several weeks. Kate was settling nicely into a routine, inside and outside of the house. She was beginning to feel if she belonged there, in the mountains, in the house, with Hawk.

Dangerous feeling, she told herself. She didn't belong there. She was there simply because of a good and kind man…who didn't even believe in romantic love.

Kate had learned of his attitude one evening while he was watching a game and she was reading a book, a historical romance novel. During half-time, after fetching glasses of wine for them both, he asked her what she was reading. Not thinking anything of his curiosity, she told him, adding a brief resume of the story. To her surprise, he raised a skeptical brow.

"What?" she asked.

"That stuff—fantasy, love till the end of time. You don't really believe in that, do you?"

If she hadn't, she was beginning to, Kate thought. Aloud she merely answered in a teasing tone, "Could happen."

"Uh-huh." Without another word, he turned his attention to the second half of the game.

"You don't believe in love?" Kate said, snagging his attention away from the TV. "What about Vic and Lisa and Ted and Carol? They appear very much in love."

"Okay, yes, I know they are in love, but they have their problems, too. It's certainly not the fairy-tale, happily-ever-after stuff." He shrugged. "Personally, I've never experienced the feeling."

Kate fought against the crushed sensation his words caused inside her. She wanted to cry out against the ache in her chest, the sense of loss and deflation. But she didn't cry out, instead lifted her head and simply said, "Too bad." Picking up her book, she walked away. "I'm going to bed."

The days sped by. They had a light snowfall in early November. The snow didn't last. They gathered at Ted and Carol's house for Thanksgiving. Hawk provided the huge turkey he had in his freezer chest.

As the season turned from chilly fall to cold winter, Kate worked with the horses until Hawk taught her how to keep the records of the ranch and the bloodlines of the horses on his computer.

Two weeks before Christmas, Hawk drove Kate into Durango. He went shopping for groceries and ranch supplies, leaving her to do her Christmas shopping. First she bought gifts for her father, stepmother and the children, and Vic, Lisa and Bella, and had them packaged and sent to Virginia and Las Vegas. Then she shopped for what she thought would be thoughtful but not personal gifts for Hawk.

As a rule, Christmas shopping had always been fun for Kate, but not this year. She simply couldn't get into the holiday mood. By next year she'd be gone—who knew where. She wasn't even sure she had done the right thing buying gifts for Hawk. She didn't even know if he celebrated Christmas.

Glancing at her watch, Kate saw that it was almost time to meet Hawk at the truck. Well, she thought, shrugging, what's done is done. She could always take back the gifts if he didn't want them. The very idea made her sad.

Kate felt a lot better about the whole holiday thing the next week when Hawk dragged a large pine tree onto the porch to dry.

When he set it up in the living room a couple days later, Kate got even more into the spirit of the holiday. If there was only to be one Christmas with Hawk, Kate was determined to make the best of it.

Christmas morning, both Kate and Hawk slept in late. Well, they weren't asleep all morning. Tossing back the down comforter, they worked up a pleasant sweat exchanging certain Christmas gifts.

Later, freshly showered and dressed, they breakfasted on coffee and Christmas cookies as they sat together on the floor to exchange material Christmas presents.

There were small items with Hawk's name on the tags: new tough leather work gloves, a braided belt and a handheld computer game. He was very obviously surprised and pleased with the handmade cable-knit sweater in the Black Watch colors, imported from Scotland, that Kate had ordered for him online.

There and then, he pulled off the sweatshirt he

had minutes before put on, replacing it with the sweater she had chosen for him.

After he had finished opening his gifts, Hawk slid a small pile of presents toward Kate.

As excited as a kid, Kate dove into the pile. Carefully unwrapping each gift, she revealed a delicate handwrought sterling silver bracelet, which she immediately insisted Hawk fasten on her wrist. The next package contained an Amazon.com gift certificate for a hefty amount, which she exclaimed over. The last package held the cashmere scarf Hawk had bought in Vegas, supposedly for his sister. The scarf earned Hawk what he declared to be a teeth-rattling kiss.

One morning a few days later, Kate had been out helping in the stables, and noticing it was time to start lunch, she headed for the house. Upon entering, she noticed at once that the door to Hawk's bedroom was open. Kate clearly recalled shutting the door before leaving the house.

Walking quietly down the hallway, she stepped inside the room, to find Brenda rifling through Hawk's dresser drawers, touching his clothes.

"What are you doing in here, Brenda?" Kate's voice was soft but icy.

"I...I..." The girl stopped trying to answer and glared at Kate. "He belongs to me, you know."

"Really?" Kate smiled.

Brenda flinched at Kate's cold expression, then lashed out in anger. "Yes, he does. He is mine. Who are you but a Vegas tramp who thought she had bagged a rich rancher?" She was breathing heavily. "Well, I'm telling you, bitch, when he's tired of his new playmate, he'll toss you out and I'll have him back."

"You've got a lot to learn, young lady," Kate said, holding on to her temper. "Hawk is my husband. Other than being the daughter of his friend, you mean nothing to him."

"That's a lie," Brenda shouted. "I'll be around long after you've been tossed out."

"Oh, Brenda," Kate sighed. "I think what you need is a swift kick in the ass to jar some sense into you."

"And I've got the boot to do it," Hawk said from the doorway. "Go home, Brenda, and don't come back until you've learned how to act your age."

"Damn you both," Brenda cried out like a spoiled kid, tears running down her face, sniffing, as she ran out of the room. They heard the front door slam.

Drawing a deep breath of relief, Hawk smiled at Kate. "Thanks, Kate. I do believe the message finally got through to her. I appreciate it."

"Anytime, cowboy," she said. "Now, what do you want for dinner?"

He laughed. She joined in with him.

The next day Jack drove Brenda to the airport to put her on a plane. She was going back to her mother's home.

Winter brought with it heavy snow. On the morning of the heaviest snowfall, Hawk confined Kate to the house. He didn't advise her to stay inside, he issued a flat order. The name Jeff immediately sprang into her mind.

"Hawk," the sharp edge of her voice stopped him in his tracks as he headed for the back door.

"Yes?" He turned frowning.

"I'm an adult, a full-grown woman. I will not be ordered around, not by you or any other man." Placing her hands on her hips, she stared defiantly at him.

Hawk's drawn eyebrows rose. "Kate, I'm only insisting you stay inside because I know how treacherous the terrain can become outside in this weather. It's for your own safety."

Kate lifted a hand to flick a shooing motion at him. "You go to work, and leave me to worry about my safety." Without waiting for any argument from him, she stormed down the hallway and into their room to make the bed. She fully expected him to follow her. Her shoulders slumped and she felt like crying when he didn't.

Damn, she didn't know what she wanted anymore. Now there was a rift between her and Hawk, but Kate knew she had to carry on. A deal was a deal. Only their deal was now a mostly silent one. They spoke only when necessary. The quiet wore on Kate's nerves. Tired of it, she went outside to stomp around in the pristine snow, slamming the door behind her.

Hawk was there waiting for her when the cold finally sent her back into the house, wet and shivering.

"Feel better?" He looked tired. He sounded tired.

Kate felt ashamed for acting out like a spoiled kid. "I'm sorry, Hawk, but I will not be penned up in the house, snow or no snow."

"I can understand that," he said, his tone inflectionless. "I don't like it myself. But when I'm working some distance from the house, will you agree to confine yourself to the path the men and I made from the back of the house to the stables? I'm sure Babycakes would appreciate your company."

Kate knew that once Hawk had given her the mare to use while she was on the ranch, he had not taken Babycakes out with him to work.

"Yes, I'll agree to that."

"Thank you." He started to turn away. "I'm going to get a shower before dinner." He glanced back at her. "That is, if we're having dinner."

The shame making her uncomfortable turned to

a flash of anger that zipped through her. "Of course we're having dinner," she said heatedly. "Haven't I prepared dinner every evening since I've been here?"

"Yes, Kate, you have." He gave her a half smile. "Thing is, I've gotten used to coming into the house to be greeted by the delicious aroma of whatever you're cooking. I don't smell a thing today."

Pleased by his appreciation of her cooking efforts, Kate smiled back at him while shaking her head in exasperation. "I made dinner earlier...so I could go romp in the snow. The meal is in the fridge; all it needs is warming up. It will be ready by the time you've finished your shower."

"Oh...okay." His smile now rueful, he retreated to the bedroom.

From that day forward there was a change in Hawk, in the atmosphere whenever they were together. Though he was unfailingly polite, there was very little laughter or teasing, and what smiles did touch his lips were strained.

Kate couldn't help but notice the only time he touched her during the day was obviously accidental. The nights were different, too. His lovemaking steadily grew a bit rough with an almost desperate intensity, driving Kate to heights of breathtaking pleasure she had never experienced, never dreamed could be experienced. Yet when she finally came down from the shattering high she felt empty and alone.

Longing for the easy companionship they had shared before, Kate racked her mind for a reasonable explanation for the change in him. Thinking a breath of fresh air might clear her mind, she took some sugar cubes and an apple then went to the mudroom at the back of the house and pulled on her boots and heavy jacket.

Leaving the house, Kate made her way along the path that was now almost bare due to the sudden shift to milder weather a couple of days ago. Entering the stables, she went straight to Babycakes' stall. The mare was obviously happy to see her as she nudged Kate's shoulder before lowering her head to snuffle at her jacket pocket.

"You know me too well, Miss Babycakes." Laughing, Kate drew two sugar cubes from her pocket and gave them to the eager horse. When the animal was finished with the treat she looked up, her big brown eyes staring right into Kate's as if sensing her unhappiness and silently asking why.

Kate's eyes and nose began to sting an instant before she burst into tears. Once again the mare nudged her shoulder. With no one else to talk to, Kate poured her heart out to her temporary pet.

"Oh, Baby, I don't know what to do." Raising her arms, Kate cradled the mare's large head atop her shoulder. "There's no one else for me to talk to. I don't know Carol well enough and I can't call Lisa, she'd get upset and that's the last thing she needs at this stage of her pregnancy. I won't call my father because I've let him believe I'm so happy and so very much in love."

Kate sniffed and, moving back, she dug in her other jacket pocket for a tissue. She blew her nose. Before she was through, Babycakes nudged her again, as though telling her to go on with her tale of woe.

Smiling, crying, she stroked the long nose, swallowed and allowed the misery to spill out. "There's been a distance between us for weeks now and I hate it." The tears flowed freely. "He told me he didn't believe in love." A sob caught in her throat. "And he told me long ago he enjoyed being alone." The horse whinnied as if in commiseration. "I'm afraid he's beginning to think of me as an intrusion into his life." For a moment Kate closed her eyes, swiping her hand over her wet cheeks.

"I'm a fool, Baby," she murmured. The mare shook her head, eliciting a weepy laugh from Kate. "Yes I am, a foolish idiot. I suggested the bargain as the perfect answer to my problem and now I have a bigger problem, a much bigger problem. I am so deep in love with Hawk I can't bear this coolness between us."

With a final sniff and a final stroke of the mare's long nose, she took the apple from her pocket and fed it to the horse. "Spring's almost here, Baby. I want winter back. I want the Hawk I knew in Vegas back." The mare finished chomping the apple and Kate turned away.

"I want, I want," she muttered, sighing as she left the stable. "And I'm talking to a horse. Sheer idiocy."

While Kate grew more quiet, more withdrawn, Hawk was wrestling with uncertainties of his own. Throughout the past few weeks the coolness in the house had nothing to do with the heating system, and everything to do with the chill between him and Kate.

Riding in late one warm afternoon in the beginning of April, Hawk walked his horse to cool him down. After grooming the roan, he stabled him then walked down the aisle of stalls to the one holding Babycakes, the mare he had given to Kate for her exclusive use while she was at the ranch. Now he couldn't think of the animal as anything other than Kate's.

Stepping into the stall of the gentle chestnut, Hawk took up a brush and began to groom her. Also, without thinking, he began softly talking to her.

"I'm in deep crap, Baby," he murmured, using Kate's nickname for the horse. "And I'm afraid you're going to be mad as hell at me." The horse nickered. "You may not believe it now," he said, as if he had heard a "no way" in the horse's noise, "but you'll understand when your mistress is gone."

The mare shook her big head. Damn, Hawk thought, for all he knew, maybe the horse did understand. Mocking himself for the very idea, he nevertheless continued talking.

"It's my fault she is going," he went on. "I deliberately built a wall of virtual silence between us." The horse snorted. "Yeah, I know, pretty stupid. But, much as I hate to admit it, even to you, I was getting scared. It started after we had a silly argument about her staying inside during the worst weather. As gentle as Kate is with you, Baby, you wouldn't believe how she blew a gasket at me for daring to give her orders."

For a moment Hawk smiled in memory of how magnificent Kate had looked in her defiance of him. Another memory flashed and he sighed.

"But it was the night I laughed at the book she was reading, calling it a fantasy of happy-ever-after and telling her I didn't believe in that kind of thing. She walked away from me, and since then has stayed away from me, there but cool and distant. I could kick myself in the ass. When she walked away a knot settled in my gut. It's been getting tighter and tighter with each passing day."

By pure coincidence, Hawk felt sure, the mare moved her large head, trapping Hawk's head against her long neck. The curry brush fell unnoticed to the ground. Hawk rested his forehead on her smooth coat.

"And now our bargain time is up, Baby. Kate's going to leave us both." A shudder ran through him. The horse shook her head. "I know, you don't want her to go. You think she's yours. Well, I don't want her to go, either. I love her. I—who has never felt anything deep or lasting for any woman—love Kate more than my own life."

Hawk shuddered again and felt a sudden sting in his eyes. Tears rolled down his face. Damn, he never cried, hadn't shed a tear since he was nine or ten. He didn't make a sound but the tears continued to flow until the mare moved her head and he noticed the wet spot on her coat.

"Sorry, girl," he drew a deep breath, scrubbed his big hands over his face and stood up straight. "I don't suppose you have any suggestions? No? I didn't think so." Stepping back out of the stall, he closed the gate. The mare stuck her head out and with a shaky laugh Hawk stroked her face. Her big brown eyes appeared sad.

"I'll see what I can do for the two of us, sweetheart," he promised. "I'll beg her to stay if I have to."

* * *

Stepping out onto the porch for a breather late one afternoon early in April, Kate felt the first mild breeze of spring. The last remnants of happiness and contentment she had enjoyed until recently with Hawk, while working, laughing, making love with him, dissolved like the small patches of snow from the last snowfall.

It was almost time for her to leave. Her six months were up. Sadness welled up in her; tears stung her eyes. Where had the days gone, one after another, fading from month to month? Kate loved spring, but she wanted winter back. She didn't want to return to Vegas or to her father's farm. She didn't want to go, couldn't bear the thought of being away from Hawk forever.

But his coolness, his near silence for nearly two months, said it all to Kate. It was time for her to go, to give Hawk's life back to him.

Tears streaming down her face, Kate squared her shoulders and walked into the house. A deal was a deal. Pain twisted in her chest as she remembered the way they had "double" sealed their deal with a handshake and two kisses.

Going to Hawk's bedroom, *their* bedroom, Kate swiped the tears from her cheeks, impatient with herself for wanting, longing to renege on their bargain.

It wasn't fully six months yet; she could wait until the end of the month. The thought wriggled its way into her head, tempting her to hang on to him every last minute.

Kate shook away the thought. It would only get harder for both of them if she lingered longer. Dragging her suitcases from the closet, she began packing her things. For a moment, she stroked the beautiful scarf Hawk had given to her at Christmas. The tears started again.

Ignoring them, sniffing, Kate continued until she had packed all her belongings but the clothes she was wearing and the those she planned to wear tomorrow, when Hawk, she hoped, would take the time to drive her to the airport.

Hawk entered the house and frowned at the lack of aromatic cooking scents wafting on the air. It was quiet, too quiet. There was no sight or sound of Kate.

He smiled softly, thinking she had probably lain across the bed to take a nap and had overslept. His smile growing sad, he went down the hallway to their bedroom, planning to take advantage of the opportunity to join her on the bed…and sleep had nothing to do with his plan.

The door was partially open. Quietly pushing it in, he stepped inside the bedroom and stopped dead.

Kate was sitting on the side of the bed, her suitcases on the floor next to her, unchecked tears running down her flushed face.

"Kate?" Hawk crossed to her in three long strides. "What's wrong? Why are you crying? And what are your suitcases doing here on the floor?"

She drew a long, shuddering breath and, without looking up at him, said, "I'm leaving, Hawk. The six months are almost up. Will you drive me to the airport tomorrow, please?"

"No." His heart was racing.

Her head flew up and she stared at him. "Oh, well, if you're too busy, perhaps Jack or Ted can take me."

"No." Now he could hardly breathe.

"Why?" She swiped a hand over her red-rimmed eyes.

Hawk couldn't stand seeing her cry. Kicking her luggage aside, he grasped her by the shoulders and pulled her up to face him.

"I don't want you to go, Kate." He heard the pained rawness in his voice and didn't care. "I want you to stay here with me."

"After the coolness between us for two months, you want to extend my stay?" The tears had stopped but her lips still trembled.

"No, dammit!" Throwing caution and possibly his hope of continued happiness away, he gazed directly into her red, puffy eyes and said, "Will you marry me, Kate?"

She blinked, then blinked again. "Hawk, what are you saying? We *are* married."

He shook his head. "I mean, will you stay married to me? Can we renew our vows to each other, for real this time?" He caught his breath. "Kate, I love you so much. If you leave me now, I'll live. But I won't like it."

Kate had the audacity to laugh…right before she threw herself against him, wrapped her arms round his neck and joyously shouted, "Yes, yes, yes, I'll stay, Hawk, because maybe you'll live if I go…but I don't know if I will. I love you." She raised her voice even louder. "I love you, Hawk McKenna. I believe I have from our first kiss."

* * * * *

"I need to ask a favor," Jasmine said, her gaze steady on his face.

What could she want? His body? That tantalizing thought flitted through his mind. He'd gladly oblige, but first he'd teach her some morning-after etiquette. "I see. Is it just me, or do you see the irony in that?"

For the first time, she had the grace to look a little discomfited. Not much, just a brief shift in her gaze, a tiny clearing of the throat. But Adam possessed the secret to unlocking that composure.

"What can I do for you, Jasmine?" he asked, settling back on the desk. He folded his arms, intrigued now that his pride had been restored.

Jasmine swallowed again. "I want you to spend Christmas with me at my family's estate in Lincolnshire," she said. "As my fiancé."

HIS VIENNA
CHRISTMAS BRIDE

BY
JAN COLLEY

Published in Great Britain 2010
Harlequin Mills & Boon Limited,
Eton House, 18-24 Paradise Road, Richmond, Surrey TW9 1SR

© Jan Colley 2009

ISBN: 978 0 263 88188 2

51-1210

Harlequin Mills & Boon policy is to use papers that are natural, renewable
and recyclable products and made from wood grown in sustainable forests.
The logging and manufacturing processes conform to the legal environmental
regulations of the country of origin.

Printed and bound in Spain
by Litografia Rosés S.A., Barcelona

Jan Colley lives in Christchurch, New Zealand, with Les and a couple of cats. She has traveled extensively, is jack of all trades and master of none and still doesn't know what she wants to be when she grows up—as long as it's a writer. She loves rugby, family and friends, writing, sunshine, talking about writing and cats, although not necessarily in that order. E-mail her at vagabond232@yahoo.com, or check out her website at www.jancolley.com.

I dedicate this book to the music of Johann Strauss II.
May you leave me in peace now that I have
written the books!

Dear Reader,

Do corporate jets land at Vienna International Airport? How do you spell goulash? Can you take a fiacre (horse-drawn carriage) from the Imperial Hotel to the Hofburg Imperial Palace? The internet is a vital, if time-consuming, tool for authors. It doesn't always get it right and is open to interpretation and local custom. I visited Vienna back in the eighties, with no room in my backpack for a ball gown and too little money to take in the Spanish Riding School, a lasting regret. But it was, and is still, an enchanting city, with its Fasching, incredible architecture and rich history.

Indulging in armchair research is no substitute for being there. My travel bug has reawakened. Until I get back to Austria, I hope I got most of the facts right in Adam and Jasmine's story. If I didn't, please write and enlighten me!

And goulash? I found five different spellings while trawling through online Austrian restaurant menus. All I know is, it's yummy!

Best wishes,

Jan Colley

One

Well, well, Adam Thorne thought as he lounged in his chair, staring at the woman who had just entered his office. Mohammed had come to the mountain.

Satisfaction plumped up his chest. The rugby ball he'd been tossing up and down stilled in his hands. She might have shown him the door last month after a magical night of passion, but here she was, standing in the doorway of his London office, in the flesh. He tamped down the urge to smile. She'd better be prepared to grovel, or stump up with the goods. He wasn't a man used to slights and empty promises.

"Hallo, Adam."

Taking his time, he gave the ball one last toss,

caught it, then slid his feet off the desk. "Shouldn't you be twelve thousand miles away, hard at work for my big brother?"

Jasmine Cooper, personal assistant to his brother, Nick, English but presently living in Wellington, New Zealand. Cool, composed and without doubt the most fascinating female in Adam's considerable catalogue.

"I had some leave owing."

Adam unwound his long frame, stood and skirted the desk, tossing the rugby ball into a nearby open box.

She walked toward his desk, unbuttoning her long black woolen coat, and he let his eyes have at her. She was, as usual, impeccably dressed in a navy wool trouser suit, saved from severity with a bright-yellow sweater and those four-inch spiky heels she liked. His eyes were drawn to her heels like a magnet. Years of ballroom dancing had given her the most sensational, mile-high legs. A savage bolt of desire rushed through him and his fingers twitched, recalling never-ending silky smooth skin, firm and strong as they locked around his waist, as he molded them with his hands....

"May I take your coat?"

He held out his hand while she slipped out of her coat, glancing around curiously. His office resembled a bomb site, littered with boxes. Adam was enjoying a leisurely last day as junior partner in Croft, Croft and Bayley stockbrokers. In the new year, he would be opening his own premises in the Docklands for a markedly different venture.

He slid the garment on to a hanger and turned back to her, indicating she sit. "To what do I owe this very unexpected pleasure?"

She lifted a graceful hand and patted at her long dark hair, tied back, as usual. Adam preferred it out, remembering how it tickled his chest as she straddled him, kissing his mouth. Her almond-shaped eyes, he'd discovered, interchanged between smoky gray and blue, depending on her level of arousal.

Today, she was poised and elegant, lightly made-up, the perfect milk and roses of a true English beauty with a warm, rich shade on her lovely lips. As if he hadn't been assaulted by the same sights and sounds dozens of times over the past weeks, he again recalled those eyes hazed with passion, her short, well-kept nails digging into his hips, urging him on. The desperate little panting noises that escaped her throat at the onset of orgasm, and which he just bet prim and proper Ms. Cooper was mortified about later.

Pity she'd blotted her copy book. Adam was still mightily displeased at the way she'd treated him afterward. It had taken six dates to charm her into bed, spurred on by her quietly confident decree that she would not be another notch on his crowded bedpost. He'd persevered because he was on holiday, his time was more or less his own and he'd enjoyed her company more than expected, considering she was nothing like the women he usually dated. If people had a type, Jasmine Cooper was nothing like his.

Hell, he'd persevered because she'd told him no.

"I just spoke to Nick last week," he mused. "He didn't mention you were coming over."

He'd also courted the displeasure of his brother, who seemed to take a personal interest in keeping him away from his P.A., going so far as to tell him that a woman like Jasmine wouldn't give him the time of day.

Adam never could resist a challenge, but his brother had been partly right, as it turned out. After an incredible night of unbridled passion, he'd been shown the door. She couldn't wait to be rid of him. Perhaps she considered him a lapse of her impeccable judgment, or thought he might be less than discreet and tell her boss. One moment, she'd been all over him—literally—the next, it was here's your hat, what's your hurry?

Adam was a master of keeping things casual but at least he did so with charm and good manners. This elegant woman in front of him may look genteel, with her cultured accent that would be at home in Windsor Castle, but she'd dented his normally robust esteem and he didn't like that one bit.

Now she sat in front of him, her hands clasped tightly in her lap. A second glance showed him how tightly. Her knuckles were white. An interesting show of nerves.

"I usually come home at Christmas."

Logical. It was Christmas Eve and she was English and presumably had family here. But why bother coming to see him when a few short weeks ago she couldn't wait to be rid of him?

"And you just happened to be passing?" he said dryly.

Her lips softened. "Not exactly."

Jasmine was a woman of few words. Well-educated, classy, she would never run away with her mouth—although he recalled one or two things she had done with her mouth that had caused him all sorts of pleasure. Adam put his desk between them, feeling as horny as a school kid. He'd been working twenty hours a day since returning from New Zealand, winding up his affairs here, hunting out investors, organizing new premises. He hadn't had a date since he got back. The London debutantes that usually peppered his crowd had had short shrift from him of late—and that, he told himself firmly, had nothing to do with the trouble he was having dislodging the thought of one particular woman from his mind. He only gave Jasmine Cooper a second thought because she'd pissed him off!

"I need to ask a favor," she said, her gaze steady on his face.

Adam raised a brow. That was rich. He'd asked her a favor, one that could make a huge difference to the success of his new entrepreneurial start-up business. She had promised to help and yet every time he'd called from London, she had frozen him out, told him she was too busy to talk.

What could she want? His body? That tantalizing thought flirted with his mind. He'd gladly oblige, but first he'd teach her some morning-after etiquette. One does not hand one's lover his pants and usher him out the door before he's even had his coffee. "I see. Is it just me, or do you see the irony in that?"

For the first time, she had the grace to look a little discomfited. Not much, just a brief shift in her gaze, a tiny clearing of the throat. His brother, Nick, liked to boast that he had the best P.A. in the country: scarily efficient, über-professional, absolutely composed. But Adam possessed the secret to unlocking that composure. All he had to do was get close to see the way he affected her.

He stood and perched on the edge of his desk right in front of her.

"If I acted a little distant after…" she began.

He kept his brow arched and his eyes on her face. He wanted that apology. "After our unforgettable night together?"

Adam smiled when she swallowed, noting the faint tinge of pink on her cheeks.

"I apologize," she said gravely. "I'm afraid I'm not very experienced in these matters."

"Which was one of the most charming and unforgettable things about that night," Adam told her. And he meant it. For a woman in her midtwenties, she was beguilingly shy and inexperienced. "Was it not to your satisfaction?" he asked, knowing the question would discomfit her, and that she had been satisfied several times over.

Her skin pinked even more and he could tell she'd embedded her teeth into the inside of her cheek.

"I'm very sorry, Adam," she told him earnestly. "It was a special night, one I'll never forget."

Adam held her eyes for a few seconds more, then nodded. He deserved no less, but the apology seemed to be from the heart and his anger dissolved. Besides, having her grovel put the ball firmly in his court. She had come to him. He wanted what only she could give him.

And presumably, she wanted him, or else why was she here? "What can I do for you, Jasmine?" he asked, settling back on the desk to give her a modicum more breathing space. He folded his arms, intrigued now that his pride had been restored.

Jasmine swallowed again and looked him directly in the eye. "I want you to spend Christmas with me at my family's estate in Lincolnshire," she said. "As my fiancé."

In the shocking silence that followed, Jasmine forced herself to keep her eyes on his handsome face. She must stay calm and controlled, act as if this was just an everyday request and not the most preposterous thing she'd ever done in her life.

Under his short, razor-textured dark hair, his forehead creased in surprise. His toffee-colored eyes were wide with astonishment. Designer stubble and sideburns normally turned her right off but the moment she'd met Adam Thorne, playboy, high-flyer, and—according to his brother—a shameless flirt and womanizer, she was mesmerized. Model good looks, a tall, lean build that looked oh-so-good in his designer suits and trendy open-necked shirts.

Now all traces of his heart-stopping smile had vanished, his full lips pursed as he stared at her intently. Lord, why had she come out with it just like that? She should have worked up to it.

Jasmine bit her lip, cursing the long flight that seemed to have loaded her brain with cotton wool and feeling less than her best physically. For some reason, a few weeks ago, this interesting and very sexy man had found her attractive. Today, she felt as dull and dowdy as the winter's day outside.

"Perhaps I should expand a little."

She never volunteered details about her family, not to Adam, Nick or anyone. It was easier that way, to shun relationships, not get close to people. She'd fled England five years ago to get away from her colorful past.

On the morning after they'd finally slept together, Adam had asked her about a magazine article she'd cut out and left on her coffee table. At the time, Jasmine was distracted, admiring his naked chest, the long line of his spine, the length and sheer fluid beauty of his legs as he walked around her lounge.

Distracted mostly by the utter novelty of having a gorgeous naked man walking around her lounge.

"That's my uncle," she'd responded to his question before realizing the danger. Adam lived in London. He might have heard something. He might mention it to Nick. She couldn't bear it if her few New Zealand friends and colleagues found out about the complicated circumstances that had dogged her all her life.

Jasmine had panicked, barely hearing him as he told her he'd been trying to get hold of the great Stewart Cooper—the subject of the article—for two months, and maybe she could get him an introduction. "Yes, probably," she'd told him, thrusting his shirt and trousers at him, making excuses that she was late for something, sorry, have a good trip back to London, thanks for everything. She had practically closed the door on his goodbye kiss, full of regrets because it had been the best night of her life and now it was spoiled.

But she hadn't worried about it for too long. Adam Thorne was hardly likely to remember her. That was one of the reasons she'd indulged herself, that and the fact he was heading back to London in the next couple of days.

He had called, as it happened, several times. She'd managed to stay cool and vague and after a couple more calls, he stopped asking how her garden was looking, had she been dancing lately and was Nick working her too hard. He only asked about her uncle.

She'd stammered that she was too busy to talk, she hadn't been able to contact him. Jasmine felt terrible, but what could she do? She'd never met her uncle. Never wanted to because of the bad blood between him and her father. And according to her father, he'd never wanted to meet her. Really, she'd done Adam a favor. Stewart Cooper, the reclusive billionaire, might never agree to see him if he knew Jasmine was a friend.

Now, she cautioned herself against telling him more than he needed to know. "Firstly, my name isn't Jasmine. It's Jane."

Adam frowned, pursing his lips, and she nearly smiled when he softly formed the word a couple of times, *Jane,* as if testing it on his lips.

Then he shook his head. "Doesn't do it for me, sorry."

"I haven't changed it officially," she told him, digging her fat traveling wallet out of her bag. She slid her passport from its compartment, opened it and showed him. "My passport and official documents are still Jane."

"Jasmine suits you better," he insisted, glancing at the passport.

She wondered with trepidation if her next words would get a reaction. "My father is a retired barrister, Sir Nigel Cooper?" She raised her brows in query.

Adam shook his head again.

She took a breath, maintaining eye contact while relief coursed through her. He hadn't heard of her father or her. She could scarcely believe it. But then, he'd only been in London four years, arriving more than a year after the scandal that caused Jane Cooper to become almost as prominent a household name as Princess Di—and not for the first time in her life. "He and my stepmother live at Pembleton Estate. It's a two-thousand acre estate in Lincolnshire. A stately home, part of which is open to the public." Again, Adam looked nonplussed, but she wouldn't expect him to be interested in English stately homes.

Now for the difficult part. "My father needs a male heir, a son or grandson to be able to keep the estate. Since my older brother died as a toddler, Father has always been very keen to see me married."

"You mean, like an arranged marriage?" Adam asked, leaning back and crossing his legs. "Do people still do that?"

"I expect he thought I'd take care of things myself," Jasmine said dryly. "Anyway, he's recently been diagnosed with a brain tumor. I'm afraid it's very advanced." The tumor was slow-growing, but her father had apparently ignored the signs for much too long. Jasmine was haunted by the thought that if she had been here, she may have seen the signs or persuaded him to be vigilant about medical appointments.

Adam made the usual platitudes of regret.

Jasmine continued, telling him her father even had a suitor for her in mind. "Our neighbor. He's an old school friend of mine."

"The wicked prince," Adam murmured.

Jasmine smiled. "He's not. He is a nice man, but I have no intention of marrying him."

She knew this must sound strange to someone who hadn't grown up in the rarefied atmosphere of English gentry, with all the tradition and history that was still alive and well in the country estates.

Jasmine looked down at her hands. "This is going to be a rather fraught visit. It's almost certainly Father's last Christmas. I…" She exhaled, feeling childish. Get it over with, she urged herself. Who knows? Adam may find the whole thing a lark.

But it wasn't. She had been a disappointment to her father all her life. She just wanted to please him, once, and have the memory that she'd done so. "I'm afraid I told an untruth a couple of months ago. I told him I was already engaged."

"And that's where I come in." He suddenly leaned forward quickly, fixing her with an intense look. "Why me, by the way?"

Because you are unaware of my past, she thought. *Because I felt guilty about the way I treated you. Because I wanted to see you again…* "I don't know very many men," she said truthfully. At least, not many that didn't pity her or think she was a laughingstock.

"And when your father asks about the wedding… where we're going to live…the pitter-patter of tiny feet?"

"We'll be suitably vague," she answered with confidence. "My father and I don't see eye to eye about some things." Most things, she thought. "Our relationship is quite distant. I am close to my stepmother, Gill. She may ask questions but probably not in front of him, and she's very discreet."

Adam's eyes never left her face. Jasmine mentally crossed her fingers and toes, knowing it was a lot to ask at such short notice. He was bound to have plans. She had thought about calling but hoped a surprise attack might have better results.

Still unsmiling, his eyes assessed her. If only she could turn the clock back and play that last morning again, or the phone calls afterward. Adam used to look at her with such regard.

He hadn't lost the habit, however, of maneuvering himself too close to her. Jasmine wished he'd sit at his desk rather than on it because he was too close for comfort. He always had been.

As if he read her mind, he suddenly sat up a little straighter. "And will your uncle be present at this family Christmas?"

She had expected him to ask. And in the scheme of things, this was the most important point of all. She kept her reply crisp. "No. He and my father have had a small falling out and it would be best not to mention him." Illness or not, the whole of Lincolnshire would hear Sir Nigel's roars if anyone mentioned his nemesis's name.

She softened her voice, plumping for sympathy.

"Since this may well be his last Christmas, I'd hate to upset him."

Adam's sharp eyes searched her face. She held his gaze steadily, waiting for his reply.

"For a favor of this magnitude," he said slowly, "and considering I have plans for Christmas…"

"Do you?"

"I *always* have plans, Jasmine." Adam smiled but there was little warmth in it. "Is there any good reason I should put myself out for you when you virtually ran me out of your house a few weeks ago?"

Friends were not a commodity Jasmine was flush with, but she had enjoyed every minute of their dates, of doing things she hadn't done before, the parry and thrust of his attempts to charm her into bed. "I thought we were friends."

She reminded herself that friends don't, as a rule, have hot, sweaty, plentiful sex in nearly every room in her house. Incredibly though, the experience had left her with such good—no, great—memories, it wouldn't worry her if Adam Thorne was her last lover ever. Who else could possibly measure up?

A shiver went through her and judging by the sudden flare of attention in his eyes, he'd noticed. She swallowed quickly. He couldn't know what steamy recollections had just filled her mind. Or how, all of a sudden, she could identify mint and orange blossom in his cologne. Or was so attuned to his breathing, her own emulated it. Nor how bloody attractive she found the way his fierce brows feathered a little on either side of the bridge of his nose.

"Friends help each other out," he murmured.

She closed her eyes and began to despair. Adam used the same voice as he had the night he finally persuaded her that she wanted him as much as he did her. Why deny each other, he'd said, when sex was such a natural and pleasurable way to show appreciation? That voice was her downfall; sultry, suggestive and warm, it coated the senses like honey on ham. Erotic images of their night together, his whispers inciting her to do things she'd never dreamed she could do, had her toes curling in latent pleasure.

For the first time—unless in her overheated state, she was imagining it—his eyes warmed a little—a lot. Adam Thorne knew exactly what she was thinking.

"Oh, I'm not discounting *that,* lovely Jasmine," he confirmed a second later, his deep, soft voice raising the hairs on the back of her neck. "Believe me, I remember every spectacular, soft, passionate inch of you."

She sucked in a breath to try to contain a pulse gone mad. Heat bloomed on her cheeks and all the way down her body. How did he do it, send her senses wild without even a touch? He used to toy with her at work, sitting on her desk, talking of nothing very much in that velvety voice of his, watching her with eyes that would tempt a saint. She'd thought it was about needling his brother or shattering her good-girl reputation. His effect on her was powerful and he knew it.

"That's not on the agenda this trip," she said, not as firmly as she would have liked. Which of them was she trying to convince?

She had to shoot him down. There were more important priorities than her own selfish desires. "I slept with you in a moment of weakness, not expecting to see you again. I wasn't looking for anything more."

Adam chuckled. "Well, I'm certainly not in the market for a relationship. But back to your 'agenda—'" he held up his index finger to indicate quote marks "—there doesn't seem to be an equitable balance of mutual reward between friends here."

Jasmine's desire seeped away. She knew what he wanted, but if he discovered the full extent of the hatred between her father and uncle, she would cease to be of use to him. She had to gloss over the family feud, at least until he was there at the estate, accepting their hospitality. Hopefully his good manners and charm would do the rest.

"All I want," Adam prompted, "is the introduction. The rest is up to me."

Seeing the determination on his face, Jasmine realized glossing over it wouldn't be enough. This man preferred something a little more concrete.

With six months to a year left to live, her father's happiness was her first priority. With no idea how she would go about it, Jasmine summoned up a self-assurance she didn't feel. "If you do this for me, I give you my word I will set it up—" She hesitated and then said firmly, "—after Christmas."

"Good." Adam got up and went back to his side of the desk. "Now that's settled, there is one more thing…"

Jasmine was already half way to her feet, preparing to depart.

"It's the annual company Christmas bash tonight. I've been too busy to find a date. Come with me."

Even as she reluctantly agreed, Jasmine had a sinking feeling about this. The more time she spent in Adam Thorne's company, the more she wanted to spend. Hopefully her good intentions wouldn't get her into trouble.

Then again, she'd had few enough opportunities to feel like a woman over the last few years.

Adam Thorne made her feel all woman.

Two

Adam picked her up in a silver Mercedes cabriolet that smelled brand-new, and took her to a trendy club only a short drive from her hotel.

"What name are we going by tonight?" he asked as they waited to be checked off the guest list.

"Just Jasmine," she said firmly, and it suddenly occurred to her she may be recognized. This was the kind of place some of her friends from five years ago might have frequented. She looked around warily, hoping that her long dark hair was different enough from the shaggy, lighter style she went with back then.

They made their way to a mezzanine, where about a hundred VIP guests of Croft, Croft and Bayley milled about. Almost immediately, well-wishers swamped them and she learned that tonight doubled as the annual corporate Christmas function, as well as Adam's farewell from the company. She looked around in amazement at the incredible interior. Every wall depicted what appeared to be a blue waterfall of vertical lines of numbers.

"Very high-tech, isn't it?" Adam smiled at her open-mouthed wonder. "Corporate clients can digitally design their own colors and atmosphere—or their brand, if they want to be boring—onto computers and have that imagery projected onto the walls for their event." He explained that Croft, Croft and Bayley had gone for a stock-exchange depiction tonight, but he'd been here when heaving blue seas seemed to crash against the walls. He'd seen panoramic landscapes of canyons that almost echoed, and meadows filled with nodding wildflowers in a gentle breeze. "You could come here every night of the week and feel you're somewhere different." He shook his head. "I liked the idea so much, I bought into it."

"You own this club?"

Adam shook his head. "Just a percentage of the multimedia company that came up with the concept."

Jasmine knew that innovative and daring ideas intrigued Adam. That was the catalyst for his start-up business, to give talented people with big ideas the means and expertise to go global.

She accepted a glass of champagne from a Santa-

hatted waitress and was introduced to too many people to count. While Adam chatted, one of the senior
partners extolled her escort's virtues. "I first saw him
on the floor of the exchange four years ago, making
money hand over fist as a day trader. A successful
trader should be passionate about markets, rather
than trading. While everyone else ran around in a
panic, Adam just sat there, watching, sticking to his
plan. I knew we had to have him."

As the night progressed, she heard much more of
Adam's ambition, how hard he'd worked to attain his
high level of success.

"The youngest-ever partner in this company,"
another partner confided. Croft, Croft and Bayley
wasn't the biggest stockbrokerage in the city, but it
was one of the oldest and most venerated. "We'll
miss him but we're too small to contain his ambition." Another of his colleagues told her that the new
business was risky but if anyone could pull it off,
Adam could.

All this left Jasmine a little confused and a lot impressed. Until today, her preconception of Adam
Thorne, based on their half-dozen outings in New
Zealand, had been of a fun-loving, sexy and rich
young man, an opinion reinforced by his brother's
declaration that he wasn't to be taken seriously. Nick
loved his brother, she knew that, but looking around
at the army of admirers, the breathtaking backdrop
of moving numbers, the copious bottles of French

champagne and decadent hors d'oeuvres, she couldn't help feeling Nick hadn't given enough credit to Adam's work ethic.

The formalities of the evening commenced as the partners wished their staff a happy Christmas and then made a special presentation to bid Adam farewell and wish him good luck for what was sure to be a stellar future. Jasmine watched the proceedings from well back in the crowd, feeling sorry for every other man in the place. It was unfair that one man should be so overendowed, not only with good looks and vitality, but success, too. Not so long ago, she'd thought Nick Thorne the most handsome man she knew. He was bigger than Adam but similar enough in coloring, athleticism and those hypnotic eyes, so she'd been as surprised as anyone when it came out recently that Nick was adopted.

But they were as different as night and day. Nick was straight-A all the way, a brilliant but conservative businessman in his expensive suits and neatly cropped hair. Jasmine tried and failed to imagine him tossing an old rugby ball around his office, or even with his feet up on the desk. Never in a million years.

Adam Thorne probably didn't even know how to knot a tie. Certainly she'd never seen him in one, not even the night last month he'd escorted her to the Royal New Zealand Ballet. Style oozed devilishly from every pore. His fierce brows and the stubble shadowing his jawline and full sexy lips lent him a bad-boy demeanor, even though his smile was a lot more ready than Nick's.

While she'd been busy daydreaming, another half hour had passed and the formalities wound up. Adam returned from the front of the room and drew her into his side.

"Very nice," he said in that low, sultry voice, leaning so close his lips almost touched her earlobe.

Jasmine shivered, knowing that he felt it since he'd placed one hand lightly on the small of her back. If that hadn't alerted her, his self-satisfied smile when he drew back did.

"What?" she asked casually. Adam Thorne was too discerning for his own good.

"Being the object of your avid attention."

So she'd been staring. "I believe it's polite, when listening to a speech, to pay attention to the speaker."

Adam's grin only widened. "You can be very *English* sometimes, Ms. Cooper."

He was playing with her. He knew the effect he had on her and was using her gratitude to his full advantage. But Jasmine had her pride and after all, he wanted something from her, too.

Aside from sex…she resisted the urge to fan her hot face and thought it best to change the tone of the conversation. "I think Nick would have been very proud of you tonight."

His surprise at her comment showed in the slight arch of one dark brow. Jasmine wasn't sure if it was the subject matter or just the change of direction but when he pursed his lips a second later, she saw that he was pleased. And that, funnily enough, pleased her.

"You'll never guess!" A young colleague of Adam's joined their small group, brimming with a sly kind of excitement that Jasmine recognized as typical of a gossip. "Which esteemed royal is in the gents', popping party pills right this minute?"

"Vincent de Burgh," someone said quickly.

"Not again!" Another member of their party rolled his eyes.

Jasmine's heart plummeted and she almost swayed on her feet. Vincent de Burgh, notorious playboy, tenth in line to the British throne, and the man whose betrayal five years ago sent her packing to the other side of the world.

Careful not to turn her head, she looked for the bathrooms, which she located on the first level. She then scrutinized the messenger's face, wondering if he was telling her in a roundabout way that he knew she had once been engaged to the very same royal louse fittingly off his face in a toilet.

The young executives compared recent stories about the troublesome royal, not giving her any particular interest. Satisfied it was just idle celebrity gossip, Jasmine relaxed slightly. Nonetheless, she couldn't afford to stay here and risk being recognized.

That Vincent was still behaving badly didn't surprise her. She'd heard he recently divorced the woman he ditched her for—her ex-best friend—and no doubt was drowning his sorrows and searching for some other rich, deluded female. The unfathomable thing was that he always succeeded, as her father had repeatedly warned her.

She turned to Adam, her mind racing. If he found out about her high-profile engagement, it would take just one Google hit to find out the rest. All she needed was tomorrow, one day, to play happy couples at the estate. Then Adam could leave "on business" and she could continue her holiday and spend some quality time with her father before she had to get back to work. She didn't expect to have to keep the pretense up for too long. Her father was getting weaker and more forgetful by the day, according to Gill. In two or three months, he might not comprehend anything, and if he did, then she would tell him that sadly, she and Adam hadn't worked out.

But if Adam discovered before tomorrow how acrimonious the relations were between her father and Stewart, she could kiss her Christmas Day goodwill mission goodbye.

Adam's eyes were on her face and she realized she'd been staring again. He had his back to the conveniences on the ground floor and she flicked a glance to the door of the men's toilets, just in time to see an older, but by the look of him, most un-wiser, Vincent lurch out.

Jasmine froze. He seemed to be looking directly up

at her but it was hard to tell with the lighting in here. After a moment, he turned toward the bar, stripping off his jacket as he did. While breathing out relief, she relished the rather nasty thought that her ex had not weathered the passing of years well. Too much good living showed in his paunch and the way his thick neck battled to be reined in by his tie. It may have been the lighting but his previously thick, sandy hair looked wispy from her vantage point on the mezzanine.

She watched as he joined a small group of men at the bar. The private function on the mezzanine had waiter service so he was obviously not part of the Croft, Croft and Bayley group. Jasmine began to breathe again.

Adam touched her arm and she brought her eyes back to his face.

"I'd like you to meet someone."

She shook hands with John Hadlow, Adam's new business partner, and his wife, Sherrilyn.

"I see why you've stood us up for Christmas, old boy," John said jovially.

Jasmine bit back a smile and glanced at Adam's face. Had he deliberately given her the impression his plans were more romantic than Christmas dinner with this pleasant couple? She apologized for upsetting everyone's schedule.

Half an hour later, she had almost forgotten about Vincent when a break in the music exposed an altercation by the stairs. She glanced over to see her ex-fiancé arguing loudly with a security man, who blocked his entrance into the private function. She spun around quickly, looking for Adam and hearing Vincent's voice clearly over the myriad conversations surrounding her. "Do you know who I am?"

Adam was a couple of feet away, talking to an attractive blonde. What to do? She could hole up in the ladies', or just pray the security guard remained aloof about Vincent's lineage. There were two stairways on either side of the mezzanine leading down. Jasmine contemplated making a dash for it down the left-hand side while Vincent was engaged with the bouncer on the right.

Her heart pounded in near panic. If he accosted her, she could claim not to know him—or she could just come clean and tell Adam the truth; that she was persona non grata to her uncle and didn't have the tiniest chance of setting up a meeting between them.

"But I just want to say a quick hallo to someone," Vincent insisted loudly to the staunch security man.

Making a decision, and hoping she wouldn't live to regret it, Jasmine walked up to stand beside Adam and slid her arm around his waist, inside his jacket. Sucked in a breath against the impact of lean, muscled torso, a very appealing male cologne and the peculiar pheromones or hormones that always had her off-kilter with this particular man. Absorbing the jolt to her senses, she bravely waited as he slowly turned his head to her. Yes, cool blonde or not, she had his full attention.

"Sorry," she said apologetically to his companion. Lifting up on tiptoe, and without removing her hand from his body, she put her lips directly onto his ear. "I think the jet lag has just caught up with me," she whispered, ensuring her lips caressed his ear with each syllable.

Adam had bowed his head in deference to his greater height. Now he turned his face and looked down into hers. His eyes burned gold, interest and wariness flickering.

Jasmine reached up toward his ear again but because he had turned his head, her cheek brushed his, thrilling her with the contact. "That," she whispered seductively, "or the champagne."

He moved as she withdrew, so that his cheek blocked hers from retreat. Triumph, query and a wolfish sort of warning blazed out from the golden depths of his eyes. If there wasn't so much at stake, she would have run to save herself. The message was clear: *Don't play with me.* Or maybe that was just her guilty conscience.

After a second's hesitation, he became all concern and solitude, making his excuses to the blonde, saying goodbye to John, shaking hands with people as they prepared to go.

And moving toward the wrong staircase. Vincent was still there, of course. She'd learned during their engagement that when he didn't get his own way, the arguments lasted for days.

"This way." She tugged on his arm, nodding at the other staircase. "I need to visit the ladies'."

They veered to the right. "You don't have to come," she told him rather half-heartedly once they were at the bottom of the stairs, glancing around fearfully in case His Royal Highness emerged from the sea of people celebrating Christmas Eve. "It's your big night, I feel guilty."

She did feel guilty about spoiling his big night, but not too guilty. And she would prefer he didn't hang around without her in case Vincent bailed him up and asked about her.

No sign of him, though, and no sign that Adam was disposed to let her disappear into the night. There was a nasty moment on the way to the exit when a photographer came from nowhere, his camera up. "The man of the hour. Quick photo for the *Out and About* magazine?"

Luckily Jasmine was able to melt judiciously into the ladies' directly beside her, hoping it would not seem ungracious.

Nothing eventuated and soon they were at Adam's car. "Feeling better?" he asked as she strapped herself in. He started the car but made no effort to put it into gear.

"Much." She allowed herself to relax a little. It was a close call but the ends justified the means and now they were safe. "I'm sorry about this. I could just take a cab…"

Adam reached over and picked up her hand. "What sort of fiancé would I be if I didn't look after you?"

He lifted her hand to his mouth and pressed his lips to the pulse point on her wrist. Her bones melted as he nibbled and sucked at the sensitive point. Suddenly, Jasmine was in real danger of keeling over and it had nothing to do with jet lag. A warm flush bathed her as she imagined a thousand arrows of fire wove a prickly scarf on the back of her neck. Her skin felt tight and stretched, her insides jumped about nervously while her mouth was as arid as the desert. "Wha-what are you doing?" she asked.

The big motor purred. Adam didn't answer right away, engrossed in driving her mad with equal parts delight and trepidation. Then he lowered her hand and spoke with the honeyed, seductive tone he'd used before. "Let's just say I'm getting into character for tomorrow." He brought her hand to his mouth again, kissing each fingertip.

Just for a moment more she wanted to enjoy this, the desire that raced through her veins, her heart beating a tattoo on her rib cage. Maybe it was jet lag, because Jasmine was a sensible woman. Why else would she seriously consider succumbing to the incredible pull to move closer, drink in the heat coming off him in waves of male scented sensuality? It wasn't right that this man should have such a monopoly on her innermost desires and be able to exploit them at will.

Summoning every ounce of concentration and willpower, Jasmine stiffened her fingers and tugged until he let go. For good measure, she turned her face to the front, knowing that his strong-boned face, those wicked lips branding her flesh, turned her on unbearably. She'd never missed sex until she'd tasted it with him.

Adam's laugh was almost inaudible in the hum of the car, but decadently amused. "I enjoy watching you squirm, Jasmine, if only because it's out of character."

She huffed out a breath, her cheeks burning. "I don't know what you mean."

She didn't look at him again until they'd pulled up outside her hotel. The moment the car stopped, she released the seat belt and opened the door, welcoming the freezing blast of air on her hot face.

Adam's eyes were still amused. "About nine?"

Jasmine nodded and closed the door.

A couple of minutes later, she swept back the curtains in her deluxe room, sank down onto a chair and looked out over Trafalgar Square and the world's most famous Christmas tree. Her stepmother, Gill, had first brought her to see the tree when she was only six or seven and she'd been many times since. Strings of vertical lights draped the huge Norwegian spruce, picking out the snowflakes as they fell. It was a magical sight, one that should have felt familiar and soothing.

She wasn't soothed. Her nerves felt chafed raw.

In the last five years she thought she'd found peace, if not happiness. From the way Adam had been talking, it wouldn't be long before he was back in New Zealand, probably Wellington, laughing and teasing and driving her mad with lust. Why had she slept with him? Far from satisfying her sexual curiosity, it had only served to make her want him more.

Three

The drive from London took longer than expected because of a thick snow flurry, but finally they arrived at the estate just in time for lunch. Jasmine's apprehension and excitement built as they passed through the heavy wrought-iron gates. She loved the drive up to the house. Fallow deer grazed in the wooded parkland. She pointed out the stud farm her father established a decade ago. Snow dusted the reeds around the lake fronting the house.

Pembleton, originally a large Georgian house, had been greatly added to in the years before the First World War and now lent itself more to the Edwardian era.

Even Adam expressed his admiration as they slowly approached the great dun-colored house, whose dimensions more resembled a terraced street than one residence. Jasmine sighed with pride. She might have grown up here and certainly had her share of bad memories of the place, but the house and setting still took her breath away.

"How many rooms?" Adam asked as they pulled up in front of the massive porticoed entrance.

"Over a hundred, though half of it is closed up."

Her stepmother, Gill, burst out of the door and raced down the steps. Sixty years young, a petite, iron-gray-haired bundle of energy and efficiency, she greeted them with a volley of warm squeals.

"Your father is having a good day," she told them, "and is quite excited about meeting Adam, even if he probably won't show it."

Jasmine didn't take offense that her father was more excited about meeting Adam than seeing his daughter. She had always been a disappointment to him, first by being born a girl, and then when she became the willful teenager who defied his wishes.

But in his distant manner, Sir Nigel did seem pleased to see her. He sat in his comfortable chair by the fireplace and inspected her for a minute or more while clasping one of her hands with both of his. Jasmine—Jane, to them—tried to conceal her shock at his frail appearance. He'd always been a burly man—that's where she got her height from, since her mother had apparently been tiny. His most notable feature had always been his booming voice but there was little evidence of it today, except occasionally when addressing Adam. He was a shadow of his former self.

Jasmine grappled with guilt. She should be here to take care of him instead of leaving everything to Gill. She'd been with the family since Jasmine was ten years old. Gill was the warmest thing about her childhood and beyond.

They ate Christmas lunch in the formal dining room, a room that had, in the past, hosted banquets for heads of state. Among many great portraits on the walls there was a Madonna and child painted by Murillo hanging over the antique fireplace. They sat at one end of the massive table for "One's table should never exceed the nine muses," Gill liked to say.

As usual there was a daunting array of food—quail; turkey, roast beef; a whole salmon, pink and delicious; vegetables of every variety and then Christmas steamed pudding and brandy sauce with Gill's folly, ancient threepences hidden within. Jasmine had pre-warned Adam of this eccentricity to avoid breaking a tooth.

Afterward, her father insisted Gill take the seal off an old bottle of port and they adjourned to the more informal drawing room.

"So you're engaged at last," her father said croakily,

settling into his chair. Adam and Jasmine sat on an overstuffed antique couch opposite her father while Gill served the drinks.

This would be the awkward part but she didn't expect there would be many questions. Her father would not care who she married, as long as his estate was looked after. "Yes, we are," she replied, trying to sound excited.

"When is the wedding? Will it be here?"

Adam's arm slipped around her shoulder and she tried not to flinch. "As soon as possible," he murmured, "as far as I'm concerned."

Jasmine's smile didn't slip but every muscle in her body tensed up and her mind raced. "We haven't had time to discuss it," she said, before burying her nose in her port.

Her father's head raised. "Well, six months, a year?"

Her heart went out to him. With a death sentence hanging over his head, of course he wanted a date to grasp on to. "We'll discuss it while we're on holiday and let you know."

"Hmph." Her father subsided back into the seat, picking at the rug Gill had put over his knees. "I'll have to announce it."

"No!"

Jasmine's sharp response had all eyes swiveling to her face. She swallowed down the panic that comment had instigated. "I'd really prefer to keep this just within the family, if possible."

Her father gave her a spiteful look. "My daughter, the procrastinator," he muttered.

She heard Adam's quick indrawn breath and couldn't look at him.

"That's understandable, dear," Gill said sympathetically.

Adam's hand slid around and surreptitiously tugged on her ponytail. "I'm all for shouting it from the rooftops," he said in a low voice that only she could hear.

Jasmine resisted the shiver of awareness that generated and kept her eyes on her father, amazed he would even suggest a public announcement after what happened with Vincent nearly six years ago. When the story broke that her fiancé and her best friend had run off into the sunset together just a month before her wedding, she hadn't been able to leave the house without paparazzi on her tail. That was when she realized she could never escape her past. All her hopes and dreams crashed in spectacular style, played out in the media, and she decided to move as far away as she could get. Somewhere where no one knew of her infamous past, and hopefully never would.

"Have you spoken to Ian recently?" her father asked, his stern gaze losing none of its sharpness despite the ravages of age and illness.

"No." Jasmine sighed. "Should I have?"

"Who's Ian?" Adam leaned forward to set his port

glass down. His brows were raised and his knee pressed against hers.

She gave him a cool glance. If you asked her, he was playing the amorous fiancé just a little too well for her liking. "A friend. Our neighbor." She had told him about Ian—the little she wanted him to know at this point.

"A little more than a friend I think," her father murmured.

Ian had been there all her life. They were the same age, had played together as children. He was her friend—until her father decided he would make an ideal husband. "He's steady, a hard worker, and boys run in that family," he declared. "Plus he will inherit the adjoining thousand acres. That gives us options to expand the estate and generate more income."

From the time she was eighteen, her father never let up but Jasmine gave no serious consideration to a union. When her past and present collided with vivid impact, Ian was there to pick up the pieces. Because he was the only one in the world who didn't look at her as if she had two heads, and because her father did all in his power to push them together, she went out with him for a couple of months and tried to think of him as more than a friend. She even slept with him, but there was no chemistry there for her.

They usually got together for a coffee or a meal on her annual trips home but she hadn't felt obliged to let him know she was coming. Besides, she knew he was in Switzerland for Christmas.

Now everyone, Adam included, was looking at her as if she was a jezebel. "He's a friend," she repeated firmly, sipping her port.

"Hmph." Her father glared at her hands. "No ring?"

"We plan to remedy that on this visit, don't we, darling?" Adam took her free hand and squeezed it. "Antwerp or Amsterdam?"

Jasmine smiled faintly and forced herself to relax her fingers, one by one, while thinking of ways to kill him.

Thankfully the excitement and port had worn her father out and he retired shortly afterward for a nap. The blazing fire and overstuffed bellies had everyone yawning. Gill rose, saying she had made up Jasmine's room. "You are staying? And for the party tomorrow?"

Jasmine prepared to say that she would stay but not Adam, and then Gill's words filtered into her brain, setting up a wave of temptation to batter her defenses. *Her* room, she'd said. Not two rooms…

Her room where she'd played with dolls, swooned over the Backstreet Boys, experimented with clothes and makeup, fantasized over real boys, sneaked Vincent into…and then howled her anguish into her pillow when he broke her heart. What was a girl's bedroom but a catalogue of the most intimate experiences of one's life?

It couldn't get any more intimate than having Adam Thorne in her room, in amongst her personal things. Heat that had little to do with the fire and more to do with that *blasted* man caressing her fingers spread through her, dampening her forehead.

And then there was the annual Boxing Day party tomorrow that the estate put on for the locals in the district. An afternoon tea and free tour for the villagers and later, cocktails and a dinner party for closer friends and the village dignitaries. The chances of getting through the whole thing without Adam discovering the depth of hatred between her father and his brother were slim. The locals loved to gossip about the inhabitants of the estate. The family feud and her personal shame were bound to arise at some point.

"Sorry," she managed at last. "I can, but Adam has some business in town."

Her "fiancé" lifted her hand to his mouth and pressed his lips to her palm. "Nonsense. It's Christmas. We'd love to stay."

Oh, she really would have to kill him. Refusing to look at him, she gave Gill a rather strained smile and shrug.

Adam was clearly trying to embarrass and discomfit her. She set her mouth. It wouldn't work. Pembleton wasn't short on bedrooms and Jasmine knew where the bedding was kept.

Gill gave her a curious glance. Her stepmother was pretty intuitive. What was Adam playing at? She'd have thought he'd be pleased to get away from the ancient old house and her overbearing father. This just didn't seem his scene.

"I think I'll show Adam part of the house," she said, rising. "And walk off some of that wonderful dinner."

Gill nodded. "If you get hungry later, there are plenty of leftovers in the kitchen. Just help your-selves. Your father usually has his tea in his room but he might come down later."

As soon as she'd gone, Jasmine turned back to Adam and kept her voice low. "Did you have to say you'd stay?"

He remained seated, looking up at her thought-fully. "I've never stayed in a stately home before... tell me about Ian."

She missed a beat. "What about him?"

"Have you slept together?"

Jasmine pressed her lips together to stop the hot retort that sprang to mind. Something in the way his sharp gaze focused so intently on her stopped her. After a long pause, she nodded.

"I see."

What did he see? That she'd slept with him, there-fore she was obliged to marry him? A smile nearly slipped out when she thought of the dent that would put in Adam Thorne's womanizing ways.

Yet she felt compelled to justify herself. "It was comfort sex. And my father has his own acquisitive reasons for wanting me to marry Ian."

"Do I need to dust off my dueling swords?"

She let another heartbeat go by, squashing down, as she often did, all the clever things she'd wish she'd said later, when she was alone. "Would you like to see the house or not?"

Adam got up, looming tall over her. She turned toward the door but he caught her arm and turned her back. "Why did you need his comfort?"

Jasmine blinked, needing to think. Overfull, overheated, overwhelmed by him…how much did he deserve to know? She couldn't bear it if all the salacious stories got back to his brother and her colleagues. Of course she missed home, this house mostly, Gill, and sometimes her cantankerous father. But New Zealand was her haven. Her comfortable art deco house in the eastern suburbs was a far cry from the luxury and tradition of Pembleton, but she felt safe there. With one careless word, Adam could whip that safety net out from under her.

From the determined gleam in his eye, she deduced the lesser of two evils would be her failed love affair, the incident that sparked the return of all the unwelcome publicity from years before. The most important thing was to keep the feud from him, for now at least.

Jasmine looked pointedly at his hand on her arm. "A broken heart, reasonably common when you're twenty."

Adam merely raised his brows.

She sighed. "Against my father's wishes, I fell in love with the man who is tenth in line for the throne. It didn't last. He preferred my best friend. They recently divorced, but the point is, for a few months, I was a lamb to the slaughter for the press. An engagement announcement—" she gave him a scathing look "—for our *pretend* engagement might bring it all up again."

Adam's face cleared. "Vincent de Burgh. That's why you were in such a hurry to leave last night—and you didn't want your photo taken."

Jasmine nodded, not realizing he'd picked up on that.

His eyes searched her face for so long she began to fidget. Finally he nodded. "Okay. That wasn't so hard, was it?"

"What?"

"To bring me up to speed. I'm beginning to think there are more secrets hoarded up in that lovely head—" he tapped her temple with his index finger "—than currently floating around the Secret service."

Adam was enjoying himself. Despite Jasmine's stuffy father, who seemed to regard her achievements and wishes as an afterthought, her stepmother was great and the house was out of this world.

The best part was making her squirm, because as he'd pointed out last night, she didn't like it one bit. Playing her fiancé gave him carte blanche to touch, to be suggestive, to tease. He almost forgot why he was here. Oh, he wanted Jasmine—or Jane, as he had to keep reminding himself—more with each passing minute but his main goal was the opportunity to meet her uncle.

The touching, being suggestive and teasing just made it all the more enjoyable—for him.

The private apartments were bright and light, showcasing plenty of marble, plasterwork, windows and gilded furnishings. It was a different story "below stairs", as the basement was known. This is where the twenty or so servants in the early nineteen-hundreds had worked, Jasmine explained. "And that doesn't count the gardeners, farmhands, garage or stable hands. Or, would you believe, the night watchmen."

History wasn't his thing, but as they slowly wandered the areas open to the public, Adam was transported back to another time. She astounded him with her knowledge. It seemed she had a story about every nook and cranny, every priceless heirloom, every brick in the house! It was all so fascinating.

"The hall of summons," she announced, pointing out the labels where forty bells hung high on faded plaster walls, some sporting the names of some of her ancestors. She showed him the cavernous kitchen, with its incredibly high ceiling, "to dissipate the heat and steam from the coal-powered range, which could eat up to a hundredweight of coal in a day."

"How do you know all this stuff?" he marveled, declining her invitation to walk up the ninety stone stairs to the maids' quarters in the attic.

"I grew up here." She ran her hand over some ancient books in the butler's rooms—*Burke's Peerage, Baronetage and Knightage* was one tome that caught Adam's eye. "And I have a degree in English history."

He straightened, surprised. "You do?"

"Uh-huh. I got interested in history when we started a family tree at school," she explained. "It took me years to finish, even though our family has only been here for a couple of hundred years." They walked up the basement stairs into the entranceway, blinking at the strong light after the gloominess below. "I enjoyed it so much, I decided I wanted to work in a museum one day."

"And yet now you reside in one of the youngest countries in the world and work as a personal assistant in a financial organization."

Jasmine laughed. "Ironic, isn't it? Maybe Te Papa would have me."

She referred to New Zealand's national museum in Wellington. Adam's interest in Jasmine doubled. She was well-educated, cultured, elegant. She oozed class, spades of it—and it wasn't something she'd learned. Rather, she was born to it, to this grand house with hundreds of years under its belt.

As she uncovered history for him, he so wanted to uncover her many layers, to know her secrets and desires and fears and dreams. Despite her culture and poise and obvious smarts, she was vulnerable, softer than the socialites or corporate sharks he normally dated.

But Adam had a feeling unraveling Jasmine's mysteries would take a lifetime.

"Don't you miss it here, all the history, the house and the countryside?"

"Sometimes."

"Will you stay in New Zealand?" he asked.

"For now," she said pensively, neither her tone nor the brief reply a confirmation.

"What do you like about it?"

She thought for a moment. "The laid-back, fair-dues character of it. The small population. A lot of things. It just seems a more open and fair society."

Adam nodded. He missed his country often—when he wasn't working fifteen-hour days or squiring some gorgeous woman around London—and was looking forward to returning, probably within the next year, and showing his brother and father that he'd risen to the top.

They'd eat his dust. So he was an irresponsible lightweight who could not sustain his incredible success. He'd show them and raise them some. And when he'd set up in Australia and expanded into the States, perhaps by the time he was forty, he'd choose a mate and start a family. And his family would come first. Adam would not emulate his parents, who had worked six days a week for most of his childhood.

Not that he was complaining. He liked his particu-

lar set of familial individuals. He'd just come out of
the womb always wanting to do better…at everything. What was wrong with that?

That night, they said their good-nights to Gill and
he followed Jasmine up the incredible silver stairway,
which apparently took three men three days to polish
in its day. They hadn't discussed sleeping arrangements but she wasn't at ease. The stiffness of her
back as she showed him the way corroborated that.
After several fruitless dates in New Zealand, he was
conversant with her resolve.

His desire for her had only increased since their
passionate encounter last month. Far from slaking his
thirst, he was parched to the bone. She'd been very
proper throughout the day, even when he pushed the
boundaries a little, touching her, whispering in her
ear, all the little nuances that hopefully had her father
and stepmother believing they were a couple.

She hadn't cracked. He admired her composure
but it only made him more determined to break it. He
thought back to some of the dark rooms "below
stairs" and imagined there was a ghost or two clank-
ing around this mausoleum—perhaps he could play
the "afraid of the dark card"…

She opened a door and showed him into a bedroom that would fit most of his town house inside.
The room and salon were tastefully decorated in
sage green, overlooking an Italian fountain in the lily
pond, and with the ubiquitous fire crackling in the

antique fireplace. This house must be hellish cold, he thought, with the number of fireplaces throughout.

"Don't tell me this was your actual room?" He touched the four-poster bed that looked the size of an Olympic swimming pool. He was amazed anyone could sleep here. The furniture and decor belonged in a palace.

"Mmm." She walked over to their bags, which the housekeeper had brought up from the entrance. Watching her, it suddenly hit Adam that she'd grown up here, this was a slice of her life, with all its pomp and ceremony and tradition.

And yet it just didn't mesh with the shy woman he knew in Wellington. Her home was comfortable, small, with a bright garden full of camellias and rhododendrons, but not luxurious by any means.

Adam blew out a long breath, it suddenly occurring to him that Jasmine was serious money. Not that he cared about having money half as much as the making of it. But with her obvious love of history, her family so ancient and well-connected, how could she turn her back on this and expect to find happiness in a country where only the odd tree dated back more than a couple of centuries?

She belonged here, couldn't she see that?

Jasmine picked up her bag and headed for the door. Adam leaned on the fireplace, knowing she was too well-mannered to leave without saying good-night.

She turned at the door, gifting him a small smile. "Sleep well."

"That's a fine way to say good-night to your fiancé," he said in a low, teasing voice.

She shifted the overnight bag into her other hand. Her eyes were wary but not hostile. "You're enjoying this, I believe."

Adam's head went up, his smile ready. He always enjoyed the chase. She should know that! "I am, I admit it."

And he wasn't just teasing. He enjoyed seeing her in her natural environment. "It's like a different world."

"Good night, Adam," she said quietly, looking into his face, and as always happened when they looked at each other, the overpowering attraction leaped to life between them, boosting his anticipation.

Then she blinked rapidly and began to back away toward the door. Adam spoke quickly. "And now you're going to leave me to the mercy of the resident ghosts and go off to some crypt somewhere, because you don't trust yourself in the same room with me."

Yes, he was disappointed. The desire he felt for her was much too intense for a woman he had already slept with. What was this hold she had over him?

Jasmine smiled gently. "The ghosts are friendly and I'll pass on the crypt, but I should be safe in the maids' quarters in the attic."

Adam nodded. "Ninety stairs should render you relatively safe, yes."

Again she turned to go, then stopped. "Thank you for this."

Simply said, classy. He *really* liked this woman—but he had to remember what his purpose here was. His whole life stretched out in front of him, time enough for distractions. But for now, he had a new business to contend with, people who depended on him.

He shrugged carelessly. "You want something. I want something."

Often he'd thought Jasmine's eyes looked sad. If not sad, then as if they were expecting something to make them sad in the very near future. Now she stood in the doorway, both hands grasping the strap on her holdall, her chin tucked into her chest, and her eyes almost silver in the firelight, filled with sadness and secrets.

"Of course," she said, and left the room.

Four

A weak sun came out on Boxing Day, so Jasmine decided to show Adam the grounds of the estate. They took her father's four-wheel drive and motored slowly around the two-thousand acres. There were a couple of hundred acres of woodland and grazing for fallow deer, the thoroughbred stud, stables and track and expansive but basically disused parklands, backed by rocky, heather-covered hills behind the house.

"Father always said he'd like to develop a golf course here. I don't know why he hasn't."

"How many staff look after all this?" Adam asked. She told him that the estate retained only a small staff of a live-in housekeeper, part-time cleaners and kitchen hands, cook, tour guide and gardener. "Plus the stud manager," Jasmine finished. "It's not nearly enough. We need an agricultural specialist, first and foremost. Gill still handles most of the administrative tasks, but she hasn't kept up with learning new techniques and technology." She turned her face to the house in the distance. "And I doubt she'll have time for the next few months."

Jasmine had many ideas for improving the estate, although her personal choice would be to concentrate on the house and heirlooms first.

"All those empty rooms could be put to such good use," she mused, her mind clicking into second gear. "An antiques center, private exhibitions, niche weekends for small groups like writers and such, small conferences, weddings…" There were endless possibilities that excited her but not, sadly, her more conservative father. "Father doesn't hold with the modern trend of opening up stately homes to the public. He's had to, to some extent, to keep up with the maintenance costs, but it's a struggle getting him to listen to any new ideas."

"With you in charge," Adam commented, "Pembleton could be a world-class venue."

She smiled at him and gazed around at the snow-dusted landscape. Perhaps absence did make the heart fonder. Or the reality of her father's mortality brought it all closer to home. She had loved the house and the land, would always love it, but the memories that remained at the edges of her mind were of distance, of being let down. She'd always been convinced that the events in her early life colored how her father saw her, ultimately as a burden and a disappointment. She had long accepted that they would never be close, and that that wasn't her fault. But after Vincent, the place became a prison. And if she'd gone along with her father's wishes to marry Ian, it would be her prison now.

They drove into the village and stopped for a pint at the local pub. She acknowledged the curious stares of the locals, a few of whom she remembered vaguely. Suddenly she was glad she lived in New Zealand. Just something so small as to be able to drink a coffee or a beer in public, without everyone speculating on your love life or your parents' tragedy of a marriage, was worth the pangs of regret she sometimes suffered when thinking about home.

"Is that little Jane Cooper?" the barmaid asked.

Jasmine trawled her memory banks. "How are you, Mrs. Dainty?"

They chatted for a minute or two about the sad state of her father's health. "Some families have their share of tragedy," the pleasant woman said, shaking her head, "but yours has had more than most."

"What did she mean?" Adam asked as they took a table by the fireplace.

Jasmine had spent a good part of the night, bedded down in a room four doors away from Adam, thinking about him. Wishing that she could separate sex from emotion, because her emotions were going haywire with him around.

She didn't regret that she'd slept with him a few weeks ago, but involving him in her family affairs could turn out to be the biggest regret of all, because despite his arrogance and his teasing, he was dangerously likeable.

She looked at him over the rim of her beer, felt the kick in the pit of her stomach whenever their eyes met. If only she could accept, as he did, that sex was the only thing between them, the only thing that would ever be between them.

She remembered what he'd said the day before about her secrets. She was full of them and experience had taught her not to confide in people.

Since she'd been here, she'd had one fright on Christmas Eve with Vincent, and now faced the prospect of Adam hearing about her past tonight at the party. She didn't think for a moment he would be unsympathetic about the rest of it, but the killer would be her non-contact with her uncle.

Jasmine decided he should know the details—with the exception of the insurmountable rift between her father and uncle. She crossed her fingers and hoped he'd feel so sorry for "poor little Jane Cooper" that he'd forget about Stewart Cooper.

Adam waved his hand in front of her face. "Are you still with me?" That wicked, expressive mouth curved. She warmed to the crinkles in the corners of his eyes.

It would be a relief to share, after so many years hiding it away as if it never happened. Even as her fingers tapped the side of her pint glass, as she inhaled in preparation of laying her life bare to a virtual stranger, she wondered, why take the risk when there was no future for them? What if he misused the information?

What if he didn't and it brought them closer?

Jasmine swallowed and looked at him steadily. "My mother died when I was fourteen, after spending ten years in a psychiatric institution. She—she never got over the fact that she was driving when my brother was killed in a car accident, not long after I was born."

Adam had been holding his pint to his mouth. Now he set it down slowly, his eyes focusing intently on her face, and put his elbows on the table. She imagined this was what he looked like when chasing a financial deal.

Or a woman… She looked away.

"They said she was suffering from post-natal depression after having me." Jasmine shrugged, her eyes flitting in an ordered way to each object on the wall behind his head, from the stag's head to the rusty old scythe to an ancient photo of Pembleton, which she must remember to have a closer look at. "Anyway, she bore it for a few years but when I was three years old, while my father was away on business, she took me on the ferry to Paris and left me there."

Adam exhaled carefully. "Left you where, exactly?"

"On the Montmartre carousel, actually." Jasmine smiled ruefully. "Going around in circles."

Thankfully, she'd been too young to remember. It hadn't dimmed her love of the horses on the estate, and she had only nice thoughts of France the couple of times she'd visited. "She came home without me. Father came back to Britain two days later and saw the news, saw me—" she cleared her throat "—on the news, and called the police."

Being only three, the media frenzy had gone over her head, but it must have been terrible for her parents. Every European country published pictures of the "poor abandoned soul" and in Britain, her parents—especially her mother—were vilified as monsters. Her father kept the details from her over the years but Jasmine picked up a fair amount from the playground at school. Her mother struggled on for another year after "the incident," heavily medicated and supervised, but continued to deteriorate. Another furor in the papers erupted when she was finally committed to the psychiatric facility, and again when she died and Sir Nigel married Gill a few years later. Every time the Cooper family name came up, the whole sad story was rehashed, most spectacularly of all when her engagement to Vincent failed. "That was when I realized that I couldn't escape my past and moved to New Zealand," she finished matter-of-factly.

Adam eyes were warm, soothing, full of compassion, but all he said was, "Wow."

"I didn't tell you this to get sympathy but you're probably going to hear bits and pieces tonight."

"Did you see your mother after that?" Adam asked.

Jasmine shook her head. "After an argument with Gill one day when I was about thirteen, I told her I wanted to see my real mother. Later, when I'd calmed down, she said I could if I wanted to and she would take me. But somehow, we never did."

Her father hadn't been so forbearing. He refused to allow her mother's name to be mentioned. It was Gill who told her that her mother was so ill and so heavily medicated, she wouldn't know her.

"Why New Zealand?" Adam asked.

Her shoulders rose. "Fresh start and about as far away as I could get."

"Does Nick know any of this?"

"No." It was as flat and final as she could make it.

He reached over the table and squeezed her shoulder briefly. "Thanks for telling me. Your secret is safe with me."

Jasmine believed him. Then again, what choice did she have? She picked up her half-full glass and took a mouthful, then pushed it to the center of the table. "Drink up. We'll be late for the meet and greet."

After the locals left the estate, full of ale, cider and the cook's excellent afternoon tea, Adam dressed for the dinner party, wandering around Jasmine's room as he did. Although it was furnished fit for a princess, and obviously hadn't been used as a regular bedroom for years, it retained some little touches of her. A stuffed toy or two, a collection of boy band CDs, a cluster of framed photos that had pride of place on an armoire that belonged in a museum, like nearly everything in this house.

One photo showed her in front of a huge Christmas tree in Trafalgar Square, if he wasn't mistaken, dated 1994; she must have been about eleven years old. Another in a silver ball gown that still hung in her closet. He knew she was a member of one of his mother's dancing clubs for a number of years.

Adam understood better now her fiercely guarded personality. She didn't let people close because those close to her had let her down, abandoned her. Those she should have been able to trust—her mother, her lover—had, for whatever reason, turned their backs on her.

There was another photo of her with a handsome, thick-set young man in muddy boots and oilskins, leaning on a rifle. Jasmine looked about eighteen and wore a smile as fresh and open as a child's. He wondered if that was the neighbor or a young Vincent de Burgh, the louse who had broken her heart.

He checked his watch and straightened his jacket, thinking at least he'd brightened up her sad eyes a bit last month. They'd gone clubbing, sailing and once for a wild motorcycle ride around the bays of Wellington.

She'd lost her breath and laughed, saying she'd never done anything like that before. She took him to the ballet and cooked for him one night at her home. And the last night, when he'd finally got her into bed, there was no sadness or tight control, only passion.

And that, he supposed, opening the door and stepping out into the hallway, was why she had chosen him for this well-intentioned scheme to convince her father they were engaged. She didn't know many people because she liked to keep to herself and with her backstory, who could blame her? Adam had made an effort, which was nothing unusual for him, but he suspected not many people in her life did that for her. Certainly not her father....

He would keep her secrets and keep her old man sweet for tonight but he wanted something, too, and he wasn't her savior. Once she had helped to bring her uncle to the negotiating table, they would go their separate ways, hopefully after a last sensational night together. After what she'd been through, he doubted she had any illusions left about love and forever, and Adam had no time in the foreseeable future to take a woman seriously.

Jasmine came out of the room down the hall and waited when she saw him. She inspected him as he approached and nodded approvingly. He hadn't expected to be hobnobbing with the gentry and had only brought a leather jacket, but Gill had come up with a smart sports jacket that fit perfectly.

"You look nice," she said, and tucked her arm through his.

"And you are ravishing, as always," he said. She wore her rich dark hair swept back in a loose French twist, long wisps trailing her shoulders. He liked the softer, less restrained look. Her trouser suit was platinum-gray, with a lacy cami underneath the open jacket and a dark green chiffon scarf looped simply around her neck and hanging down to her waist. Emerald and diamond studs glinted at her ears, her only jewelry. Simple, elegant, classy. "Very country," he murmured as he escorted her proudly into the formal dining room. And from nowhere came the fleeting thought that if he ever was to take a woman seriously, it would be this woman....

The English gentry knew how to eat. It seemed compulsory to showcase every meat known to mankind on the same groaning table. The old historical dramas that showed Vikings and warriors at table, gnawing on a massive hock, were not so far removed from today, cutlery and table manners notwithstanding.

Jasmine's father sat at the head of the long table of thirty guests. Most were older, all of them local, but there were a couple of people around Jasmine's age that he learned had attended the same schools. She stayed close to him during the dinner and they were both relieved that her father did not mention the engagement. Adam was introduced as "Jane's friend."

As dinner was cleared away by the attentive staff,

everyone adjourned to the large room called the orangery, a kind of insulated and robust conservatory, with underfloor heating, impressive sculptures, exotic plants and lots of glass. In the less formal situation, Jasmine's attention was avidly sought. Everyone wanted to know how she liked New Zealand and when she was coming home. Left to his own devices for the first time, Adam engaged in conversation with a blustery gentleman whose brick-colored complexion increased alarmingly with every glass of port he was able to snag from the circling waiters.

"Oh, yes, I've known the family all my life," the man said, his eagle eyes already scoping the progress of the next waiter. "Tragic story, Sir Nigel's wife and all."

Adam nodded absently, his eyes searching for Jasmine, bored by the man's inebriated waffle. He prepared to make his excuses when he suddenly heard the name Stewart Cooper. He raised one eyebrow, signaling his interest.

"Both brothers loved the same woman, you know," the man confided while Adam braced himself against the alcoholic fumes wafting from his companion's mouth. He waved a meaty hand in Jasmine's general direction. "Her daughter takes after her in looks. One only hopes not in morals or mental health."

Adam turned to face the man and stepped forward, backing him up against the wall a little. He wanted to hear more but didn't necessarily want the rest of the room to hear. "Really?"

The man needed no more encouragement. By the time he was finished, Adam knew every detail of the troubled marriage of his pretend fiancée's parents. Every twisted betrayal and tragedy, and the aftermath of bitterness that lived on today.

She'd duped him. He set his glass on a passing waiter's tray and went looking for her, his mood black. He'd been set up. Jasmine—or Jane—had no intention of helping him with his goal. How could she, when there was such a bitter rift between her family and her uncle that he would probably rather do business with a badger than any friend of hers?

The English rose had some major explaining to do. He found her coming back to the orangery, having just said good-night to her father. He waited until Gill led the frail man away, then turned on Jasmine, his anger close to the surface.

"What is it?" she asked, her brows knitting together.

Adam grasped her arm firmly. "I need to talk to you, *darling,*" he gritted, walking her away from the party. "Somewhere private, I think."

She led him into a nearby room that must have been an office or library, as there were wall-to-wall books. The drapes were open and the bright lights of the party across the courtyard lit up the falling snow in friendly sparkles.

Adam didn't feel friendly at all. "How long did you think you could go on playing me for a fool?"

Jasmine drew the drapes and switched one small

lamp on by the desk, but the cavernous room was still dim. She turned to face him, a resigned look in her face. "What did you hear?"

She wasn't surprised, probably why she'd clamped herself to his side all night, he thought angrily. "That your mother was sleeping with both brothers, but when she got pregnant, she chose your father because he inherited the estate and Stewart got nothing. That the baby—your brother—was your uncle's child, not your father's. That she was so unhappy with your father, she was running away to Stewart on the night of the accident that killed his son."

Jasmine held his gaze for a long moment, then swallowed and looked away. "I don't know for sure that any of that is true," she said quietly.

"You've never met him, have you?" That realization only angered him more. "I bet he doesn't want anything to do with you. Why would he? Yet still, you promised me you'd set up a meeting."

"And I will try, as I promised, after Christmas."

Adam gave a derisive bark of laughter. "Don't do me any favors, sweetheart. If he knows I'm at all connected with you, he'll probably laugh me off the planet."

Jasmine brushed her hands over her face and rubbed her arms. Her face radiated guilt. "I'm sorry."

"You're sorry." He reached out and grasped both ends of the scarf she wore, watching her eyes widen.

"Not good enough, I'm afraid." He tugged on the scarf until Jasmine had no option but to take a step forward, and another.

"I'll get what I need, with or without you," he growled, referring to Stewart Cooper, "and I'll take what I want, as well."

She tottered another step forward, her mouth rounded and surprised and infinitely appealing. "What you want?" she whispered breathlessly.

Adam's anger sizzled under his skin, aggravating him to a fever pitch of desire. He tugged her relentlessly forward, his eyes lighting hungrily on the delicate line of her shoulder exposed by the scarf as he seesawed it over her skin. Her pulse pumped and jerked in the hollow of her throat, mirroring his, he'd wager. The tip of her tongue shot out quickly to moisten her lips, capturing his avid attention. He had no idea where the hell they were, but he wasn't averse to taking her right here, against the towering dusty bookcases, not twenty feet from where her peers partied on, oblivious.

"*You,* lovely Jasmine." Adam bent his head to stop an inch away from her mouth. Her eyes filled his vision, hazed over, too dark to be gray. "As soon as possible," he breathed, watching her beautiful lips part slightly. "As often as possible." He closed that last inch, his tongue flicking out to sweep her lower lip. "You owe me that, at least."

She shivered. Her front bumped up against his,

ratcheting up the tension a little. Her breath escaped in a rush and she immediately gasped in another. From past experience, he'd say Ms. Cool, Calm and Collected was about to lose it, and he remembered every thrilling erotic detail of the last time she'd lost her composure.

Nothing wrong in helping her along. Adam let go of the scarf and put one finger in the waistband of her trousers. Her front bumped him again, all knobs and bone, soft and hard, bumping together, burning for more. His other hand circled the back of her neck as he tilted her face up and finally crushed his lips down on hers.

She opened for him immediately. He pulled her hard against him, dipping into her mouth with a hunger that blasted away any finesse he might normally employ, or that she might expect. Her scent was rich in subtle passion; the warmth and smoothness of her skin incited him to go deeper, push more insistently. Adam considered himself an experienced lover who always had his partner's needs in mind, but with this woman, all bets were off. He wanted more fiercely, needed more of everything she could offer.

And he wasn't the only one. Her tongue delved in and out of his mouth, maddening him. Her hands clutched and kneaded his shirt and she strained against him, her sighs loud in the dim room. Just as hungry, just as needy as he.

He maneuvered his hand inside the camisole and

slid up toward her breasts. Jasmine's spine tensed like steel and she pushed her front out hard against him. Her head fell back, breaking the kiss, and she moaned softly as his fingers caressed the underside of her firm globe. Heaven help him, she was so sweet, tasted so sweet.

And then a harsh white light flooded the room. Her eyes snapped open and locked on his, full of alarm. Adam cursed under his breath and looked toward the door. A man he didn't recall seeing at the dinner party tonight stood there, framed in the light from the hallway.

They stared at each other, or more correctly, Adam glared at him, he stared at Jasmine and Jasmine— after a quick glance at the intruder—stared at Adam's throat, her lips moving in soundless surprise.

"Can I help you?" Adam asked, the warning in his voice implying he'd like to help him into next week through the closed windows, if necessary. He took his hand out from under Jasmine's top reluctantly, away from her glorious breasts that still rose and fell robustly.

It was an older version of the man in the photo in her room. Adam studied his pale and surprised face, impatiently waiting for his explanation. What, did he want to watch?

"I'm not sure," the man said, his voice infuriatingly vague. "I thought I'd found my fiancée but it can't be her, because you have your mouth and hands all over her."

Five

Jasmine's eyes closed in distress. Ian! What on earth next? And why did he have to say *that,* of all things?

Her hands dropped from Adam's shirt, trembling with interrupted passion, shock and now shame. She began to straighten her clothing, not sure which of the two of them she most did not want to look at. She felt, rather than saw Adam's head slowly turning her way, and licked her chafed and sensitive lips nervously.

"What did he say?" he asked her softly.

Jasmine covered her mouth with her palm, exhaling. Excuses clamored to be let out: He didn't mean it, it's a joke, I was going to tell you… She took a step back from him, looking over at Ian, who looked as confused and embarrassed as she felt. Her heart clenched in sympathy. She walked quickly to him, put her hands on his shoulders and kissed his cheek. "Why aren't you in Switzerland?"

Ian studied her face, looking somewhat relieved. "My father called to tell me you were back. You might have warned me. It was no mean task, getting flights at this time of year."

She stepped back from him and glanced at Adam. His eyes bored into her face, one dark brow raised. He looked ready to explode.

Jasmine exhaled, agitated. She hated being agitated. "I'm not engaged," she said to the room in general, not looking at either of them.

"To me or him?"

Oh, the softness of his voice, like a velvet noose…

"Well, technically—" Ian ventured.

She shot him a venomous look, willing him to shut up, then turned back to the smoldering man a few feet away. "It's not what you think."

"Oh, you don't want to know what I think."

Scathing, angry, disgusted. Arrows of displeasure pummeled her. Coming on top of learning about her family history, this could be the last straw for them.

Jasmine couldn't bear not to see him again, not to be held or kissed by him again….

With a last hard look at her, he stepped forward. "I'll be off, since I'm surplus to requirements."

"Adam, I can explain."

"I've had enough of your explanations." He brushed past her, pausing to look into Ian's face. "You're welcome to her, mate. I've even warmed her up for you."

Shame coursed through her and she hurried after him. Ian grabbed at her arm as she passed and she spun on him. "Why did you have to say *that?*"

"We need to talk. Your father's dying. You can't keep putting it off."

Jasmine shook him off, her eyes on the tall, angry figure striding away down the hallway.

"Talk to me, Jane."

The agitation in Ian's voice stopped her at the door but she didn't turn around. "I have to go after him. Please, Ian, just wait for me here."

He let out a petulant sigh. "I've been waiting all my life. When is it going to end?"

"A few more minutes," she said with her back to him. "I promise."

She found Adam in her room, tossing clothing and toiletries into his small overnight bag. If only he'd left this morning, as she'd intended. His face was closed and angry. She could barely believe he was the same man who had kissed her so passionately just a few minutes ago, as if he'd die if he hadn't.

"Please don't go." She stood in the doorway, twisting the ends of her scarf in her hands. "It's all a mistake."

"It sure is." He took off the borrowed jacket and laid it on the bed. "Thank Gill and your father for their hospitality."

"Listen—" she said hurriedly; his bag was already packed and he'd picked up his leather jacket— "what he said…it's not really true. It was just a silly pact we made five years ago before I left to live in New Zealand."

"Jasmine—*Jane*—get this through your lovely head: I don't care. I've had enough of your silly games and your secrets and your lies. I have wasted all the time I'm going to."

"You have every right to be angry, but—" she walked to him swiftly and took his hand in hers "—please let me explain."

With his dark glower and black leather jacket, he looked dangerous, unapproachable, but she had to try. She thought too much of him to just let him walk out, maybe forever.

Besides, she had to think of her job should his displeasure get back to Nick. Suddenly Jasmine was tired, mentally. So many revelations today after years of holding it all in.

With a deep breath, she started at the beginning. "My father has always wanted Ian's family land adjoining the estate, mostly because he's worried about developers getting their hands on it. Ian is a farmer; he wants to farm the estate. Anyway, as I told you in your office, my father needs a male heir to keep the estate after he's gone."

"Or what?" Adam interrupted brusquely.

At least he wasn't leaving. "Or it passes to Stewart." There was a long silence while he digested that. This was the tricky part, because now he knew how irreconcilable the differences between the brothers were. What use would she be to him?

In front of her, Adam shifted impatiently. She'd lose him if she didn't get on with it. "When I met Vincent, my father strenuously disapproved. His connections aside, he thought he was a money-grabbing opportunist." Sage words as it turned out a short time later.

"Because of his high profile in the tabloids, I came in for a lot of interest but it wasn't until he ran off with my best friend that…" Jasmine closed her eyes to blot out the headlines. "Everything you heard tonight about Uncle Stewart and the love triangle, my mother abandoning me and going mad. Poor little Jane, everybody leaves her, they said. I was a national joke."

She gulped in air, reliving the horror of the paparazzi at the gate, being followed everywhere. "My father was beside himself with shame." It had taken her years to forgive him for his cruelty in those dark days. "He said the only thing I could do to make it better was to marry Ian. The press would lose interest and we'd all be left alone. And the estate would be safe from Stewart."

But there must have been a bit more life in her. She

couldn't bear the thought of staying and being at the mercy of the press all her life. And she couldn't bear the thought of waking next to a man she didn't love every day. Jasmine had been hurt badly by the actions of her mother and lover, but something inside her wouldn't let her give up on life and love just yet.

"I tried to love Ian, I really did, but I just couldn't make myself go through with a wedding. I had finished my degree but had plans to work in the history field or at least do some more study, but the publicity didn't let up. In the end, I took the coward's way out. I ran away."

Was she imagining it or had Adam's hand, sandwiched between hers, softened and warmed? "When I left, Ian and I made a silly promise that if neither of us was married by the time we were twenty-five, we'd marry each other." Twenty-five had seemed a lifetime away when she was twenty. Jasmine knew Ian felt more for her than she did him, but he didn't love her, either, not the way she wanted to be loved. They were friends and he wanted the estate. "I honestly thought he'd find someone else in my absence."

"But he didn't."

She looked up and saw that Adam's expression wasn't any friendlier than before.

"It was a stupid agreement, entered into at a time when I was overemotional and just wanted to be away." She squeezed his hand between hers, imploring him with her eyes to believe her.

Unmoved, Adam retrieved his hand from hers. "He seems to be taking it seriously enough."

Jasmine swallowed, feeling him cool and close up. "I'll talk to him tonight."

Adam gave her another hard look, then walked away from her toward the window. He pulled the drapery back. The snow was still falling. She clutched at the hope that he wouldn't be able to leave because of the weather.

"You're full of surprises, aren't you, *Jane?*"

"The only lie I told was assuring you I could set up a meeting with my uncle."

"Oh, but you've been very economical with the truth." He turned, his gaze dark as night. "These little games, playing hard to get a few weeks ago, making promises you have no way of keeping, telling me half truths—I didn't expect it of you."

Jasmine's heart fell. His attention, his admiration had surprised her from the first. It was a nice feeling, and it saddened her to lose it. "I've been such a disappointment to my father," she said quietly. "I wanted to please him just once before he died."

Adam shrugged and turned back to the window. "I don't particularly like the way he treats you, but the ultimate way to please him, if you want to throw your life away, is to marry Ian." He paused. She saw him tilt his head at the reflection, knew he was watching her in it.

"As you know," he continued conversationally,

"I'm not in the market for marriage. I certainly won't stop you."

She shook her head miserably. It wouldn't be fair, to herself or to Ian.

Adam's disappointment in her lanced her heart. Right from the start she'd been determined not to get involved with him. He hadn't seemed to mind her reticence; he'd just set about seducing her over a period of weeks. She loved the attention—and the company. Even while fending him off as nicely as she could, she dreamed of him, vivid, addictive dreams that left her hot, turned on and uncomfortably aware of her loneliness. The reality, when finally she couldn't bear to push him away, was so much better than her dreams.

Adam might be a career womanizer but he'd always made her feel special, as if she was worth the wait. However, she had no hold on him now; he'd sampled the goods, and because of her actions, he was disappointed in her.

The fight left her. Jasmine hung her head, the design on the carpet blurring as she studied the floor. "I'm so sorry, Adam. And grateful, for everything." Her shoulders rose and fell helplessly. "I wish I could make it up to you."

Two large black shoes appeared in front of her feet. She looked up in surprise, not hearing his approach.

His eyes were cool, his lips set in a thin line.

"Oh, you'll make it up to me, all right," Adam said

softly. "I want you, God help me." His thumb brushed the corner of her mouth and continued slowly on along her bottom lip. "Don't bother adding to your litany of lies by denying that you want me, too."

She took a deep, shuddering breath in, hoarding it. Excitement gripped her in hot, sharp claws.

"And I intend to collect," Adam continued, his finger tracing her chin, down over the edge, and kept going to the hollow in her throat.

Jasmine's head rolled back a little, all her senses focused on his stern, searing eyes, his wicked mouth and the finger burning a path down her front.

His eyes never left her face, watching her struggle to breathe, to contain the soaring desire that only he could invoke. He brought his hand back to her chin, cupping it, studying her like an exhibit. His voice became businesslike. "I'll send a car for you on Thursday, at noon. Bring your passport and pack enough for a couple of days."

She blinked, her mind a flurry of nerves, desire and confusion. Maybe a little relief that he still wanted her. "Where…?"

Adam smiled grimly. "I have no idea yet." His fingers on her chin firmed and his smile became a scowl. He bent his head so that his mouth was very close to hers. "But make no mistake, wherever it is, we will be together." His fingers gentled and then he released her. "Don't even think of letting me down."

Jasmine tried to formulate a reply but her mind

was in a spin. The most galling thing to accept was the excitement dulling her senses, thickening her tongue, sending that howl of triumph through her blood. Not indignation, defiance, or even fear. And that was not a good sign.

With one last hard look, Adam turned to go. But at the door, he swung back to her. "There is no question you have suffered in your life. No one could blame you for having abandonment issues." He paused, his eyes pitiless. "But for God's sake, if you don't intend to marry him, put that poor sap out of his misery."

Six

Three days later, she found herself on a private executive jet, wondering what on earth she was doing. Where was Adam? The car had arrived at noon, driven her to an airstrip just outside London, and a flight attendant had bustled her up the steps and into a seat and taken her passport away for checking. Now the engines began to roar, and there was still no sign of him.

This wasn't her intention. After he'd left the party, Jasmine realized Adam was right. She'd been keeping Ian hanging, giving him hope. Afraid that she'd lose the only friend she had if she stripped him of that. After all, hadn't everyone else let her down?

Her heart-rending talk with Ian had convinced her that she was about to be humiliated again. He'd checked Adam out, said his playboy status was on a par with Vincent's. Adam himself had told her he wasn't in the market for a relationship.

Jasmine recognized the danger of losing her head and her heart to Adam Thorne. This madness must be nipped in the bud before someone—she—got really hurt. So yesterday she had taken the bull by the horns and gone to see her uncle, telling only Gill what she was up to.

The flight attendant returned with her passport and checked that her seat belt was buckled.

"Is Mr. Thorne here yet?" Jasmine asked.

The woman shook her head. "You are our only passenger today."

"But—" Jasmine's mouth fell open. "Where are we going?"

"Vienna," came the reply.

Vienna? In one second flat, she forgot her resolution and soared with excitement. She'd never visited the city before and yet felt she knew it intimately. Courtesy of her love of ballroom dancing, especially the waltz, she had dreamed for years of attending a ball in the Austrian capital. Each year, Vienna staged around three hundred balls, and tonight—New Year's Eve—was the opening ball of the season, the Kaiserball, the greatest of them all. Jasmine nearly passed out with excitement and recalled telling Adam on one of their dates that it was a lifelong ambition to attend this particular ball.

He'd remembered. Her throat closed up. Emotions she didn't want to acknowledge rose up and begged to be acknowledged.

But she'd only come to tell him about her uncle. She had fulfilled her part of the bargain and when the car had arrived at Pembleton, she'd gotten into it with no intention of going away for a dirty weekend. Determined not to be tempted, she hadn't even packed a bag. She didn't expect a fight about it. After all, it was what he'd wanted all along. She was only the consolation prize.

The reception she'd gotten from Stewart Cooper had overwhelmed her. Far from being spiteful or angry at her unannounced visit, he seemed hungry for her company. Hungry for some connection to her mother. He had never loved another soul.

Jasmine liked him. For all his money, he cut a sad and lonely figure. He told her he'd visited her mother every single week in the ten years she'd been in the psychiatric institution.

"I would sit and hold her hand," he said sadly, "looking at her face while she stared out of the window. She never looked at me and never spoke. I think she was so wracked by guilt—the car accident, abandoning you, hurting Nigel—that she couldn't bear to see me. But I couldn't bear not to see her."

Jasmine had wept, haunted by the thought of it.

She hadn't known her mother well and had good reason to despise her. But the thought of this kind, sad-eyed old gentleman holding her mother's hand, week after week, year after year, when she wouldn't look at him or speak to him…it was so terribly sad.

Her uncle hoped to see Jasmine again. He also promised to check out Adam's business. If his advisors were in favor, he would contact him directly.

Jasmine sat back in her seat as the plane took off, her mind racing with excitement and confusion. Was Adam already there? Please God it was the Kaiserball she was going to. If so, how could she resist anything he asked of her?

And what was she going to do for clothes?

"Danke schoen."

Adam left the boutique having purchased the gown and arranged for it to be delivered to the hotel. He checked his watch. She would be landing in an hour. He had time to shower, dress and leave her a note. And the gown.

He hadn't been able to resist. He'd intended to take her shopping since she'd have no idea of the event they were attending. Luckily he knew a savvy travel agent who'd not only managed to find tickets to the coveted event but also, through a late cancellation, to get him a suite at *the* hotel in Vienna. Considering it was New Year's Eve, the man deserved a medal.

Quite by chance, he'd seen a creation in the window of a boutique that took his breath away—at least, when he imagined Jasmine Cooper's curves poured into it. God knows she didn't deserve it, but after all, it was for his pleasure, not hers.

She'd made him crazy with all her heartbreaking secrets. Maybe—just maybe—he felt a tiny bit guilty about the sex-as-payment thing. Not too guilty, but once he started on the arrangements, the whole thing took on a mind of its own. He was setting the scene for sex, that's all, and he would give her a night to remember.

He couldn't wait to see how she looked in her finery. His step was light, his smile ready as he entered the opulent Hotel Imperial and headed for the elevators. On impulse, he doubled back and with his rudimentary German, asked the clerk to order a horse-drawn carriage for tonight. The princess was going to the ball in style.

Jasmine stood outside the fabled Hotel Imperial, her mouth hanging open. This was supposedly one of the most romantic hotels in the world. Her day just got better and better.

The flight was uneventful and speedy—or that might have been her mind racing. The only hitch came as she walked uncertainly into the airport, wondering where Adam was. Wondering if there was some cruel joke afoot.

But there was a man with a sign: *Fräulein* Cooper.

And a short drive later, here she was, so excited she could barely contain it.

She checked in, her heart soaring when told they were expecting her, and asked for a map and a directory of clothing stores. Her head told her to entertain the possibility that she wasn't going to the ball—she'd find out in a few minutes—but she needed underwear, toiletries, something to wear tomorrow.

She followed a personal butler to the suite booked in Adam's name. He opened the door with a flourish and left her alone.

Jasmine was too awestruck to wonder where Adam was. She shed her coat, handbag and shoes where she stood, walked out into the middle of a star-patterned parquet floor, and just stood for long minutes, taking it all in. It was too much! If she expired right this minute, she could not be happier.

Opulence of a degree she'd never encountered transported her back to another age. Crystal chandeliers glittered from the high ceiling. Rich silk covered the walls behind gilded frames holding precious nineteenth-century oil paintings. Antique chaise lounges, bowls of flowers and fruit—she nearly cried out when she saw the perfect Biedermeier armoire. Everywhere she looked, a new treasure delighted her.

After an age, she walked into the bedroom with some trepidation. Surely such perfection could not be improved upon. She was wrong. The huge canopied bed somehow didn't dwarf the room, perhaps because of the impressive height of the ceilings or the massive Baroque-framed mirror opposite. Elegant casement windows flooded the room with light and looked out over the Musikverein, one of the finest concert halls in the world and home to the Vienna Philharmonic.

By the time she got to the bathroom, Jasmine's senses were exhausted but it boasted every conceivable luxury, she was sure. Plus a sign that Adam had been here, a damp towel on the rail and his toiletries on the double vanity. Further checks revealed clothes in the closet, a used cup in the sink and an English newspaper open on a sofa.

She sat on a plush chaise lounge and took out her phone, assuming he would have the same number he'd used in New Zealand. But on a whim, she called Gill instead of Adam.

"You'll never guess where I am."

Gill squealed when she heard. Jasmine floated around the suite again, trying to describe it. Finally, she remembered to ask after her father.

There was an ominous pause. "He's not having a good day. He talked to Ian who painted a rather grim picture of Adam's character and also said you've given him no hope of you two marrying someday."

Jasmine sighed. She knew her father would be upset to know there was no hope of her and Ian marrying. Why couldn't he see how unreasonable it was to try to force her in this day and age?

She snorted and looked around. What day and age was she in again?

A knock at the door sounded. "Gill? I have to go. I think Adam's just arrived back." She told her stepmother she would be back in a couple of days and opened the door to find the butler holding a very large flat box.

"Fräulein Cooper?"

"*Ja?*"

She took the box and he waved away her tip. Jasmine pulled off the ribbon and tissue paper, humming with excitement. Her breath caught in her throat when she saw the color of the gown. She'd describe it as thistle, a pale purple but with a depth that surpassed lilac. It was strapless with two ruched panels in the front, so that the full overskirt raised up, revealing lilac gauze underneath. The bodice sparkled with Swarovski crystals. It was the most beautiful thing Jasmine had ever seen. She lifted it carefully, noting the hand-wrought hanger, and rushed to the bedroom mirror, holding it up against her.

In the image, her average gray eyes were shining and looked almost indigo. One hand held the dress against her front while she hurriedly scooped her hair up with the other. Her happiness knew no bounds. Adam had bought her a gown. What else was she to think but that Cinderella *would* go to the ball!

But where was her prince? She remembered her

phone and regretfully hung the gown in the ward-
robe. She had just walked out of the bedroom when
another knock sounded. The butler with another box.
Jasmine just stood there, looking at him stupidly,
and the poor man had to walk past her, place the box
on the table and close the door behind him.

A white fur cape. Correction, faux fur. And not
quite white, a smoky pale gray. The perfect accessory
for the gown.

Accessories. She'd need gloves, shoes, a strapless
bra. Maybe some earrings…how much time did she
have? It was then that she noticed the envelope on the
exceptional Baroque writing desk. Of course, he
would think with her love of antiques that she would
have looked there first, but the whole suite was full
of such treasures. She slid a single heavy page from
the envelope. Handwritten, brief:

Your carriage will be waiting downstairs at 7:00
p.m. I'll see you by the Grand Staircase. A.

Jasmine checked her watch and got moving.

A couple of hours later, she staggered into the
suite, laden with bags. Shower, makeup, hair…no
time for an appointment with a *ballfrisuren,* the hotel
hairdresser specializing in ball hairdos.

She'd have to make do herself. Humming *Die Fledermaus,* she threw herself into her preparations.

At five minutes before seven she left the suite,

walked out of the hotel and was guided into a horse-drawn carriage. Of course…

They moved slowly down the Ringstrasse toward the Hofburg Palace. A light snow fell, and the city glittered. Everything was so perfect, Jasmine felt she might die with happiness. And the first nerves were starting to bite at the thought of seeing him again. He had been so angry with her.

She hadn't expected him to be so thoughtful. Or generous. She'd heard Adam was well off, but this excursion must have cost a small fortune. How could she ever repay him?

Unease slipped below the mantle of joy cloaking her, just for a moment. She knew exactly what he expected for payment. But surely he knew that all this trouble and expense wasn't necessary. Her acquiescence to Adam Thorne came as cheap as one touch, one look into his eyes.

Then the lights of the palace showed through the snow and her nerves evaporated. The fairy tale continued. They slowly approached the great palace, from which it seemed a thousand windows glowed. Jasmine floated toward the entrance, along with hundreds of others in their beautiful clothes, and finally she was inside.

Lord, how would she ever find him? There must have been a couple of thousand people milling around, all craning their necks, waiting with a muted air of expectancy.

She looked for the staircase and took stock. The men were all in black or white tails or dinner suits. Jasmine moved in the direction of the great marble staircase and then, wonder of wonders, there he was, head and shoulders above everyone else, even though he leaned against a wall. His dark good looks magnetized her eyes. Perfect—except there were still about a thousand bodies between them.

Luckily the Imperial Guards chose that moment to conduct their changing of the guard ceremony and the crowd mostly stilled so she was able to push her way through, looking up every so often to check on his location. Her apprehension grew as she neared. Would he like the gown on her? Was he still angry? But she couldn't believe he would go to all this trouble and expense if he did not intend her to enjoy it.

She paused about ten feet away to admire him. The elegant black dinner suit draped his tall, lean body, caressing his broad shoulders and slim hips. With his trendy haircut and trademark stubble, he hardly fit the mold of one of the imperial family, but he stood out like an emperor with his presence and vitality. A perfectly tied bow tie completed the package. She drank the sight in and tucked it away to last her the rest of her life.

As if on cue, he half turned. His head raised, as if scenting the air, and then his eyes found hers and sucked the breath from her lungs. He straightened but did not walk forward to meet her. A commanding presence in a sea of people. The crowds and the opulence, even the orchestra faded away and to Jasmine, they were the only two people here. Holding his gaze, her confidence surging, she moved toward her prince as if in a dream. They stared at each other, his stern demeanor softening into admiration. Finally Jasmine could breathe again.

She felt more beautiful than she had ever felt in her life. In that one long look, he'd given her back her pride, her self-confidence, her belief in herself as a desirable woman. All the things she'd lost years ago. He took both her gloved hands and just looked at her as if seeing her for the first time.

A fanfare rang out and there was a hush while everyone waited for the official welcome by the actors playing Emperor Franz Josef and Empress Sisi. The spell was broken. Adam inclined his head and offered her his arm. They made their way up the marble staircase to the state chambers, Jasmine's eyes devouring every detail: myriad twinkling lights, beautifully set tables, huge urns of carnations everywhere. A silk-liveried waiter showed them to their table and finally, she could sit, take off her cape and say hello to the man who had made this all possible.

He passed her a glass of champagne.

"I'm—speechless," she said, and then, because she wanted to clear the air so they could enjoy themselves, she asked if he was still angry.

He shook his head, his eyes on her face. "It's your night, for now."

The implication was clear but Jasmine didn't mind. She was too happy to mind that she was here because she owed him. "Don't worry," she smiled. "I promise not to turn into a pumpkin at the stroke of midnight."

He gazed at her, his eyes rich with approval.

"Adam, all of this—" she raised her gloved hand, indicating the sumptuous surroundings "—it's too much. This—" her hand swept down the front of her, and his eyes followed "—and the hotel. It's like a dream. I can't believe I'm here."

He turned in his seat to face her, his hands clasped in front of him. "Tonight we're going to indulge our every whim."

A bubble of desire popped in her veins. Every muscle tightened and warmed. Adam noticed, she knew, because his eyes sharpened and again roamed slowly down her body. Her arms ached to wrap around him, to feel the burn of his beard on her face, the strength of his arms around her.

"Don't think about it," he said softly. "Just enjoy."

"It's perfect, Adam." She leaned close and touched her lips to his. "Thank you."

He gave a short laugh. "You won't thank me when I step on your toes."

They served themselves from the sumptuous buffet and watched the opening polonaise where beautiful girls in white gowns and boys in tails strutted and stepped expertly in formation. "It's a sort of debutantes' dance," she explained to Adam. "I was reading about this ritual before the major balls in Vienna that turned me on to ballroom, when my friends were all into pop or sports. Now it's my only social life."

"Poor lonely little dancer." He smiled. "Perhaps you should take up surfing or watching rugby."

"Typical Kiwi bloke. I don't dance to meet men. It just gets me out of the house."

"Perhaps you haven't danced with the right men," Adam said enigmatically.

As she wondered what he meant, the dance master called out the words that everyone was waiting for— *"Alles Waltzer!"*

Adam stood and offered his hand. "Shall we?"

Jasmine's smile stretched wide. "I would be honored, sir."

In between courses, they danced to Strauss and Mozart in each of the seven ballrooms. A Viennese waltz was much faster than other waltzes, and once it was learned, every other waltz seemed pedestrian.

From the moment Adam took her into his arms, Jasmine realized that this would be a dance like no other. He wasn't quite the best dance partner she'd ever had, and anyway, the finer points of the waltz were somewhat lost in the crush of people. But dancing with him was like making love with him. He was all she could see and feel. His eyes never left her face, bathing her in such intensity that she moved on autopilot, which, thankfully, she was proficient enough to do. She forgot about her feet and concentrated on feeling the music on the inside and absorbing his presence on the outside. His hands under her palm and on the small of her back were warm and dry and as they moved together, so did his hands, causing starbursts of delicious friction on her skin that effervesced to every nerve ending.

She remembered how she felt after they'd made love for the first time. Sensitized, energized, pulsing in small bursts of sensation that she never wanted to end. She felt his breath on her face, his muscles bunched under her fingertips and the length of his legs when they brushed hers occasionally. Her body became his instrument, to lead and spin and twirl at will, an extension of his own.

Her anticipation grew as one dance flowed into another and another. Adam Thorne exuded sexuality and could turn her on even in the midst of thousands of people. And if that was his intention, he was exacting his payment early in the evening but strangely enough, it wasn't more than she wanted to give.

Seven

Adam could not take his eyes off her. The pleasure he took from her enjoyment of the evening was unsurpassed by anything he had known, which perplexed him because of his selfish reasons for doing it. He crushed it down in case the feeling became addictive, and then where would it all end?

Her enchantment was to be expected. What was unexpected was how enthralled he was watching her eyes sparkle—no sign of sadness now—her lovely mouth curve in yet another delighted smile as each new image or dance or bar of music registered and gave her joy.

His instincts about the color and style of the gown were spot-on. Her pale skin and dark hair and brows

lent the delicate shade of fabric a richness that anyone else would have overpowered. Dusky gray eyes
and her hair pulled back in a classic, elegant chignon
completed a picture that would stay with him for a
long time.

And yet what arrogance he'd displayed to choose
her clothes. What vanity to set the scene as he had.
But what pleasure to see her happiness, especially
knowing that this woman did not usually allow herself to get carried away.

What anticipation he had of the night to come…she
looked amazing in that dress, but he wanted her out
of it more with every minute that passed. His body had
been reminding him of that all night.

Just before midnight, the orchestras faded away
to the chimes of the giant bell of St. Stephen's as
it rang the old year away. Adam stood behind her
at the stroke of twelve and as the crowd erupted
into applause, his hands dropped onto her bare
shoulders and Jasmine turned and smiled at him.
Everyone was smiling, some were kissing and hugging and shaking hands, some had moved between
the tables and began to dance to the first strains of
The Blue Danube waltz, heralding the New Year in.

He and Jasmine stared at each other and he saw
his desire glow in her eyes, darkening them to a shade
deeper than her gown. He knew now why he'd
bought it. He stepped closer and bent his head, keeping his eyes open.

"Happy New Year, Jasmine."

She raised up to meet him, whispering something, her lips soft and fragrant and perfect. He tasted her upper lip with the tip of his tongue, tracing the outline of her mouth, and she leaned even closer, sighing, her mouth moving under his. His hand on the small of her back tightened, drawing her close, and they kissed until they were breathless.

When Adam drew back, he felt on a more even keel, even though his breath was ragged and he was as hard as rock. Normal service had been resumed. She wanted him. He wanted her. She would go where he led, just like on the dance floor.

They stayed to watch the New Year operetta and the Fledermaus Quadrille, a highlight for Jasmine. It was late and the ball would go on for hours yet, but Adam was suddenly tired of people. They left the Imperial Palace. The night was cold but clear and they decided to walk along the busy Ringstrasse back to the hotel.

Jasmine was hungry since she'd professed to be too excited to eat much of the buffet at the ball, so they stopped at a *Wurstelstand* for the Viennese equivalent of hot dogs. The streets were packed with party hounds. She almost skipped along, tipsy on champagne and excitement, humming at patchy intervals. Adam held her arm tightly, mindful of the earlier snow, the uneven paving stones and the spiky high heels she insisted on wearing.

The drinking establishments were mostly over-flowing but not far from the hotel, they were drawn by a beautiful voice. Jasmine headed down a cob-bled alleyway and they stopped by a tiny bar where inside, a black woman crooned a Tina Turner ballad very credibly.

Jasmine pulled on his arm, facing him. "Let's go in,"

"With that smudge of mustard on your mouth?" He reached his thumb out, but thinking better of it, bent his head and licked the spot with the tip of his tongue.

In the freezing chill under a rusting old street lamp, Jasmine shifted restlessly, inhaled a ragged breath, and magic of a new kind entered her face.

Adam stilled, instantly, viciously aroused by the sudden flood of awareness darkening her eyes. All his senses clamored for more and he bent his head again, caging her face with both hands, sipping now at her lips. He tasted the piquant mustard she'd eaten, garlic and spices from the sausage, a crisp fruity hit of cham-pagne. It all fed his hunger and he deepened the kiss.

Jasmine's eyes closed while her lips parted. She was still now, but he sensed her blood, her muscles, her very cells reaching for him, as palpable as if she'd raised her arms and pulled him close. He thrust his tongue into her mouth, holding her cheeks firmly, exulting at her response as the tip of her tongue played with his.

"Let's not." His eventual response to her question about going inside the club sounded hoarse and raw.

A desperate need swamped him and he couldn't wait another minute. He pressed against her, his thighs bumping hers as he turned and pushed her toward the hotel.

Another couple entered the Hotel Imperial's elevator with them and they exchanged New Year wishes. Adam's eyes bored into her as he discreetly tugged at the fingers of one of her gloves, easing it all the way off. Jasmine leaned against the wall, unable to look away and shivering with anticipation and nerves.

For a moment on the street, she'd wished they didn't have to go back to the hotel. Not because she didn't want him—she did, desperately. But that meant the fairy tale was over. They were now leading up to the real reason they were here. Payback. She had done a deal with the king of deals.

She knew she'd be compensated handsomely. She'd already enjoyed his prowess in the bedroom, her body's response to him. But for a few hours, she'd chosen to believe she was living this dream because he really felt something for her, rather than collecting on a contract she had failed to honor.

She hid a smile behind her hand when he wrapped the glove around his neck; the spoils of war. She was really in trouble here. She liked him, enjoyed him so much. The anticipation when he looked at her, held her face in his hands…payback never felt so good, even though she should be running for her life.

He opened the suite door and stood back while she entered, stiff-backed, her stomach tight with nerves. Adam cast an interested glance at the bags from her shopping expedition still strewn around. Flustered, she began scooping them up, but he caught her hand and the bags stayed where they were.

He lifted her hand by the finger of her glove and without breaking eye contact, he tugged until the silk slid smoothly down her forearm, making her tingle.

"Shall I call the butler to help you off with your gown?" he asked, his eyes glinting.

"I think we can manage." And then she smiled sweetly. "Did he help with your tie?"

Adam bared his white teeth and hooked a finger in her cape, tugging until she bumped against his front. "My lips are sealed, but I gave him a very good tip."

He cupped her face and bent his head to feather her lips with kisses, undoing the clasp of her cape as he did. He slid his hands inside the fur and skimmed up her back, stroking over her shoulder blades. Then he settled in for a deeper, soul-touching kiss she felt all the way to her toes.

Jasmine loved the way he kissed. A complex mix of tease and command. Of pleasing himself and invitation. His kiss invited her to be passive, free to enjoy and be taken. But it also incited her to hum blissfully in her throat, to allow her impatience to come to the fore, tearing off the cape and tossing it blindly at a sofa a few feet away. She would shudder about that tomorrow but right now, she just wanted one less obstruction between them.

Again he used his thighs to walk her backward toward the bedroom, still with his mouth locked on hers. His fingers ran down her bare arm and clasped hers and he danced her into the room, spinning her once, twice, three times, closer to the bed every time. The ball continued, only to a much more private composition than Herr Strauss ever devised.

When the backs of her legs bumped the edge of the bed, Adam drew back and switched one bedside lamp on. His face fell, he sighed, looking at her hair, and then he began to take down her hair, pin by pin.

A guilty laugh escaped her. "Sorry." Why hadn't she left it down? Thank heaven the dress had a zipper and not a hundred buttons!

He smiled distractedly, intent on his work. "Don't ever apologize for making an effort to please me."

Ditto, she wanted to say, but she reached for him instead, knowing she, too, had her work cut out. Black tie involved far too many clothes—and buttons. The tie was easy but there was still the waistcoat, braces and the stiff-fronted white shirt whose buttons were not cooperative with her fumbling fingers. His hands left her hair and landed on hers to assist in guiding the buttons through the damnably unyielding holes, while he somehow managed to shrug out of his jacket and take the waistcoat with it.

He finished with her hair. It spilled around his

hands and he ran his fingers through it, smoothing it down over her neck and shoulders and cleavage. Her skin burned wherever he touched. She sucked in a breath and tried to ground herself, feeling her knees dangerously close to buckling. Not only that, but her tight breasts were dangerously close to pushing out the bodice of the dress. It didn't help when he bent his head and took her mouth again in a deep, carnal kiss, igniting a storm inside. And when he moved his mouth lower, nuzzling her earlobe, down the slope of her shoulder and across the front of her cleavage, she swayed a little, almost afraid to breathe.

"Breathe," he commanded softly.

She sucked in a breath obediently and her head cleared a little.

Adam straightened, his hands on his shoulders. "I can honestly say," he murmured, sliding his hands around to her back, "I have never wanted anything as much as I want to see you out of this dress." He found the fastening on the zipper that ran the length of her back. Slowly, slowly, he pulled the fastener down, his knuckles grazing her back, his body sizzling her front. She had time again to think about touching him, in between congratulating herself for the new lingerie. Good move, she thought, her hands slipping inside his open shirt to skim across the smooth, warm skin of his chest and abdomen. She leaned forward and pressed her lips to his sternum, running her hands over long, curved pectoral muscle, using the edges of her teeth on his nipple.

The gown swished down to her feet with a pretty rustle. Jasmine stepped daintily out of it, still in her heels, and it occurred to her she should never have walked across the parquet floor in heels. She eased them off now and started to bend to pick up the dress but Adam had hold of both her hands and kept her upright. She stilled as he stepped back, his eyes sweeping her body, ablaze with stark hunger. Down over the ivory front-clasp bra, to the matching panties and the thigh-high shimmering stockings that had—as the saleslady promised—actually stayed up with their silicone grippers, even after dancing the night away.

His head moved in a half shake, his tongue swept his bottom lip and there was a crease between his eyes that looked like a frown of concentration rather than displeasure. Jasmine raised her head, about to ask what was wrong. But when he lifted his eyes to hers, she felt again as she had at the Palace. Beautiful. Desirable. His.

He shucked off his shirt and undid the fastening of his dress trousers. Without the braces to hold them up, they fell to the floor in a pile and he added to the mess by kicking off his footwear. Jasmine bit back a smile at the snug-fitting gray hipsters, all out of shape and probably stretched way past the manufacturer's most stringent seam tests. The sight distracted her so that she didn't even worry about the expensive clothing scattered drunkenly around the antique carpet. When Adam crushed her to him, his hands molding her body against him, she forgot everything except the burn of his skin, his hard planes against her soft curves and the texture of his tongue as she eagerly drew it deep into her mouth.

His hands stroked over her, cupping the back of her neck, spreading the pleasure down the middle of her back, over the curve of her behind and down the back of her thigh. She shifted restlessly, needing more, needing everything. He raised his head, his eyes hooded and dark, leaving her mouth wet and feeling puffy. He cupped her breasts, weighing and squeezing until her world shrank to focus solely on the soft slope of her breast, the way each tiny bump around her nipple seemed to raise and pulse, begging for touch. Oh, sweet heaven, when his mouth finally closed over one taut bud, when he drew her into his mouth and sucked. The sensation was so primal, so deeply wrenching inside, her mind screamed "more!" It wasn't possible to be this close to release when he hadn't touched her intimately, when he hadn't even touched her breasts except through the silky bra she wore.

Suddenly, he bent her over the crook of his arm so she lay back against him, her legs stretched out, the backs of her heels on the floor. One arm was trapped by his side, the other clutched ineffectually at the muscles of his upper arm. But he held her so easily and his dark smile was all reassurance. "Relax," he ordered in response to her sharp intake of breath.

He pinged the front-clasp bra with one touch and it slid apart. *Now,* she thought, *please now, touch me…* His hand swept down her body in one stroke, taking her panties on the downward sweep, leaving her naked except for the stockings. Stroking unhurriedly, he kissed her mouth and throat, turning his head often to look down her body, laid out before him, trembling for him. Her breathing came in gasps. He held her helpless in one arm like the dip of a tango. She ordered her limbs to relax but her whole insides clenched like a vise, even more so when he began to lavish his mouth on her breasts. And all the while, his hands worked magic from her knees up to her inside upper thighs, firm, sweat-inducing strokes that reminded her he knew exactly how to play a woman.

Her eyes were open, staring at the impressive arched ceiling, wondering if this was the famous former chapel. A smile surprised her; the imperial family that may have worshipped here would not be amused at the way Adam was worshipping her. Perhaps they'd answer her prayer for release, for his touch *there* where she needed it as he circled and stroked and drove her mad. Helpless to touch him back, her head lolled over his arm, his bunched muscles her pillow. Helpless to do anything but try to absorb the millions of sensations he evoked.

A strangled pant erupted from her throat when finally he cupped her, his palm pressing firmly on her pubic bone, his fingertips teasing. The more he pressed down, the more tension built inside. She squirmed uneasily, almost afraid of the storm of sensation, the lurking torment that awaited her. Scrabbling back the fragments of her mind, she remembered her precarious position, her heels having little purchase on the floor and her mind in splinters on the ceiling. His fingers glided over her most intimate flesh, unerring, unhurried, firm yet tender, expertly applying pressure where she needed it most. And someone heard her prayer.

Her legs clenched, her throat constricted. Her breath stopped altogether. As she hovered at the edge of release, his clever fingers and his clever mouth intensified and tipped her over. The climax crashed into her, squeezing her eyes shut, emblazoning every cell in her body with streaks of ecstasy, holding her taut and shaking for brilliant eternity.

He continued to ply her with such exquisite touch until the blood cleared from her brain and she gradually became conscious of the coolness of her wet nipples, the aftershocks still rippling through her and her deadweight on his arm.

She opened her eyes and Adam was watching her, his eyes filled with dark purpose. He lifted her, his arm tensing so that her grasping hand nearly slid off. He straightened, bringing her upright. Boneless, liquid, she could only hope her legs would hold her up.

* * *

That her legs held her up surprised him. Then again, she had seriously beautiful legs, long, strongly muscled, smooth as satin. And those stockings were the sexiest thing he'd seen. Her sigh resonated with satisfaction and he couldn't help but mentally beat his chest with pride. He'd done that, put that smile there, stolen her breath and her mind for moments that stretched into the stratosphere.

He wanted more of her satisfaction, he wanted those legs around him. He needed to be inside her, all over her, to see and feel her response again and again. Her dancer stamina would be put to good use tonight.

He hurriedly shucked off his underwear and reached down to grab a fistful of condoms where he'd stashed them earlier in the bedside table. Her eyes lit up when he tossed them on the bed. She reached up and looped her arms around his neck, pressing her body along the whole length of his. She smelled amazing, her elegant but subtle fragrance mingled with sex, the sharp drugging scent of her own climax on his fingers.

Without preamble he tipped her onto the bed and rolled to his side next to her. He raised up on an elbow and fed his eyes, his senses with her. She was sensational, a vision of pale marbled skin, well-proportioned, glorious breasts, her tiny waist and flared hips giving her a feminine delicacy for all that strength. Her flawless skin glowed and was so smooth, he couldn't keep his eyes, hands, lips off her. How his blockhead brother failed to properly appreciate the sexy beauty right outside his office for five years was beyond Adam. He'd known from the moment he saw her that under the crisp business suits and severely tied-back hair, there was great beauty, a lush-for-loving body, and a response to him that drove him wild.

She smiled, a slow curve of her lips, her eyes bright with anticipation and a playfulness he hadn't associated with her before. She'd told him he was only her third lover and he'd believed it because she'd been shy and unsure, unused to showing her body or touching a man.

While he was still thinking about that, he suddenly found himself flat on his back. She rose up, a sexy phoenix, her long dark hair falling over her shoulders, her perfect breasts jutting out above him, begging for his touch, and those damn naughty stockings with their thick band of lace at the top now straddling his waist.

"You want to play, beautiful?" he murmured, sliding his hands up over her hips and settling on her waist.

"A little." She took his hands off her and arranged them by his sides.

Whatever the lady wants, he thought, narrowing his eyes. She began to run her efficient, questing hands over him and within an embarrassingly short time, he was squirming impatiently, feeling his excitement build fast, too fast. He began to count as a distraction. One elegant fingertip circling his nipples, ten nails scraping over his stomach. One lush pair of lips sipping at his mouth, the tip of her tongue delving and teasing, while he shifted, bringing his straining erection into contact with her shapely backside. He put his hands on her hips, pressing her back.

Her mouth moved all over his body, starting fires everywhere. He let his head loll back, not too far. He was enjoying the show too much not to watch, but the strain of holding back was immense. Her hair tickled his chest as she dragged her head down, bending from the waist, going lower while he went higher. His hand scrabbled around on the bed for a condom, finding one and tearing it open with his teeth.

Jasmine raised her head, distracted by the noise.

"Put it on," he said hoarsely, holding it out to her. He couldn't wait a moment more. They could take it slow next time….

She straightened and took the pack from him, slowly extracted the contents and held it up daintily between index finger and thumb. Adam closed his eyes. She was killing him in tiny, torturous increments.

She rose up on her knees and wriggled down a little so his jutting erection was between them, then tossing the condom onto his stomach, she began to fondle, light, teasing caresses interspersed with slow, firm, two-handed strokes. His mind blanked. The air punched out from his lungs and he began to sweat.

Sweet torture, he couldn't take much more, but on she went until he thought he'd explode in her hands.

He grabbed the condom and held it up to her. "Put it on," he growled. Then he grasped her thighs, prising them apart, and exacted his own punishment, dipping his fingers inside her heat, feeling her clench around him, her thigh muscles tight and hard. Good. That got her attention. Adam liked to play as much as anyone but he was wound too tight, had wanted her for so long. They had all night to indulge her playful side.

He ground his teeth as she smoothed the condom over his flesh with such painstaking care. Finally she scooted forward and raised up over him. He thought he'd expire as she eased him into her hot body to the hilt. She stilled, settled, stretched while he filled his hands with her breasts. There was something just so damn right about this, the way she looked, felt, responded to him.

She began to move her lower body in a torturously slow circular motion, her waist twisting, her breasts firm, her body gloving him tightly.

It was bliss but the need to thrust, to take, to plunge overwhelmed him. He reared up and flipped her onto her back, swallowing her squeak of surprise with his lips. He thrust his tongue into her mouth at the same time he thrust into her body. She arched up as he filled her, panting his name, matching him stroke for stroke, lifting those lovely legs to wrap around his waist. All playfulness melted from her eyes and they filled with a steely resolve as intense as his. Release became the only goal for both of them. He tried to hold on for a few moments more, wasn't confident as his own release clawed at him, gripped him hard.

He grabbed a nearby pillow and pulled her up, shoving it under her hips. The different angle was electric, deep, amazing. Her eyes shot open; she gasped and tightened her legs around him. He thrust again, taking them to another level, higher and hotter and more consuming than anything he'd ever experienced. He felt her walls, gloving him so snugly, begin to ripple. He tore his mouth from hers and watched her shatter, sob her pleasure and relief, and followed her into endless pleasure.

Eight

Adam sat on a chair a few feet away from the bed, watching Jasmine sleep. It was after ten. He'd pulled the drapes to find the quiet streets looked clean with crusted snow at the edges, and sun shone down from a blue sky.

He'd been woken by a text from John, his friend and business partner in London. There had been a phone call for Adam from a man claiming to be an advisor of Stewart Cooper's. When told Adam was away for a couple of days, the man said he'd call back.

Adam looked over at Jasmine's sleeping face. Over the past couple of months, he'd left several messages and e-mails, but hadn't been able to breach the eccentric recluse's inner circle. He didn't want to wake her; they hadn't gotten to sleep until well after four. But it was driving him crazy, wondering if she had anything to do with the billionaire's sudden change of heart.

Not that he could tire of looking at that face. Adam doubted he'd ever forget the way she looked last night in the lovely gown, or out of it, for that matter. Now her warm, walnut-colored hair spilled over her face and the pillow, the ends twirling like gift-wrap ribbon.

He tilted his head, listing the many faces of Jasmine Cooper. So far in their brief acquaintance, he'd seen her mussed from a motorcycle ride, all conservative glamour for the ballet, crisp and tailored at work, elegant and regal last night, and hot, naked and very discomposed a few hours ago.

Jasmine Cooper with her different faces, her secrets and her very sexy body, was one interesting lady. Who would have thought that Nick's bookish personal assistant would burrow her way under his skin so completely? Too completely, perhaps. Adam could not afford the distraction of secrets, different faces and sexy bodies right now, sexy bodies excepted. For the next few months, it was nose to the grindstone all the way.

Thankfully she'd be returning to New Zealand soon. What with the fake engagement, her uncle and her working for Nick, it seemed he was becoming inextricably entwined in her life.

Which should worry him more than it did....

His cell phone beeped and he swore softly and flipped it open. It was John wanting an ETA tomorrow.

"Business on New Year's Day?" Jasmine asked sleepily.

Adam's head snapped up. She'd lifted her head up off the pillow and looked fresh and pink-cheeked. He finished his text and closed the phone. Picking up the cooling cup of coffee he'd poured from the breakfast tray the butler had delivered, he walked over to the bed and offered her the cup. "Did you contact your uncle about me?" He sat on the edge of the bed and restrained himself from brushing a wisp of hair from her face.

Jasmine blinked rapidly. "Umm." She slurped at the coffee, made a face and handed it back, then struggled into a sitting position, dragging the sheet up over her. "Why?"

Adam watched her, amused at the secretive face she wore. "Apparently he phoned, wanting to talk to me."

She nodded, her eyes wary. "That's good, isn't it?"

"That's very good." He caught her chin in his fingers. "You did that for me?"

She nodded and looked away. "I owed you."

He stilled, hearing his words, his demand on her lips, devaluing the night they'd just shared. "And yet you still came."

The tip of her tongue appeared and she moistened her lips. "I—didn't intend to. I didn't bring anything except what I was wearing and a handbag."

Hence the shopping spree, the bags he'd noticed spread all over the suite.

"You were going to stand me up?" His brows lifted. "Mind telling me why?"

She raised her eyes to his for a long moment and then shook her head.

Adam breathed out, strangely relieved. Something in her troubled eyes told him he didn't want to know why. Not now, when he had to keep this casual. "What changed your mind?"

She looked down at her hands, breathing out carefully. "I asked the flight attendant where we were going." The milk-and-roses complexion leaned heavily in favor of the roses. "It was New Year's Eve…"

Adam nearly smiled. "So you arrived at the airstrip—"

"I expected you to be there," she interjected.

"—at the airstrip," he continued, "intending to tell me where I could stick my weekend away because you'd done what I asked."

Her pink and guilty countenance confirmed it.

"But when you discovered it was Vienna…"

She gazed around at the opulent suite, chewing on her bottom lip. "I hoped…I remembered telling you in New Zealand that I'd always wanted to go to the Kaiserball."

"And you couldn't resist?"

She shook her head.

Adam stared at her, unsmiling, for a few moments longer, enjoying her guilty discomfort. Then he began to chuckle. "And here was me thinking it was my irresistible sex appeal and scintillating charm."

Jasmine's shoulders dropped, her eyes meeting his at last. Her lips twitched. "I'm not sure about the charm, but maybe the sex appeal...."

They smiled at each other. Then he reached out and caught her chin again. "Thank you." He knew how worried she was about her father's declining health. Risking his displeasure wasn't something someone like Jasmine would take lightly. "Going to see your uncle can't have been easy."

Her smile faded a little. "It wasn't so bad. I liked him."

"I appreciate it." He brushed her mouth with his. "Get dressed. It's your day for sightseeing. Anything you like."

Several hours later, they left the world-famous Kunsthistoriches Museum.

"Another lifelong ambition achieved." Jasmine sighed happily. "This is the best New Year ever!"

She hadn't stopped prattling for hours, showing off her knowledge of Austrian Baroque art and sculptures and the many other treasures in this massive museum. Poor Adam. She gave him a sidelong glance. He would probably much prefer a bar or the

Lipizzaner horses. Or, her heart skipped a beat, being holed up at the hotel with her.

"I'm sorry if I bored you." She took her gloves from her pocket and began to put them on. "I guess museums aren't your thing."

No, from what she knew and had heard of Adam, culture, history and tradition would not be his first choice of entertainment. But he'd borne their woefully quick trip to this great museum with good humor.

"Not at all," he said loftily. "Seeing it through your eyes has been a revelation. Your knowledge amazes me."

Jasmine preened a little. She really must do something to add to her degree, a postgrad art course or something.

"Like I said over Christmas," Adam said, turning his collar up against the crisp late-afternoon air. "You have all this passion for history and yet you work for a financial company, typing letters and picking up my brother's dry cleaning."

She slipped her arm through his as they walked out onto Maria-Theresien-Platz, trying not to be miffed by his summation of her job. She did more than type letters and run errands. Nick and his father traveled a lot, there were always flights and hotels to book, conferences to register for, soirées and functions to organize…and she realized that it may have been challenging for the first year but she could manage all of that now standing on her head.

"I enjoy my job," she insisted. "I like being orga-nized. Nick pays well and the staff are nice."

The staff kept to themselves and that was the most important thing. As personal assistant to the boss, she was treated with respect and held at arm's length and that suited her fine. No embarrassing family secrets slipping out over social occasions.

Adam squeezed her arm. "I'm not knocking the job, I'm just interested in your reasons."

Her reasons were completely justifiable and she didn't feel the need to explain. She'd endured scandal and pity and finger-pointing all her life. She wanted privacy. It wasn't hard to understand.

"I think maybe you're running away," he contin-ued after giving her plenty of time to answer him. "Burying yourself in an unsatisfactory career to es-cape a bit of bad publicity."

"What's the alternative?" she demanded, trying not to sound testy. "Stay in England and be subjected to a media frenzy every time I step outdoors?"

He squeezed her arm. "You're exaggerating."

She booted at the snow crunching underfoot. Then she sighed noisily. "You're right, of course."

What happened last time seemed a million miles away, and it was stupid to let the past intrude on their winter wonderland now. Jasmine put it out of her mind. She pulled him over to admire the statue of Maria Theresa, the Holy Roman Empress of the Habsburg dynasty, and mother of Marie Antoinette.

"Did you know," Jasmine said, her enthusiasm for history drowning out any residual pique, "she had sixteen children?"

Adam grunted, craning his neck to look up the tall edifice.

"Rumor has it," she lowered her voice conspiratorially, "she asked her physician to stop her falling pregnant and he told her to take an apple. 'Before or after?' she asked, and he said, 'instead of.'"

Adam chuckled and patted the stone pillars that surrounded the statue. "*She's* not running away from a bit of gossip, is she?"

Jasmine laughed. Their eyes met, held and heated while insane thoughts of reproduction and birth control and Adam, naked and holding an apple, careened through her mind. Freud would have approved of the analogy: Adam, apple, sin...

Something in her face must have offered an inkling of her thoughts because his eyes darkened to a luscious molten caramel and filled with awareness. Her smile faded as an all-consuming deluge of desire buffeted her, turning her bones to water. They stood in the middle of the plaza, staring at each other as people walked around them, uncomprehending of the desire that pulsed between them.

She turned her head, looking in the direction of the hotel. They were only three or four blocks away. The back of her neck dampened with the need to get her hands on him.

Adam tightened his grip on her arm. "Hotel," he muttered. "Now."

They ran the relatively short journey without another word. The moment the elevator doors closed, Adam pulled her into his arms and kissed her hungrily. Even last night, she'd never known such burning need.

"Hurry, hurry," she whispered against his mouth as they watched the floors slowly pass. Finally they spilled out into the passageway and rushed to their room, only to find their way blocked by the service trolley. They hadn't left the suite until after midday, so the housemaid was still in attendance.

They looked at each other, panting as if they'd just run a marathon, while the woman, wide-eyed, waited for instruction. The polite thing to do would be to go downstairs, have a drink on the turn-of-the-century sofas in the secluded bar and let the woman finish her task. Jasmine couldn't wait and by the look of impatient anguish in Adam's eyes, neither could he. She flicked a glance through the suite to the bedroom—the bed had been made, at least.

He produced a handful of euros and thrust them into the woman's hand. She nodded and pushed her heavy trolley into the passage, turning to shove a bundle of towels into Adam's hands as he shut the door.

Alone at last, and Jasmine's mirth erupted in a snort. "Poor woman. She was speechless."

"I gave her a good tip," he muttered, backing her

against the wall, seemingly more interested in getting her out of her abundant clothes. He yanked at her scarf until it slid off and was halfway through the buttons on her overcoat by the time she stopped laughing.

They tore into each other, even while she wondered why this urgency, this overpowering need? After the hours spent making love every which way last night, her desperation now stunned her.

She shivered as he roughly stripped her of each outer garment, leaving her in panties and her ankle boots. With every success, as he threw the offending article aside, he captured her mouth in a hungry, lustful kiss that shook her to her marrow. A whirlwind of activity, he tugged at her braided hair, using both hands to free it.

"Bed," he ordered, turning her with his hands on her shoulders and propelling her ahead of him, stripping off his own coat as he went. He didn't stop when they got to the bed and tumbled her down in front of him. Jasmine scrambled onto her hands and knees and began to move up toward the head, but suddenly his fingers closed around her ankle. She twisted her head around and her heart went into overdrive when she saw the fierce need on his face, his lips parted, breathing heavily. A touch of apprehension fluttered through her. This was dark and edgy, not the polished seduction she'd come to expect. She fleetingly thought of how she must look from where he stood, her backside waving in the air, her silly ankle boots with the high heels probably in danger of ruining the antique bedspread.

Adam's fingers tightened around her ankle while with his other hand, he unzipped his trousers. And then he began to pull her slowly back toward him.

The sight of her nearly naked on her hands and knees and still in those boots nearly undid him. Her hair spilled over her shoulders in a riot of waves, kinked up by the braid she'd worn. When she twisted her head around to look at him, her eyes were huge with desire and apprehension. He sucked in air and called on all his powers of control to calm his breathing, needing to slow this down, reassure her. But dear God, he was riding a savage hunger.

Holding her gaze—and her foot—he drew his zipper down then used the same hand to extract his wallet and take out a condom. He let go of her foot for a moment to slip on protection but kept his eyes on her face. Then he pulled, dragging her inch by inch back to the edge of the bed to where he waited, still in his shirt with his trousers around his ankles.

Her back arched, her hands flat on the bed. He let go of her foot, leaned right over her back and slid his cold hands under her body. She gasped and tensed, sucking her stomach in and thrusting her breasts right into his hands.

Adam's body settled on hers, his legs taking most of his weight. Calling on all his shredded control, he buried his face in the fragrance of her hair and nuzzled and nipped her neck. She shuddered under him as he caressed her, her bottom pushing up against him, driving him to distraction. Somehow he slowed things down to a simmer, stroking and kneading her breasts until she was like a sea beneath him, a writhing, moaning sea. He moved one hand down her body and stroked her leg, from calf to buttock and back, paying particular attention to the back of her knee, an exceptionally sensitive area for her, he'd learned last night.

She moaned his name, and his control shattered. Nothing else mattered, his goals, his business, only this, taking her, making her his, surrendering to mindless passion and taking her with him. He nudged her legs apart and stroked her intimately, swearing when he felt her scalding heat.

She heard the muttered oath torn from his throat, felt his fingers on her, in her, and lost it. From the very deepest part of her, something broke, something that walled in her reason, her dignity, and she cried out and it was guttural and hoarse and long. Her body arched up like a bow, gripped in such an intense rush of sensation, she couldn't contain it. Oh, and he knew just how to prolong it, how to nurture the ecstasy, wring out every drop for what might have been a minute or ten. When she finally floated back to something resembling consciousness, she trembled inside and out with sweet release.

He slid his hands up her arms and linked his fingers with hers and made love to her from behind. She purred and pressed back into him, depleted but eager to please. The slide of him in the unfamiliar angle, the thud-thud of his heart beating on her back, the speed with which her own excitement ignited again and surged to equal his all collided in an apex of wonder when he suddenly withdrew and turned her.

"I want to see," he groaned, plunging his hands into her hair, holding her face still. Jasmine welcomed him in again, looking up into his eyes, and then felt her heart stutter, slide, leave her adrift for a few seconds. Something nagged at her, something was wrong inside, and yet he felt so right. She pushed the niggling feeling away, rising to meet every thrust, feeling her climax rushing upon her, wanting it so desperately. But his eyes stared down and it seemed to her she could see too far in, see his soul or hers or both, and they were melding together, becoming one. With dizzying certainty, Jasmine knew she had fallen in love.

The jagged edges of her pre-orgasmic mind filled her with hope but also foreboding. But her body surrendered to a flood of aching pleasure, wiping her mind blissfully clear of anything else.

Above her, Adam became one large, rigid muscle, burying himself one last time with something between a howl and a bellow. He collapsed, breaking eye contact at last, and after a minute, she gingerly removed her fingernails from his bicep.

He wrapped her up and held her close and they waited for their breathing to return to normal. But try as she might, Jasmine could not stop the errant notion of love from invading her thoughts. To distract herself, she made a list: where they would go for dinner; whether they'd have time to visit the Liechtenstein Museum before the flight tomorrow…but it was no good.

What was wrong with her that she couldn't separate sex and emotion? The whole male population managed that standing on their heads. Anyway, it wasn't love. It was lust. People thought and said things of no consequences in the throes of passion.

She couldn't be falling in love with Adam Thorne. She just couldn't.

He shifted a little, turning his face toward her. She concentrated on the row of half-moons indented into the smooth flesh of his bicep and ran her fingertip over them. "Sorry," she whispered. "I scratched."

Adam grinned. "Always happy to sustain a wound in the pursuit of a good time."

She didn't smile. She was thinking how relaxed he seemed, how she liked that. How she must not go there.

Adam's finger tipped her chin up. "What's up?"

"Nothing." She pretended to concentrate on his arm, licking her fingertip and rubbing it over the tiny marks. "Everything's perfect."

He exhaled noisily, a sound of satisfaction, contentment. He began playing with her hair, twisting a long strand around his finger. She sensed he was leading up to something.

"Have you and Nick ever…?"

Her head jerked up and she stared at him in astonishment. "Why would you ask that?"

Adam kept his eyes on his fingers combing through her hair. "You have to admit, you two seem tailor-made for each other."

Jasmine's indignation spilled over. "Perhaps his fiancée would disagree."

If he noticed her cool tone, he didn't defer to it. "Jordan's sensational, but on the surface, she doesn't seem his type."

That hurt. "She's more *your* type, you mean." Which was a pretty clear indication that she, Jasmine, wasn't Adam's type. Jordan was beautiful, stylish, loved clubbing and didn't seem to mind her every move being courted by the press.

Adam's smile only made her heart sink lower. "Perhaps, if one can have a 'type.' You didn't answer my question."

Jasmine exhaled, knowing her indignation was justified, but a fragment of guilt rose to the surface. She thought hard before answering. What good would it do to tell him that indeed she had believed herself in love with Nick for about three years? She had prayed that one day, he would look up and see her as more than his personal assistant. But she'd never have acted on it unsolicited.

That state of affairs changed the second Adam Thorne walked into the offices of Thorne Financial Enterprises about two months ago. The heartbeat gone mad, sweaty palms and neck and complete incapability of stringing a sentence together, convinced her that what she'd been feeling for Nick was friendship, affection, gratitude for being a great boss. She'd only felt that way about him because he was very much her "type"—conservative, solid, a constant presence in that she saw him every day. And there was no question she was lonely. There were few people she counted as friends in Wellington and none as lovers.

No point divulging that former affection now, when he was happily engaged and she was sleeping with his brother.

"I think a lot of Nick," she said rather stiffly, "and I hope he counts me as a friend, but neither of us would take our professional relationship lightly."

"He needs his head read, having you there every day and not acting on it."

Her heart skipped a beat while she wondered if he'd seen right through her. He continued. "But I'm glad, because I wouldn't like it."

"Can't stand the comparison?" she asked a little snidely.

"Oh, I think—" his voice warmed "—I know who'd win that one." His finger unraveled the long strand of hair and then landed in the dip between her breasts. Despite the instant, piercing arousal as he ran his finger slowly down between her breasts, it rankled to be considered a pawn in the competition that was the largest component in the relationship between the two brothers. The anger was good because there was no way she could be in love with such arrogance.

"He has set the bar quite high with Jordan, hasn't he?" she asked sweetly, then immediately lost track when his fingertip circled her nipple. Her very hard nipple.

Adam licked his lips, eyeing up her breast hungrily. "I don't mind losing out to him in the marriage stakes," he murmured. "At least for the next ten years or so."

His dark head bent lower. Jasmine closed her eyes, accepting it. He'd given her no reason to expect more than a temporary fling.

His tongue swiped across one nipple and despite the leaden weight she felt on her heart, she shivered with delight.

"I'll tell you what's perfect," Adam said, matter-of-factly, cupping her breasts. "*These* are perfect. Feel free to scratch."

Later that night, Jasmine persuaded Adam to take a cab out to Grinzing, the wine suburb of Vienna. "I want to go to an *Heuriger,* a sort of wine tavern with a cellar. They sell their new harvest."

"So long as there is food."

They walked into a rustic tavern with a green branch tacked to the door, sniffing appreciatively as they entered. The room was rich with the aromas of roast pork, pasta and paprika-flavored goulashe-soup. The menu was buffet, the tables unadorned wooden benches—a far cry from the sumptuously furnished Hotel Imperial, but she liked the disparity—and an old man played *The Blue Danube* on an accordion in the darkest corner.

They ate a leisurely meal, followed by the ubiquitous *apfelstrudel*. Jasmine was determined no rogue feelings would spoil their last night together. They were still on fairy-tale time.

"The flight's at midday tomorrow. Is that all right?"

No. She nodded.

"I need to go in to the new office, but why don't you stay with me tomorrow night?"

Her heart leaped. Don't get excited. He just wants more of that crazy sex....

Adam had spent the afternoon teasing her. Miss Prim and Proper Cooper, kneeling on a bed that belonged in a museum, wearing nothing but high-heeled boots. He told her it was the sexiest thing he'd ever seen.

"Okay," she replied, hoping he couldn't see her blush in the dim room. "If my father is all right."

They talked of how long she was staying in England and when his next trip home might be.

"Will you come home for Nick's wedding?"

He nodded. "Of course. April, isn't it?"

He sat back in his seat, his healthy tan showcased by his open shirt collar, the sort of man who turned heads wherever he went. Jasmine felt blessed that for a couple of short days, he'd only had eyes for her. "You'll be best man, I suppose."

He grinned. "I always am."

Jasmine shook her head with a wry smile. "You're very competitive, you and Nick, aren't you?"

"Dad always set us against each other. Everything was a competition. He'd actually pay us to win—the most tries at rugby, the best grades." He grinned. "The most broken bones, girls… Not that we needed much encouragement. That's what boys do when left to their own devices."

She raised an interested brow. "Left to your own devices?"

He shrugged. "My parents were hardly ever there. We had live-in nannies or caregivers. Dad traveled a lot, setting up the bank in the major centers. Mum was doing the same, building her chain of dancing clubs. We saw nothing of them through the week and even on weekends, after rugby or whatever, we'd be dragged around their respective empires to amuse ourselves while they worked."

Jasmine had no idea his home life was like that. She knew Randall, his father, quite well and liked him, for all that he roared like a bear when anything went wrong.

Adam must have seen the concern in her face. "Don't get me wrong, we had a good life. We wanted for nothing and we pretty much knew our parents loved us. We just didn't share things as a family."

Jasmine knew all about that. Being an only child—especially a female—meant her father tended to overlook her existence, although once Gill came along, she had no complaints.

Adam looked around the tavern and pointed out two tables with children in attendance. "Parenting has changed a lot since then. I'm sure our generation—or the next—will do much better."

And he'll probably never know, she thought sadly, gazing at him. Not if he didn't intend on marrying for the next decade.

Adam scratched his head, looking perplexed. "I wonder if Nick decided to settle down and have a family because of the adoption thing."

It was only a month ago that Nick had discovered he had been "adopted" by his parents when they believed they could not have children of their own. Adam had later come along to disprove the diagnosis.

"Are you so against marriage you can't believe that other people actually want to do it?" Jasmine countered. "To share their lives with one special person and want to have children with that person?"

When he shot an interested, considering look at her, she really wished she hadn't started this.

"I'm not against marriage and kids at all," he said

slowly. "But I'm going to make a hell of a lot better job of it than my folks. I won't even consider it until I'm financially secure enough not to have to work all the time. *My* family will come first."

Jasmine moistened suddenly dry lips. Since this was probably the end of the line for them anyway, she may as well ask. "And ten years is the benchmark?"

"I'm going global. Even if that only means say, five more countries after England, it's still a year or two scoping each one out, setting up, tracking growth. There is no way I'd consider marriage while all that's going on."

Jasmine had her answer and told herself it was no more than she'd expected.

Nine

Jasmine stared out at the dull shade of gray as they landed, remembering the gorgeous sunny day they had woken to in Vienna a few hours earlier. She tried to be happy, knowing this magical weekend was etched on her heart forever.

Adam had sent for a car and as the driver loaded the bags and they settled in the back, his cell phone rang. "Holiday over." He sighed. "Welcome home."

His expression lightened considerably a minute later when his business partner told him Stewart Cooper wanted to see him at his house at four o'clock.

"He wouldn't want to see you unless his advisors

had checked you out and he was interested," Jasmine enthused.

Adam leaned forward and conversed with the driver. "I'll drop you at my house." He handed her a key. "I have a good feeling about this, and I want you there to celebrate."

The car dropped her at his town house. "I'll keep my fingers firmly crossed for you," she told him as they kissed goodbye.

She let herself in and set her bag on the floor. Now she was alone, she indulged a girlish sort of high, waltzing around his lounge, reliving the wonderful memories of Vienna. The hotel. The ball. The music.

Adam.

She hoped his meeting went well and suspected he didn't need her prayers. He would succeed in his endeavors, she had no doubt. He was so determined with all his goals mapped out and she knew he would reach every single one, even if just to rub his brother's nose in it.

The music in her mind faded away and her steps slowed. He still had all his boxes to tick and no time for love. Could she handle this as a temporary relationship, feeling the way she did about him?

She wandered around the living room of his stylish three-bedroom town house in West Greenwich. She hadn't expected the city playboy to have a garden and backyard. Then again, he was a Kiwi and if he was anything like the New Zealanders she knew, he'd have spent most of his childhood out-doors. Most Kiwi men were sports mad. Sure enough, when she peered down the length of his neatly cut lawn, she spied a set of cricket wickets jammed in the ground.

A city playboy. Hadn't she been here before with Vincent? Light years apart in character but the les-son had been drummed into her. One woman was not enough.

She checked out his fridge. Adam obviously wasn't a cook; it was a desert in there, although there was an open bottle of New Zealand chardonnay. Why not? She found a glass and poured, her organized mind list-ing the pros and cons of sleeping with Adam Thorne.

Sex. Wow. Double wow.

His generosity, vis-à-vis Vienna. The fun they had, a commodity sorely lacking in her life. He knew pretty much all of the bad stuff now, the sticky stuff that she never talked about to anyone. He was a great listener. Quick to make her feel special and admired. Pretty good dancer—and sexy with it. He would be returning to his home country in the not too distant future. And she liked his family.

She only had so many fingers, so turned her mind to the cons, but was interrupted by her phone.

It was Gill and she sounded stressed. "No, no, he's fine," she answered Jasmine's worried inquiry after Nigel. "Well, not fine. Agitated. He wants to speak with you."

Jasmine heaved a sigh of relief.

"I'm sorry, love, I've put my foot in it," Gill continued in a low voice.

Apparently Stewart had called the estate, looking for her. In one of those quirks of fate, because he hardly ever answered the phone, Sir Nigel had today and learned that she'd gone to see her uncle. To him, it was a betrayal. To calm him down, Gill told him the purpose of Jane's visit wasn't to reunite the family or to go behind his back. It was about Adam's business. "Now he's worried that if you marry Adam, and Stewart goes into business with him, he will somehow manipulate Adam into handing over the estate to him one day."

Jasmine pressed her fingers to her temple. Her plan to please her father before he passed away had backfired. Why had she lied? She sat down on the sofa and waited tensely for Gill to put her father on the phone.

A couple of hours later, she sat in the same chair. The house was in darkness and it was cool enough to make her shiver. She got stiffly to her feet, wrestling with remorse, longing, regrets.

"I'm dying," her father had reminded her needlessly, several times. "It won't be long now, less than a year."

That "bastard"—his brother, Stewart—had taken his wife. He'd ruined all their lives. He'd get his hands on the estate via Adam and once he did, she and Gill would be tossed out like yesterday's rubbish. "Beware his tentacles," her father warned, when

Jasmine murmured she was sure her uncle wouldn't do that. "He wraps them around lovingly then he squeezes and never lets go. Look at your mother."

Jasmine promised her father she wouldn't contact her uncle again. At least, she thought, until after he'd passed away.

He then started on Adam's womanizing ways, alluding to what he called "frequent" snippets in the papers about his conquests. He'd obviously been talking to Ian. "He'll humiliate you just like Vincent did."

Yes, she thought. He would. He was dangerous because of her escalating feelings for him. She'd already told him more about her life than she'd ever told anyone. She'd also given him more of her body than anyone else and had a feeling she was about to wrap up her heart and hand it to him in a beribboned box.

Her father had finished by declaring that cancer or not, he would burn the estate to the ground before he'd let his brother get his hands on it.

Jasmine's misery and guilt went bone-deep. She should have told her father the truth about the sham engagement. She'd so wanted him to be proud of her for once. But something stopped her, some stupid naïve little part of her held on to the hope that Adam would realize he loved her, too.

Two hours sitting in the dark, mulling it all over had clarified things. Who was she kidding? Her father was right, she would get hurt. Adam Thorne was not permanent. She wasn't the one to turn his head, make him reevaluate his life. He loved his life as it was, the challenge of business, the fun, the competition. He would smash her heart into little pieces, and after the battering it had taken in her life, she didn't think she could take any more.

Jasmine drained her glass and went to the writing desk in the corner of his living room. She switched the lamp on and found some writing paper. She would leave a note; it wasn't as if he'd care. And then she'd go home and somehow find the courage to tell her father the truth about the fake engagement.

Adam tucked the bottle and his briefcase under his arm and put his key in the lock just as the door opened from the inside. Jasmine stood on the other side, her overcoat buttoned, a mustard-colored scarf coiled around her neck, one glove on. Her eyes were wide and surprised.

"Sorry I'm late, it went on longer than I expected, but—" he raised the bottle "—I'm hoping that champagne will get me off the hook."

She lagged behind, saying nothing as he moved into the kitchen. Maybe she was just going out to get something to eat. Adam was tired but exhilarated and he couldn't think of anyone he would rather celebrate with. "It's freezing in here. Aren't you going to ask me how it went?"

"How did it go?" she asked dutifully from halfway across the room.

"It's a deal!" he declared, setting the bottle down on the bench.

Jasmine did smile, eventually, but it didn't exactly light up the sky. "He's with you then? That's wonderful, Adam."

He frowned. *"That's wonderful, Adam?"* She wasn't exactly jumping for joy. "I think we can do better than that, can't we?" he chided, taking off his coat and tossing it over a bar stool. "You were the one who set things in motion, weren't you?" Her uncle had been amiable but had gotten straight down to business and they didn't discuss Jasmine. "Champagne?"

He noticed a piece of paper folded in half lying on the bench, but was distracted by the obvious effort Jasmine was making to widen her smile.

Something was off. He frowned down at the piece of paper. "What's this?" he asked, turning to scoop two flutes from the cocktail shelf behind him. By the time he'd turned back, she'd sidled around to his side of the bench, her eyes on the paper.

Adam was closer. He set the two flutes and the bottle on top of the paper, then unhurriedly went about opening and pouring, wondering about the troubled expression on her face. He'd expected more excitement from her. Surely she knew how much having Stewart Cooper on board meant to him.

Keeping his eyes on her face, he handed her a

glass and saluted her with his. "To the launch of Thorne-Hadlow Investments in the very near future," he announced.

Jasmine raised her glass and touched it to his.

"First thing tomorrow, I'm going to start organizing the launch party. This show is on the road!"

Her eyes slid off his. Something was very definitely wrong. She hadn't removed her coat. "Where were you off to just now?"

She swallowed. "I was— I have to get home."

He thought of her father, his failing health. "Home the estate or home New Zealand?"

"Pembleton," she replied listlessly. "My father found out I went to see Stewart. He is furious with me."

Adam was instantly concerned. "I'm sorry. I'll come with you, tell him it was all my fault."

Jasmine gave a bleak smile. "He won't listen, I'm afraid. He thinks if you go into business with Stewart, he'll use you to get his hands on Pembleton after Father passes away."

Now he was confused. "How would I do that?" He was obviously missing the big picture.

She studied the bubbles in her untouched glass. "After we're married…"

Concerned, confused and now confounded. "*After* we're married…?"

She didn't seriously harbor hopes that this engagement would morph into a real one any time soon, did she? Adam thought she was fantastic. He'd enjoyed their weekend as much as she had and was already planning another, but marriage?

Her lips tightened. "That's why I'm going. I have to put his mind at rest, come clean about the engagement."

He relaxed a little. "You had me worried there for a moment." He tugged on her scarf. "You can do that tomorrow."

This was supposed to be a celebration and Adam had spent the last hour since leaving the meeting thinking of just how he wanted to celebrate. He knew one thing, he couldn't get enough of this woman. "Take off your coat," he ordered, "have some bubbles and let's celebrate." He leaned toward her and nuzzled at the side of her mouth.

Jasmine huffed out a breath and turned her head away. "No, I— Don't, Adam."

He was barely listening, intent on tasting her lips again. She smelled amazing, looked amazing. Being close to her put more bubbles in his blood than the very best French champagne. "I bet I could persuade you…"

Jasmine stepped back like a scalded cat, raising her palms at chest height between them. "No!"

The sharpness of her voice surprised both of them. Adam realized this went deeper than guilt about lying to her father.

He put his own glass down and noticed the piece of paper again, still under the bottle. "What's this?" he asked, tapping it with his index finger.

Jasmine inhaled and held out her hand. "May I have it, please?"

Holding her gaze, he lifted the bottle and picked up the single sheet of paper. "Why?"

"It doesn't matter. You're here now." She made a half-hearted grab for the paper but he moved it out of her reach.

"Let's see…what sweet nothings…?" He opened the paper, an ominous feeling darkening his mood, and cleared his throat. "'Adam,'" he read aloud, "'Thank you for spending Christmas with me and for an unforgettable weekend. I loved every moment. No doubt I will see you in New Zealand from time to time.'" He sent a scathing look to her pink face. "'*Best*, Jasmine.'"

Best? That was low. They'd spent the last two days being as intimate as two people could be, and he only warranted a "Best"?

She said nothing, her face a picture of guilt.

"Dumped by note," he murmured, his quiet tone belying the anger starting to sizzle in his blood. "That's classy."

The expensive wine left a vinegary aftertaste. His satisfaction in landing the biggest defining achievement of his career ebbed away.

"I'm sorry," Jasmine said quietly. "I had no idea what time you'd be back."

"So you thought you'd just sneak away like a common thief."

Being dumped was a novel experience for Adam. It stung, he decided. He didn't like it. He thought he'd done everything to ensure she had a good time and this is how she repaid him. Worse, he was being dumped on what should have been one of the most satisfying nights of his life. "You're really something, you know that?"

"You got what you wanted, didn't you?"

Adam's head went up and he glared at her. Maybe he deserved that at the start, the old "you owe me" flung back in his face. But what about Vienna? Not that he begrudged a single penny, but he'd paid handsomely for his demand. Her lack of appreciation angered him.

He inclined his head stiffly, his eyes sweeping her body. "On all fronts, yes." He'd never had better. The sex was off-the-planet sublime.

Jasmine sighed heavily. "Well, they were your words. You said you'd take what you wanted, and you did and it was—" her voice hitched and her eyes were strangely brilliant but Adam was wound too tight to care "—wonderful," she continued. "Really wonderful."

"I aim to please," he bit out while at the same time, images of how she'd looked at the ball, in the gown he'd bought her, pummeled him. Especially the laughter and excitement and magic in her eyes.

Those eyes watched him now as if waiting for something. Did she think he was going to make her feel better about giving him the heave-ho, offer some platitude or other like, *Hey, don't worry about it, it was only sex, right?*

She looked away and began to pull her gloves back on. "Adam, I hope we—you—"

"Can still be friends?" he asked with a lightness he didn't feel. He raised his glass and tossed the contents back in one. "Sure, baby."

His tone, the careless response to her question, the unintended sharp report of the base of the flute banging down on the bench between them, made her flinch. What did he care? It was a relief, really. Now that New Year was over, his focus needed to be on the business.

A good five seconds passed before she spoke again. "Please don't tell Nick—everything."

Her words slashed at his pride. So that was her primary concern, after her father. She didn't want Nick to know his chaste personal assistant had gotten down and dirty with his disreputable brother. As if he'd want Nick, of all people, to know he'd been tossed aside by her. His brother had warned him repeatedly not to mess about with her feelings.

Who cared? He was off the hook. "Consider your debt paid in full."

So much for celebrations. Adam topped his glass up as she closed the door behind her.

Ten

Adam, his partner, John, and their new receptionist sat in his corner office on the prestigious Docklands site. They were open for business but, far from being excited, Adam stifled a yawn. He'd been working twenty-hour days to get to this point, as well as organizing the launch party next week, unpacking here at the new offices, hiring staff and fielding calls.

Lots of calls. The word had gotten out that Stewart Cooper was the principal investor in Thorne-Hadlow Investments. That started an avalanche of interest from some of the country's wealthiest business icons, clamoring to be included. The fledgling company's projected equity would far surpass their initial estimates at this rate, proving Adam's instincts about how vital Stewart's credentials would be correct.

"Promotion for the launch…" John said, rifling through his notes. "Everything is in hand, thanks to Lettie here." He indicated the bespectacled young lady beside him. "You're going down to sign the contract and pay the deposit on the venue today, aren't you?"

She nodded. "As soon as we're finished here. Have you finalized the guest list numbers?"

This would be a smallish but classy event at one of London's most prestigious clubs. Adam guessed that many of those who'd accepted personal invites to the launch were only coming in the hope of catching a glimpse of the notorious Stewart Cooper. They would be disappointed. The former pop-star manager hadn't been seen in public for a decade or more and Adam was fairly sure he wouldn't make an exception for Thorne-Hadlow.

He'd also invited Jasmine—a gesture of apology for his churlishness a week ago. Of thanks for her intervention with her uncle.

Of just plain wanting to see her face, hear her voice. Touch her, anywhere and everywhere.

"I have the reporter from the *Mail* here any minute for a bit of promo. Be prepared to have your photo taken."

Adam grimaced. "The offices are a mess." There were furniture boxes everywhere, his people sat at desks with wiring all over the place and no phones, and the entrance on the ground floor was wide-open. "Where is that security company?"

"I'll call them before I go," Lettie said, rising.

"Rome wasn't built in a day." John grinned at him. "Things will fall into place. They always do, with you on the job."

Adam grunted and watched his friend leave. It was nice to be given credit but it was primarily John's belief in Adam's ability to attract investment that had got them this far. Just a few short months ago, a lot of the big players they approached had run the other way. He owed John for keeping the faith.

He owed Jasmine, too. Without her, he doubted her uncle would have been interested. Once the launch was over and things started to settle down a little, he would give her a call. He'd hate her to return to New Zealand thinking badly of him.

He stood at his office window, looking out over the white disc of the O2 Dome in the distance, and finally allowed himself to acknowledge that he missed her. He'd lashed out because she hurt his pride and he wasn't used to that from anyone. Subsequently, he'd taken her slight far more seriously than it warranted.

A deep, booming voice broke into his thoughts, followed by John's voice, surprised and inquiring. Adam turned just as Stewart Cooper himself marched into his office with John on his heels.

The man who never left his house in the Lake

District, a virtual recluse, shunned by his family and denied his birthright, stood framed in Adam's doorway. And he did not look pleased to be here.

Adam moved to meet him but didn't smile. He was obviously in no mood for pleasantries. Adam thought again how frail Jasmine's younger, taller father looked in comparison to the physically powerful man approaching him now.

Stewart stopped at the desk, his legs braced like a fighter, and fixed Adam with a glower. "I came to tell you that if you marry my niece before her father dies, the deal is off."

Adam's vision deserted him for a second. He bit down on a howl of protest that lodged in his throat, and then unclenched his fists. Who the hell did this bloke think he was to demand whom he could or could not marry? If he thought that was the way Adam did business, he had another think coming.

Behind the big man, John's mouth dropped open. Adam ignored him, fuming inwardly. Damn, but this woman and her secrets were proving to be a monumental pain in the rear. He'd like to go just half a day without thinking about her.

"Well?"

Adam forced his mind on the facts and away from Jasmine's face. He recalled her saying her father needed a male heir to pass the estate on to. If that didn't eventuate, presumably the estate would go to Stewart, the next of kin. Bloody family feuds! His own family had just been through the wringer in New Zealand because of a stupid historical feud. Didn't people have anything better to do with their time?

Stewart Cooper and John still waited expectantly. Adam's good business sense kicked in. The word *no* was his least favorite word in the world but Stewart was a vital link to their success. Without his money, and more importantly, his involvement, Thorne-Hadlow would be just one more angel investment company. John and Adam weren't interested in small businesses; they were playing with millions of pounds to start up innovative companies that were going global. And marketing and management for global IT and technology required massive investment—and massive risk.

The big Englishman watched him through cold gray eyes that had similar color to his niece's but none of the life. "I'm waiting for an assurance from you that this engagement won't proceed."

How had he found out? Surely Jasmine had told her father by now it was all an act.

John moved into view behind the bulk of their visitor. Adam squared up to his task. If he ordered him out, he'd be wasting five years of planning and hard work, not to mention the fortune that he personally had sunk into this project. He had John to consider, one of life's good blokes with two young kids and a large mortgage. And for what? A pretend engagement that she—Jasmine—had instigated?

Besides which, hadn't she dumped him last week?

Adam cleared his throat. "The engagement is off, Stewart. I won't be marrying your niece."

Stewart's piercing eyes bored into him for a few seconds more then he snapped off a nod. "Good man. Nothing personal, you understand."

His entire demeanor changed in an instant and he became the affable man Adam had met at his home last week on his return from Vienna. "My lawyer will be in touch in the next day or so." He shook hands heartily with both of them. "Boys." And was gone, as unexpectedly as he had come.

"You were engaged?" John turned to him, looking mystified.

"Long story," Adam said, shaking his head.

He told himself he had done the only thing he could have under the circumstances, but a hollow feeling of distaste perplexed him. It was as if he'd dishonored her by going along with her uncle's preposterous demand. Which was ridiculous. Jasmine would not want his business undermined. And there was no engagement. It wasn't as if they'd announced the union anyway. Only her father and Gill knew about it, and maybe Ian. Anyway, she would have set them all right by now, and Stewart was certainly not going to open his mouth about this conversation.

Realizing he wasn't going to get an explanation from his partner, John looked at his watch, frowning. "Where's that bloody reporter?"

Left alone, Adam ordered himself to stop worrying about Jasmine and get back to trying to track down the phone people.

The phone began to ring at seven in the morning. Jasmine jerked awake as her father's booming displeasure seemed to reach every corner of the house, taking her back to the Vincent debacle before his illness. The return of his voice at top notch was not a good sign.

She hurried into the small yellow drawing room where her father spent most of his days, wrinkling her nose against the smell of sickness that was beginning to pervade the room.

Her father was agitatedly pushing newspapers all over the table when he looked up and saw her. "Here she is," he erupted. "My *infamous* daughter."

Jasmine's heart plummeted. What had she done to disappoint him now?

His anger at her for approaching his most hated enemy had abated only slightly since she'd told him the engagement between her and Adam was off. He behaved exactly as she'd expected and spent every minute lauding Ian's virtues.

Now, he tossed one of the newspapers across the table to where she stood. Jasmine looked down. "Poor Jane Dumped—Again!"

"Try another," her father said acidly, tossing more papers. "And another."

She closed her eyes briefly, her shoulders slumping. *My worst nightmare…*

Taking a shaky breath, she forced herself to open her eyes.

"The Heiress and the Playboy—History Repeats." She winced at the next one—"Poor Little Jane—Abandoned Again" while Gill shushed her father at the other end of the table.

Trembling, she sank into the nearest chair as the words on the newsprint swam in front of her eyes. Her father vigorously filled her in, saying that Adam had indeed humiliated her, humiliated all of them. Her uncle had threatened to ditch his investment if Adam didn't ditch her. And ditch her he had in double-quick time.

She barely heard her father's "I told you so"s as her mind sank into anguish and her heart with it. It was happening again. She didn't know if she could bear it. She'd angered Adam with her clumsy farewell and shouldn't have been surprised by any callous disregard for her feelings. But why choose the public arena? He must have known how scarred she was by her past, the lengths she'd gone to to get away from all this.

I think you're running away, he'd said in Vienna.

"When will you learn," her father lamented, "that love is for fools? Anyone with half a brain knows that."

Predictably, he started up about Ian again as she sat numb with shock. How Ian would never let her down, he would protect her from all of this. Finally, her stepmother persuaded him to subside and he left the room, muttering that Jasmine was as bad as her mother.

Gill sat down beside her and flicked her fingers over the papers. "Take this with a grain of salt, love. It states 'unnamed sources.' I bet no one even spoke to Adam, or they misheard or misunderstood and didn't bother to confirm it with him."

She nodded slowly, thinking that cautious hope was better than no hope, even if it wouldn't change the outcome. Perhaps he hadn't knowingly humiliated her. He could be hard, but cruel? She refused to believe she could have lost her heart to a cruel man.

Remember Vincent, her memory taunted her...

She leaned her head back on the chair and stared, unseeing, out the window, waiting for the pain to come and clamp her insides with rusty jaws. "I suppose you think I should marry Ian, too," she whispered.

Gill squeezed her arm, kept her hands there. "There's a lot to be said for compatibility, security."

Jasmine stared at her for seconds, finally seeing what she'd been blind to all these years. She grabbed on to it—anything to sway her mind from her own humiliation. "You don't love my father, do you?"

Sir Nigel never displayed affection, except perhaps to his horses, and she'd wondered if he was even capable of love. But she'd always assumed Gill saw something in him to admire. Surely they must share some kind of bond to stay together all these years.

Gill's eyes showed gentle understanding. "I married for love first time around. He left me. When I came here, I recognized that Nigel and I could be of use to each other. I could bring you up properly and manage some of the workload around here. In return, he would give me security, prestige, a little luxury." She smiled, and Jasmine's heart squeezed. "And I got to have you, honey, to watch you grow. That alone was worth the price of admission."

A tear rolled down Jasmine's cheek and Gill, wonderful comforting Gill, reached out and wiped it away. "He's not a bad man. He was terribly hurt by your mother and in his way, he doesn't want to see you hurt."

Too late, Jasmine thought. Still, there was no need to worry anymore. Her heart was dead to the possibility of love now.

All through that long day, unable to stop herself, she tracked the progress of the story on Internet sites and TV. On signing into her work e-mail address, she was dismayed to find the story breaking on the main New Zealand news page because of her Kiwi connection. It was the middle of the night there but she imagined her boss, her work colleagues, the one or two friends she had warmed enough toward to share a coffee with occasionally, all waking up to the news that she was not who she purported to be. The real Jane Cooper was so much more interesting than the efficient, reserved Jasmine.

It was all laid out in grotesque clarity: her mother's affair with Stewart, the questions around her dead brother's paternity, the car accident, abandonment and her later broken engagement. "Misplacing one fiancé was unlucky," one scribe gleefully proclaimed. "Losing two is careless."

Whatever Adam's part in the story, her uncle's actions had wounded her. She thought they'd connected in some way, felt he wanted to expand on that. But it appeared Stewart was just after the estate and his revenge.

Ian came around, but she did not want to see him and Gill sent him away. The phone didn't stop ringing. The story, even with no fresh legs to run with, seemed to stutter on: inane comments from anyone who might have known her at school, staff at her mother's psychiatric facility, even a couple of locals that had attended the Boxing Day party and who looked thrilled to find themselves being interviewed on television.

Jasmine knew one thing. She couldn't go back to New Zealand and face Nick and her colleagues. With a heavy heart, she composed and sent e-mails to him and to an international moving company to pack up her house.

Gill showed Adam into one of the unused rooms, where he found Jasmine unpacking some of the estate's forgotten antiques. From the look on her stepmother's face, he wasn't the most popular man in Britain at the moment. The atmosphere in the house was ghost-cold.

He found Jasmine sitting in the middle of a ring

of chests and boxes, with piles of packing foam and wood chips scattered around. She held a small, square silver object in her hands and was carefully turning it this way and that. She wore a black cowl-necked jumper over gray pants and both garments were liberally spotted with packing debris and dust.

When she heard his approach, she looked straight at him, her sharp inhalation straightening her back. Adam stood still, stunned at the pain reflected in her eyes. Hating the knowledge that he'd put it there.

She finally looked back at her prize. "Solid silver card case, Victorian, early eighteen-fifties. Made by Alfred Taylor, a silversmith of Birmingham."

She carefully put the case into an open box.

Adam stepped forward quickly. "What can I do?"

Her blink of surprise at his concern shamed him. Did she really think he was that callous?

"You shouldn't be here," she said quietly. "It will be worse if anyone sees you."

There was no censure in her voice or her eyes, but Adam needed to tell her it wasn't intentional, he hadn't seen it coming. "We had a reporter coming to the offices for some promo for the launch. I suspect he saw Stewart coming in, decided to eavesdrop, and then disappeared."

With the reception area in a state and Lettie out anyway, no one had noticed anyone lurking outside Adam's office while the conversation with Stewart took place. There were so many publications doing the rounds, they couldn't be sure of the original source. The fact that the reporter supposedly covering the launch hadn't shown for his appointment suggested he was the culprit, but there was no way the editor was admitting to anything. "I knew nothing about it until I saw it in the papers."

The guarded acceptance in her eyes made him feel worse, if that was possible. The weight of culpability with each new publication or Internet site or TV broadcast was heavy indeed. How could he have exposed her to this? He knew what it had cost her in the past. No matter how miffed he was at her dumping him, he wouldn't have wished this particular personal nightmare on her if she was his worst enemy, because he knew how far she'd run to put it behind her last time.

Jasmine picked up a lumpy object and began peeling back layers of Bubble Wrap. Adam paced, not looking at her, but so aware of every move she made, the way she bent her head to study the object—some sort of bronze cannon—her concentration so intense, he knew she wasn't seeing it at all. All her senses were on him.

Suddenly he whirled and squatted down in front of her. He rested his hands on her knees. "Marry me."

Jasmine nearly dropped the cannon. "Wh-what?"

"I can't change what's happened but I can make things better."

Her gray-blue eyes had a rosy tinge in the dimly lit room, suggesting recent tears.

"How?" she asked. "How could marrying you make it better?"

Adam sighed. Maybe it couldn't, but he felt so useless. "I wouldn't be abandoning you." He squeezed her thighs, not sure which of them he was trying to convince more.

"You've been talking to Nick." There was an accusatory tone in her voice.

Adam didn't deny it. Both his brother and father had called to castigate him as soon as the story broke over there. They'd taken turns to berate him for his lack of responsibility, his carelessness in hurting a fine woman like Jasmine. When would he learn he couldn't just continue to sail through life, letting people down, never thinking of consequences? Adam had been lucky to escape with his hearing.

They had some valid points. He should have taken more care with Jasmine's particular set of circumstances. His brother would never have gotten into this situation, but if he had, he would take full responsibility.

"We might be all right. We're friends, aren't we?"

They were. Not only that, but the sex was amazing. Many marriages survived on less.

"And when my uncle finds out you've gone back on your word? Your business?"

A muscle twitched in his cheek. That had kept him awake all night, but he'd contributed to this mess. He had to clean it up. "I don't think it will come to that, but that's my problem."

"Why, Adam?"

Her quiet question reminded him of all the things that had gone through his mind when Stewart made the demand. Watching the news break yesterday illustrated that he was no better than her mother or her ex. The publicity may not have been intentional but still, he'd hung her out to dry as nonchalantly and effortlessly as they had done before him.

"Because I hate that it's made things worse for you. I hate that I've made you sad. You've suffered enough."

Jasmine smiled. He warmed to see it. "Thank you, Adam," she said quietly. "That's very kind, but it won't be necessary."

Despite his earnest desire to help, relief washed through him—followed by a sharp jet of green suspicion. "You're not going to do anything stupid, are you? I won't let you marry Ian…"

Her nostrils flared. "That's not for you to say," she said sharply.

She had told him that after what happened last time, the pressure her father put on her to marry the neighbor drove her away. No way would Adam let that happen.

"But, no," Jasmine said in a more reasonable tone. "I'm not marrying anyone." She looked down at his hands, still on her knees. "You owe me nothing, Adam. The engagement was my misguided attempt to give my father some pleasure before he died."

Adam wondered how the old man had taken this.

As if she'd read his mind, Jasmine smiled ruefully. "And you can imagine the pleasure he is feeling today."

"I bet," he said feelingly. In his limited acquaintance with Sir Nigel, he could almost feel the wind of disapproval and censure from here.

"We're even," she continued. "I did you a favor, you did me one. It was my stupid idea that caused all this trouble. My fault, not yours. You did everything I asked of you—" she covered one of his hands with hers "—and more. You gave me Vienna."

She lifted her hand from the all too brief caress and brushed at her top. With her pale face and hair tightly tied back, the shadows under her eyes, she looked so much less, somehow, than the night of the ball. Not less beautiful, just faded and smaller than before. Adam's heart squeezed in his chest. He would make this up to her, he promised himself. Somehow...

He rose to his feet, for once in his life unsure of what to say, to do. "Nick said you'd resigned," he said to the crown of her head.

Jasmine merely nodded.

"Why, Jasmine? You love that job and you love New Zealand."

She exhaled and looked out the window. A minute ticked by before she answered. "I do. But the Jasmine over there is not the real me. She was just a front, born to hide my problems." She looked at him, her eyes clear. "I haven't got it all worked out yet, but I need to be here for my father. It would be a mistake to leave England at the moment. There are things I started here that I never got around to finishing." She paused, choosing her words carefully. "In fact, there is a lot of unfinished business in my life. I think it's time I faced up to it."

Eleven

Adam checked his watch for the tenth time. Where were they? His most important guests had flown half-way across the world to be here tonight, and yet the party had been going for an hour and there was no sign of them. John and the events manager of the Café de Paris kept shooting him raised-brow looks, reminding him that the venue was booked for another event in an hour.

No one was more pleased than Adam when Nick said they were coming. He'd made a flip comment like he was just keeping an eye on his investment, but Adam knew his brother was behind him all the way. It hadn't been as difficult as he'd imagined, going cap in hand to Thorne Financial Enterprises and asking them to underwrite the new company's debt, should some or all of his big investors pull out.

"Why would they do that?" Nick had asked.

"Because I'm going to tell Stewart Cooper that he can stick his investment where the sun doesn't shine," Adam had replied.

After leaving Jasmine last week, he knew he'd missed a golden opportunity. He'd needed a little more time to get used to the idea that he loved her. Some last-gasp vestige of confirmed bachelorhood had its claws into him still. She'd have been nuts to accept his pathetic proposal.

"The natives are getting restless," John said at his elbow.

With a last look around, Adam followed his friend to the front of the gathering. Sure, he was disappointed Nick hadn't made it but that was nothing compared to his disappointment that Jasmine hadn't showed. Hardly surprising, given the media contingent here.

As he stepped up onto the small stage, he ran his fingers over the tiny box in his pocket. Before the night was out, he'd have a private audience with her, and the second chance he hoped her generous nature would allow him.

Someone handed him a microphone and he called for quiet.

"I'm Adam Thorne, and this—" Adam clapped a hand on his partner's shoulder "—is John Hadlow.

We are pleased to welcome you all to the international launch of Thorne-Hadlow Investments."

He looked out over the sea of heads at the business icons, friends and invited media, and launched into his well-rehearsed speech. He was midway through when he caught sight of his brother and father right at the back and breathed a sigh of relief.

"There are many people to thank. It's been a long road, but without my family's support, and that of a few select friends, we wouldn't be here today."

He finished his short speech and stepped back so John could say a few words. His former mentor, Derek Bayley of Croft, Croft and Bayley, was next and that concluded the formalities. The hundred guests continued to graze on the food and drink provided and Adam began to work his way through the crowd of well-wishers to the back of the room, simmering with impatience. He'd say a quick hello and then flag the family meal he'd arranged downstairs in favor of a couple of hours' drive and some unfinished business at Pembleton Estate. This time he would do it properly, give her reasons she could live with.

A plethora of camera flashes lit up the back of the room. Adam craned his neck and saw the tall figures of Nick and his father, head and shoulders above the throng of people. A swish of gold fabric and blond ringlets by Nick's shoulder confirmed the photographic interest. Nick's fiancée, Jordan Lake, stopped traffic wherever she went.

Adam stopped abruptly, his eyes snagged on a deep-red off-the-shoulder dress, close to his father. He stretched tall, but with half the crowd turning and moving to see what the fuss was about, he could only pick out parts—long, blood-red baubles at her ears, a flash of white teeth, glossy dark hair pulled back in a stylish twist. The cameras flashed again and Adam's heart gave him a kick.

Jasmine. A strong impulse to melt into the crowd and escape gripped him. Was he ready for this? Matrimony? Love? It went totally against his life plan, the goals he'd set, his vision of his future. All the valid reasons why not had hammered through his brain at regular intervals for days.

The crowd noise around him hushed and the people in front stepped aside, their eyes moving between him and Jasmine with fascinated expressions. Adam stood as if in the spotlight, wishing he were anywhere else in the world, until she half turned and saw him.

A small, uncertain smile played across her face. Adam's heart slowed and swelled and for the first time since the day he met her, he felt at peace.

It was hard not to make a dramatic entrance at the Café de Paris; the opulent decor, impressive staircases and air of grandeur demanded it. Jasmine forced herself to hold her head high but in reality, if she wasn't firmly supported by Randall on one side and Nick and Jordan on the other, she would have bolted at the first camera flash. As it was, she sagged at the second.

"I'm right here, girl," Randall rumbled in her ear, holding her arm firmly. On the other side, Jordan's eye-catching beauty and vivacity pulled a few of the cameras off her face, for which Jasmine was grateful.

They were late. That was her fault. She'd argued loud and long against going, but her surprise visitors to Pembleton wouldn't take no for an answer. They'd caught most of Adam's speech but she barely heard a word. The pain was too raw, her nerves stretched to breaking at the prospect of more denigrating publicity in tomorrow's press.

She had spent the last week keeping busy to take her mind off Adam and his kind-hearted marriage proposal. This afternoon, Nick had looked over the business plan she'd put together for the bank and pronounced it excellent. She'd spent hours working on her lists, talking to her father and Gill and prioritizing the multiple ways to best drag Pembleton into the twenty-first century.

As Adam stepped down from the dais and headed in their direction, she thought how ironic that he had offered the thing she wanted most—marriage to him—and she had turned him down. Accepting his proposal, born of guilt and pity, would be as bad as accepting Ian, who only wanted her for the estate. Jasmine vowed to forget about love, marriage and children and concentrate on her father in the short term and Pembleton in the long.

Suddenly the crowd parted and Adam walked toward them, tall, confident, larger than life, and his eyes on her face. She forced herself to breathe, told herself over and over that she could do this, she could be friends with him on this auspicious occasion. But oh, it would be so much easier in a less public forum, without oafish reporters loudly querying the current status of their relationship and cameras going off left, right and center.

In the interests of public relations, she offered him a smile and he smiled back and ran his hand down her arm. "I'm glad you came," he murmured in her ear, leaning close.

"Shall we go?" Adam turned to the others. "I've booked a table downstairs." He glanced at Jasmine. "It will be quieter down there."

They ate a relatively private dinner with a couple of Adam's friends and the family. Randall was, as usual, the loudest and best company. Jasmine warmed to see how he had taken to his daughter-in-law-to-be. After all the angst between Randall and Jordan's father, Syrius, she could scarcely believe how close they'd become in such a short time.

But as soon as dessert was cleared away, Nick began yawning and making jet lag excuses, belaboring the point so much that Jasmine quickly saw through his act; her boss was determined that she and Adam be left alone. Maybe he hoped Adam could talk her into coming back to work.

The Thornes and entourage left. Adam put her coat around her shoulders and suggested a walk. The night was crisp and cold, with no wind.

"Uncle Stewart didn't come?" she asked, pulling her gloves on as they began to walk slowly toward nearby Trafalgar Square.

Adam shook his head. "I didn't expect him to."

A phone call from her uncle a couple of days ago had thrown Jasmine into a quandary. She had made a promise to her father, but Stewart begged her to come. The old man felt terrible about the publicity he'd unwittingly sparked.

While speaking to him, she realized that he was lonely and wanted nothing more than to belong to a family. Now she told Adam a little of Stewart's history. "His father kicked him out of home very young because he wanted a career in the music industry, not the done thing for an English country gentleman."

Her uncle had discovered and managed what became one of the world's biggest glam rock bands in the seventies. The predecessors of punk, glam rock bands were the outcasts of the music industry with their makeup and glitter and rocky ballads, but a handful of artists had huge success. "He met my mother in the mid-seventies when he was riding high," she continued. "Naturally her parents hated her going out with someone so anti-establishment, so they had to sneak around and she pretended to be going out with my father instead. And then she got pregnant and my father married her."

"Did he know who the father was?"

"I've never had the nerve to ask him," Jasmine said quietly. Talking about personal matters was not the done thing around her father. "Stewart lost everything, his own family, the love of his life, his son. I'm not surprised he's bitter. He's so alone."

"Are you going to keep in touch?"

Jasmine nodded. "Yes, but I'll have to be discreet. I don't want to upset my father. He'll never make his peace with Stewart now."

"You don't know that. By all accounts, Dad and Syrius are making an effort for Nick and Jordan's sake. Enough, at least, to sit down together at a family engagement dinner."

Jordan had told her as much. Syrius and Randall had been close friends before the accident that had put Syrius's wife in a wheelchair and robbed him of his son.

They walked onto Trafalgar Square, her eyes automatically gravitating to where the Christmas tree had been until a few days ago. She sighed. Another year older, but wiser? She didn't think so.

She clapped her cold hands together. "I've broached the possibility of Stewart coming to live at Pembleton when Father passes away—provided Gill agrees, of course. I feel disloyal but…it was Stewart's home, too, you know? I feel he has as much right to be there as I do."

Her uncle had no intention of kicking her and Gill out after her father died, even though she had failed to marry and provide a male heir. She glanced sideways at Adam. Best not to mention the word *marriage* in present company.

Adam pursed his lips thoughtfully. "What did he say?"

Jasmine's eyes misted with emotion. Stewart had nearly wept when she'd asked him. "He would dearly love to see Pembleton again. I think he would enjoy being involved and I could certainly use the help."

She'd told Adam over dinner about the improvements she'd instigated in the redevelopment of Pembleton Estate. She had already hired the contractors to develop the golf course. The events program could wait for now while she concentrated on setting up the new Antiques Center.

"I've asked him to tell me about my mother, let me get to know her through his eyes, because I never really knew her at all."

Stewart had said he would gladly oblige in return for having the pleasure of watching Jasmine's children grow, but she decided Adam didn't need to know that.

"And is he going to tell you about your mother?" he asked.

She nodded. "Maybe it will fill a hole in both our lives."

Jasmine recognized that she'd closed herself off from the world, afraid of reaching out to people. Perhaps that stemmed from her mother's abandonment, perhaps not, but she knew she had some growing to do.

Adam stopped and leaned against one of the famous lion bronzes, flanking Nelson's Column. "I think you'll be very happy there, amongst all your old relics."

"I'm going to try," Jasmine said.

He was right about her passion for history. Pembleton could be her museum. It would take years to unpack, catalogue and restore the treasures packed away. Now that she'd resigned and made arrangements to pack up her Wellington house and put it on the market, she needed to keep busy and to heal her heart. That particular relic would be packed away safely, perhaps never to be exhibited again.

Given her love for the man watching her right now, that was a bleak prospect. Feeling the need to lighten the mood, she craned her neck and peered up the length of Nelson's Column.

"Do you know why some rum is called Nelson's Blood?"

Adam shook his head, looking interested. Jasmine admired his tolerance for her historical prattling.

"When Admiral Nelson was killed," she began, "the ship's officers preserved the body in the crew's vat of rum and halted their rations. But when they got to England, they found the body well preserved but the vat empty. Unbeknown to the officers, the crew hadn't liked giving up their daily tot and so had drilled holes in the vat to get at their rum."

Adam pulled a face. "Well, that's certainly set the scene for romance."

Jasmine tilted her head but her query died on her lips when his eyes locked onto hers and became serious.

Her heartbeat began to rattle. Oh, please, not another of those great, addictive surges of longing. She'd tried sleeping with him without losing her heart. It hadn't worked.

Adam reached out and took her hand in his. "Marry me, Jasmine," he said simply.

Jasmine closed her eyes, cherishing the words but wishing that they came from his heart and not some warped sense of responsibility.

"We've been here before." She sighed.

"No," he murmured. "We haven't."

When she opened her eyes, Adam stood in front of her, holding a tiny red box. Her mind howled foul—it was unfair of him to tempt her so much when she was at her weakest. Inhaling, she called on all of her composure to crush the surge of hope that burst within her. With more poise than she knew she possessed, Jasmine raised her eyes to his, but could do nothing about the hitch in her breathing.

"Adam, we discussed this. I won't marry for the wrong reasons. Otherwise why not just marry Ian and be done with it?"

Adam squeezed her gloved hand. "What about

the right reasons?" He paused and then inhaled deeply, working up to something. The pressure on her hand increased. "Such as love?"

Jasmine blinked and felt frozen in time. Was he saying that he loved her?

He held out the box. "Open it."

She eyed it almost fearfully, then shook her head. There was too much longing, too much dashed hope for her to take that step.

He opened it. She tried, she really did, not to look at it. Instead, she searched his face, looking in vain for sympathy, the anguish and guilt she'd seen a few days ago. There was only strain etched around his mouth and his serious, waiting eyes.

She looked down and blinked several times. The stone was huge, a perfect cushion-cut diamond surrounded by smaller round diamonds. The band was handcrafted platinum, delicately millegrained around the square shoulders. It was a true Edwardian antique or at least, manufactured to a very high standard of reproduction. Either way, it was the most beautiful ring she'd ever seen.

She ghosted a step closer, unable to take her eyes off it.

Adam cleared his throat. "Jasmine, last week I couldn't say the right words. I would never marry anyone I wasn't head over heels about. But I made a real mess of it and you were quite right to turn me down."

She looked into his eyes and saw that he was completely serious. The tension overwhelmed her; the desire to believe him was immense. After all the secrets and games between them, could it be true that Adam Thorne wanted her for no other reason than love?

Adam lowered his arm and as he did, the ring box snapped shut. Jasmine couldn't help the tiny moan of protest and longing that slipped out.

He noticed. Smiling, he lifted her hand and wrapped her fingers around the box, covering both with his hand. She looked up at him and opened her mouth to speak, but he put his index finger on her lips. "Just let me get this out."

He was nervous, she realized incredulously. She had to bite her lip not to smile, not to pat his arm and tell him he was doing fine. Amazingly, wonderfully fine.

"I wanted you at first because you were so—cool and unattainable. And because Nick said I couldn't." A quick smile flashed over his face. "I like needling Nick. But then I got to know you, all your secrets and intrigues, all the sadness and disappointments. And then, Vienna."

"Vienna." Jasmine sighed against his finger. Where she had free-fallen into orgasm and the explosive knowledge that she loved him desperately at the very same instant.

"I agreed to Stewart's demand because my pride was hurt," Adam continued, "knowing deep down that it was wrong, it wasn't what I wanted to do. But I couldn't get my head around it. I mean, what engage-ment? It was a sham, and anyway, you'd finished with me. There were other valid reasons but I knew—I knew I'd let you down just like your mother and just like your ex. And I knew it would come back to haunt me."

Jasmine's heart went out to him, humbled that he, too, had suffered so much.

"After the publicity hit, I felt that marriage was the right—the only—thing to offer, but still I couldn't ad-mit to myself, let alone you, that I loved you. I'm so sorry for that."

"I so very nearly said yes." Jasmine exhaled sadly and reached up to place her hand on his cheek. The leather glove against his stubble scraped dully. "It's not like I have high expectations. But I love you so much, I couldn't stand to tie you into a marriage be-cause you pitied me."

There was no guilt or pity in his eyes now. He turned his head and pressed his lips against her fingers. "Then say yes, because love is the right reason, the only reason."

His hand squeezed hers around the jewelry box, reminding her of its presence. Joy and hope, waiting in the wings for so long, began to fill and warm her from top to toe. Yet, caution—an innate part of her nature these last few years—still whispered questions in her mind. "And Stewart? Maybe I can talk to him?"

"I've talked to him already, told him that's not the way I do business. He's thinking about it. In the meantime, I've asked Nick to underwrite the debt if the other investors pull out. It's a risk I'm prepared—and equipped—to take."

Jasmine's mouth dropped open. "You asked Nick for help?"

"He didn't mention it?"

She shook her head, full of wonder.

"Probably still in shock," Adam said, smiling.

For Adam Thorne to ask his brother for help was unbelievable. Nick was the very last person in the world Adam would admit to that maybe, just maybe, he didn't have the deck stacked. "That must have cost you."

"You have no idea." He ran a hand along his brow.

Jasmine liked his family so much. When she'd refused point-blank to go to the launch tonight, Nick had pulled rank quite forcefully.

"You haven't worked out your notice," he'd warned. "That still makes me your boss. Now, get dressed!"

Now she smiled at his brother. "I get the impression Nick wants me back at work."

"Nick will like the idea of you as his sister-in-law better, trust me," Adam told her confidently.

Nick's sister-in-law. It sounded wonderful.

Just one more thing stopped her from giving in to the impulse to jump on him and scream her delight, and get that gorgeous ring on her finger before he changed his mind—or they were mugged. "Where would we live?"

"There is room at that dusty old manor for me, isn't there?"

"Of course." She blinked. "But you always intended on going home, setting up there."

He nodded. "There will be some teething problems, especially initially. I know I said I wanted everything perfect before I married, but we can work out these things over time." He took both her hands. "All I know is, you need to be at Pembleton for now, and I need to be with you."

"It's not like we don't have support, good support, here and in New Zealand," she agreed. Gill was very capable if given direction and when her father passed, there would be Stewart. "I think a wedding will perk Father up, give him something extra to mutter about."

Adam pulled her into his front, their hands in between them. "As soon as you like," he said solemnly. "Sooner."

Then he bent close. "I think it's customary in deals of this nature to seal the contract with a kiss."

They kissed, a long sweet kiss, full of friendship and forgiveness, hope and love. Jasmine felt the remnants of her reserve and caution melt away.

"Just one thing worries me."

He pulled back, putting on a long-suffering look.

"You like excitement. Fast cars. Clubs and fine food. Travel and stock-market drama." She cocked her head. "Isn't playing an English gentleman in the countryside going to be rather tame?"

Adam all but rolled his eyes at her. In reply, he pulled her glove off and she watched, thrilled to bits as he slid the beautiful ring onto her finger.

"Let's see," Adam murmured, holding her hand up and bending each finger closed as he ticked off his points. "Fake engagements. Royal fiancé's. A scandalous past. An eccentric billionaire." He paused, but Jasmine was too caught up in the glitter of the diamond on her hand to notice.

"The sight of you in nothing but ankle boots on an antique canopied bed…"

She glanced up at his face, his wonderful, loving smile, and matched it with one of her own.

Adam squeezed her fingers. "Jasmine Cooper, if you promise to try and make life marginally less frenetic, I promise to love, cherish and try my best to keep up with you."

* * * * *

Desire™

2 in 1
GREAT VALUE

FROM PLAYBOY TO PAPA! by Leanne Banks

Surprised to learn he has a son, Rafe demands the child live with him and he suggests his ex-lover's sister comes too…as his wife.

TEMPTING THE TEXAS TYCOON by Sara Orwig

Noah will receive five million dollars if he marries within the year—and a sexy business rival proves perfect…

BOSSMAN'S BABY SCANDAL by Catherine Mann

What's an executive to do when his one-night stand is pregnant and his new client hates scandal?

EXECUTIVE'S PREGNANCY ULTIMATUM by Emilie Rose

Flynn Maddox thought he was over his ex-wife until he learned they were still married—and that she was trying to have his baby!

Mini-series – Kings of the Boardroom

CLAIMING HIS BOUGHT BRIDE by Rachel Bailey

To meet the terms of his inheritance, Damon convinces Lily to marry him. But he plans to seduce her into being more than his wife on paper.

SEDUCING THE ENEMY'S DAUGHTER by Jules Bennett

She was the enemy's daughter. Business magnate Brady Stone set out to seduce corporate secrets from her, but was she worth more to him than his revenge?

On sale from 17th December 2010
Don't miss out!

*Available at WHSmith, Tesco, ASDA, Eason
and all good bookshops*

www.millsandboon.co.uk

1210/51

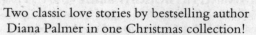

OUTSIDE OFFICE HOURS...

THEY'RE WORKING ON ROMANCE!

Bought: One Night, One Marriage
by Natalie Anderson

Always the Bridesmaid
by Nina Harrington

Confessions of a Millionaire's Mistress
by Robyn Grady

Available 17th December 2010

www.millsandboon.co.uk

M&B

REAL MEN:
Rugged Rebels

Men who work
hard—and
play harder!

*Available 17th
December 2010*

REAL MEN:
**Boardroom
Hot-Shots**

Business titans
by day…kings
of seduction
after hours!

*Available 7th
January 2011*

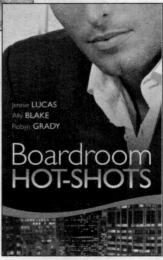

"Did you say I won almost two million dollars?"

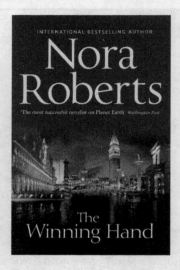

Down to her last ten dollars in a Las Vegas casino, Darcy Wallace gambled and won!

Suddenly the small-town girl was big news—and needing protection. Robert MacGregor Blade, the casino owner, was determined to make sure Darcy could enjoy her good fortune. But Darcy knew what she wanted; Mac himself. Surely her luck was in?

Available 3rd December 2010

www.millsandboon.co.uk

are proud to present our...

Book of the Month

St Piran's: Penhally's Wedding of the Year & St Piran's: Rescued Pregnant Cinderella

from Mills & Boon®
Medical™ Romance 2-in-1

ST PIRAN'S: THE WEDDING OF THE YEAR
by Caroline Anderson
GP Nick Tremayne and midwife Kate Althorp have an
unfulfilled love that's lasted a lifetime. Now, with their
little boy fighting for his life in St Piran's Hospital…can
they find their way back to one another?

ST PIRAN'S: RESCUING PREGNANT CINDERELLA
by Carol Marinelli
Dr Izzy Bailey is single and pregnant when she meets
the gorgeous neo-natal nurse Diego Ramirez. When
she goes into labour dangerously early Diego is there to
rescue her… Could this be the start of her fairytale?

Available 3rd December

Something to say about our Book of the Month?
Tell us what you think!

millsandboon.co.uk/community
facebook.com/romancehq
twitter.com/millsandboonuk

2 FREE BOOKS
AND A SURPRISE GIFT

We would like to take this opportunity to thank you for reading this Mills & Boon® book by offering you the chance to take TWO more specially selected books from the Desire™ 2-in-1 series absolutely FREE! We're also making this offer to introduce you to the benefits of the Mills & Boon® Book Club™—

- **FREE home delivery**
- **FREE gifts and competitions**
- **FREE monthly Newsletter**
- **Exclusive Mills & Boon Book Club offers**
- **Books available before they're in the shops**

Accepting these FREE books and gift places you under no obligation to buy, you may cancel at any time, even after receiving your free books. Simply complete your details below and return the entire page to the address below. You don't even need a stamp!

YES Please send me 2 free Desire stories in a 2-in-1 volume and a surprise gift. I understand that unless you hear from me, I will receive 2 superb new 2-in-1 books every month for just £5.30 each, postage and packing free. I am under no obligation to purchase any books and may cancel my subscription at any time. The free books and gift will be mine to keep in any case.

Ms/Mrs/Miss/Mr _____ Initials _____

_____

Surname _____

Address _____

_____

_____ Postcode _____

E-mail _____

Send this whole page to: Mills & Boon Book Club, Free Book Offer, FREEPOST NAT 10298, Richmond, TW9 1BR